DEAD
WRITE

DEAD
WRITE

DEAD WRITE

A JESSICA KALLAN MYSTERY

Susan C. Richards

**CAVEL
PRESS**
Kenmore, WA

A Camel Press book published by Epicenter Press

Epicenter Press
6524 NE 181st St.
Suite 2
Kenmore, WA 98028

For more information go to:
www.Camelpress.com
www.Coffeetownpress.com
www.Epicenterpress.com
www.susancrichards.com

This is a work of fiction. Names, characters, places, brands, media, and incidents are either the product of the author's imagination or are used fictitiously.

Cover design by Timothy Goulet
Design by Scott Book and Melissa Vail Coffman

Dead Write
Copyright © 2021 by Susan C. Richards

ISBN: 978-1-94207-838-8 (Trade Paper)
ISBN: 978-1-94207-840-1 (eBook)

Printed in the United States of America

In loving memory of my parents,
Jean and Phil Richards.
I miss you still.

ACKNOWLEDGMENTS

AND HERE WE GO WITH BOOK TWO. Publishing a book is a unique journey, like none other I've ever had. Lucky for me, there have been amazing guides along the way to help me get to this point.

Endless thanks to the following people for assistance and direction in the production of this book:

To my agent Dawn Dowdle of Blue Ridge Literary Agency for getting me started down the right path.

To my editor, Jennifer McCord of Camel Press who helps me sidestep the obstacles along the way.

To Tim Goulet and Rod Richards of Echo Creative for web guidance, feedback and more support than I deserve. And to Tim for his outstanding cover designs.

To Phyllis Lindberg for invaluable research and brainstorming—again and again.

Special thanks to Rebekah Beach, MD and Robin Michaels, PhD.

To my family and friends for their continuing love and encouragement—especially my rabid contingent of nieces.

And last, but by no means least, to all the wonderful readers who took a chance on Jessica Kallan and Ethan Miller the first time around, you are much appreciated and you are what makes this fun.

CHAPTER ONE

STANLEY GROVELAND, DIRECTOR OF COMMUNICATIONS AT St. Josephine's College, stood across the room from me, surrounded by a small group of middle-aged women. In the five years we'd been apart, he hadn't changed at all. He was still so damn handsome it made my teeth ache. Tall with dark curly hair and killer blue eyes the color of the ocean.

The women listened, hanging on his every word, obviously enchanted by whatever story he was telling them. I remembered that feeling. When Stanley talked, and his eyes looked into yours, you felt like you were the most important person in the world at that moment.

He'd been my first real love—my first real I-would-lay-down-my-life-for-you love. I fell hard. I'd wanted us to be together forever, but life—and Stanley—had other plans, and we'd both moved on. Now, seeing him again, I realized how much I'd missed him. Unrequited love and unfulfilled desire bubbled to the surface and blindsided me in a way I couldn't have imagined. Maybe it's true, maybe you never get over your first love.

My current boyfriend, Matt, was a great guy. I was happy with him—I was crazy in love. But Stanley would always be Stanley and I couldn't deny the intensity of the feelings I'd once had for him.

I pulled my thoughts away from Stanley and forced myself to concentrate on the others in the room. I was supposed to be working. Thirty people were packed into a classroom in the Humanities Building at St. Josephine's College for Women in central Missouri. In July. Everyone was sweating except the nuns.

Mother Abigail sat on a gray metal folding chair in the corner, watching, a look of disdain on her smooth face. I don't think she approved of people sweating.

Sister Imelda, Mother Abigail's assistant, came up beside me and placed a warm hand on my shoulder. "I think it's going well, don't you?"

Plates of hors d'oeuvres sitting on the tables congealed in the heat, an unappetizing glaze had formed over the smoked salmon, a hardened layer covered the deviled eggs. Salmonella was definitely in someone's future if we didn't wrap this thing up soon.

I smiled. "Yes, I think it's going very well."

St. Josephine's College was the final stop on the book tour for my boss, best-selling author, Ethan Miller. Only five weeks from its release date, his latest book, *Don't Look Back,* was breaking sales records and getting reviews like he hadn't seen in years. As a popular novelist, he'd taken the biggest gamble of his career, writing an autobiographical account of a murder that had taken place on his estate in Southern Missouri decades ago. The critics raved and his fans fell in love with his unbridled candor about how that tragic event had taken its toll on his writing, his life and his family. Ethan was making a comeback.

And now, here we were, hot and tired with one week left on the book tour before we could head for home.

For reasons, I've yet to understand, planning our itinerary had fallen on Ethan's main, well only, research assistant—me. Coming to St. Josephine's had never been on my radar. Until two months ago I hadn't even heard of the small liberal arts college. When the stop on campus was originally suggested, I objected. My objections were overruled.

Constance, Ethan's ex-wife number three, had been traveling with us. Constance thought this weekend from hell at St. Josephine's would help Ethan's book sales, humanize him to the masses with a week-long writing workshop, and raise some money for her alma mater all at the same time. Apparently, this would be the trifecta of book promotions.

Weeks ago, when we'd been planning the book tour, Constance and Ethan were still in the throes of rekindled love and she'd had a lot of influence over his decisions. Now, things weren't going well between the two of them, and we were stuck in the middle of nowhere, with a bunch of hopeful nuns.

A woman with spiky, bright-orange hair, stood on the fringe of Stanley's matronly audience. I'd seen her at Ethan's press conference in St. Louis two nights ago and when we'd arrived at St. Jo's the previous morning, she was waiting as our RV's lumbered onto the campus and came to a stop in front of the Admin Building.

Her name was Ginny Andrews, I learned, as she stepped forward to introduce herself to me when I disembarked the motor home. I'm not sure why I'd been chosen as her point of contact, but it didn't much matter, I guess. I smiled and shook her hand. After five weeks of traveling with Ethan's entourage, I was just trying to get through the next seven days without killing anyone. Everyone in our group was on my list of possible targets. Currently, Ethan and Constance vied for first place.

It was obvious that Ginny had once been very pretty, maybe thirty-some years ago. I pegged her as a homecoming queen in a small rural high school. She talked in long run-on sentences, her voice a chronic monotone, and before I could extricate myself from her life story, I found that I was right, she had indeed been homecoming queen.

A young man, his back against the whiteboard watched Ethan move about the room, his gaze intent on my boss. He, too had been in St. Louis two nights before.

After working as a researcher for Ethan for over a year, I knew he got emails from fans, but I had no idea he also had groupies—at least the two who had followed us from St. Louis.

The young man looked out of place in the roomful of women. Besides Stanley and Ethan, the only other men in the room were Ethan's son, John, and his Business Manager, Dan Ketner, who stood next to the classroom door, eager to bolt, as soon as Ethan started to wrap things up.

Most of the women present were signed up for Ethan's writing workshop on Monday—which we'd thrown together at the last minute at Constance's insistence. It was by invitation-only for a select group of alumnae. I glanced around the room, not sure why any of the ladies would be interested in a workshop on Creating Believable Characters, unless they had hopes of a late-in-life writing career.

Ginny pulled away from Stanley's group and moved in to lay claim to Ethan's arm. He pasted his best PR smile on his face, bracing himself for the inevitable question, "Mr. Miller, where do you get all the wonderful ideas for your books?"

Ethan shot a glance my way, that said, *get me out of here.*

He started in with his canned response. I moved toward the window to stand in front of the fans, blowing hot air in off the parking lot.

Ethan's youngest son, John, was perched on the windowsill.

I nodded my head toward the young man standing by the whiteboard. "Do you know him?"

John glanced in that direction. "No. Should I? Wait. He does look a little familiar. No, never mind."

"He was in St. Louis last night. I just wondered if he was . . . somebody."

John pulled his damp shirt front away from his skin. "Not a clue," he said. "Tell me again what we're doing here?"

"Your mother insisted a weekend of publicity for your father's latest book and the writing workshop next week, would be a great fund-raiser for her alma mater."

"And?"

"I don't think any of these people have pockets deep enough to support a scholarship fund."

"Why doesn't Ethan just write them a check and we can be on our way?"

"Yeah? Tell that to your mother."

Constance flitted gracefully, from one sweat-dripping group to the next, as if she was hosting a cocktail party for celebrities. Ethan Miller was easily the only celebrity in a hundred and fifty-mile radius, the rest was just a room full of hot, droopy people, waiting for this painful ordeal to be over.

Ethan slid out from Ginny's adoring hand resting on his forearm, and made his way to me. "Jessie, get me the hell out of here," he whispered in my ear.

I held up my hand. "Everyone," I said loud enough to be heard over the commotion. They stopped talking and looked at me. "Thank you so much for coming today. I want to remind you that the golf outing starts at nine tomorrow morning, followed by a picnic lunch in the arbor. Before we wrap this up, we have time for one more question for Mr. Miller."

Mr. Miller was already inching toward the door, a smile painted on his face as he looked out over the group, hopeful that no one had anything else to say.

The young man who'd followed us from St. Louis, stepped away from the whiteboard and moved toward the center of the room. He was probably somewhere in his thirties, tall and gangly, with straight brown hair and Harry Potter glasses on his round face. "I have a question." He turned toward Ethan. "Mr. Miller, did you know that you are my father?"

Okay then. I wondered if this would be the end of my brief career with the great Ethan Miller. Even though the visit to St. Josephine's College had been Constance's idea, I'd been the contact person to set this thing up. Ethan had made it clear from the beginning, that if there was one slight hiccup in the whole week, I would pay.

And now there was a hiccup. A really big hiccup.

All the ladies in the room, including five nuns, turned toward Ethan. Mother Abigail raised her eyebrows in obvious disapproval.

Ethan moved out from behind Sister Imelda. "Young man, I have no idea who you are, but I can tell you unequivocally that I am *not* your father."

"Really? Then you don't remember my mother, Lois Westenfeld?"

Dan Ketner started to choke, his face turning bright red as a coughing fit overtook him.

I could almost see the wheels turning in Ethan's head. I imagine, after decades of womanizing, all the names and faces ran together after a while.

And just before all hell broke loose, I heard John say, "Uh-ohhhh."

CHAPTER TWO

CHAOS ERUPTED. ALL OVER THE CLASSROOM in the Humanities Building at St. Josephine's College for Women. The young man and Ethan squared off in a shouting match, the alleged son of the best-selling author, shouted accusations. Ethan, never one to hold his tongue, shouted his denials right back.

Ethan was bigger and had more volume, but for some reason, the only voice I heard was Constance, shouting down both of them, her flawless face veiled in anger.

Finally, Stanley stepped forward. I still don't know how he did it, but he managed to get their attention long enough to quiet everyone down, then herded Ethan and family and the young man from St. Louis out of the Humanities lecture hall past the twenty or so women, who were waiting to hear the lurid details of Ethan's past. Disappointment hung on their faces as he marched us out of the room.

Heat waves shimmered up off the blacktop. We made our way to the Administration Building and up a flight of stairs, Stanley pushed open an office door with the title, Director of Communications, stenciled in bold black letters on the opaque glass above his name. The room felt hotter—if that was even possible—than the Humanities building.

Stanley stood behind his walnut desk, trying to mediate some kind of temporary cease-fire between the warring factions. He wasn't having much luck.

"Young man," Constance said, "how old are you?"

"Thirty-two."

"Thirty-two?" She did a quick round of math in her head. "Thirty-two!" she screamed at Ethan. "*We* were still married thirty-two years ago!"

Ethan held up his hand. "Constance—"

She cut him off. "I want to know who that woman was and what the hell you were doing with her. Oh, never mind—I guess we all know what you were doing with her!"

"Constance!" Ethan bellowed. "If you will shut up for just one minute—"

She was in his face then. "Do *not* tell me to shut up." She swung back. Her hand flew toward Ethan's left jaw. He reached up and grabbed her by the wrist before she could make contact.

Stanley moved quickly around his desk to Constance's side, taking her by the arm, "Mrs. Miller, why don't you take a breath before you do something you'll regret." His voice was calm. He led her to a chair as far away from Ethan as possible, then nodded to John and the alleged son, to be seated between the two of them.

I stood by the window, surprised by Stanley's finesse. This wasn't the young college boy I'd fallen in love with. He'd picked up some impressive negotiating skills in his years in San Francisco.

Dan Ketner leaned a shoulder up against the door, his eyes intent behind his round wire-rimmed glasses, as he watched the young man claiming to be Ethan's son. Sixty years old, his hair more gray now than brown, he was slim and not particularly muscular. If his plan was to stop the young man, should he decide to leave, I don't think he could do more than slow his progress for a second or two.

Stanley moved back around his desk and took a seat. "Let's look at what we're dealing with here." He turned toward the young man. "What's your name?"

The young man stuck out his chin and looked at Ethan. "Ethan Miller, Jr."

Constance started to rise. John put out a hand to stop her.

Ethan-the-original said, "Do you have a birth certificate, young man?"

He took a folded piece of paper from his front shirt pocket, started to hand it to Ethan, then stopped and handed it to Stanley. Ethan rolled his eyes.

"Well?' Constance asked.

Stanley looked at her and then Ethan. "It says here that the father is Ethan Miller."

Constance started to rise from her chair and again her son stopped her. "I knew it," she said to Ethan, her jaw clenched. "Where did you meet the little floozie?"

Ethan Jr. jumped up. "That's my mother you're talking about. She was not a floozie."

Stanley motioned Ethan Jr. back into his chair.

A look of annoyance settled on Ethan's face. "You don't know anything, Constance." He turned to Stanley and held out his hand. "Let me see that."

Stanley reached across the desk and handed him the birth certificate.

Ethan read it. "If this is indeed a legal birth certificate, then there's no way I could possibly be this young man's father." He handed it back to Ethan Junior.

There was silence.

"You sound pretty sure of that, Mr. Miller," Stanley said. "I'm not saying you're lying, but . . ."

"My son, John, is seven years older than you are," Ethan said to his namesake. Always the flair for the dramatic, he paused for effect. We waited. "I had a vasectomy before John was born."

Constance narrowed her eyes. "Wait. What?"

There was a supercilious grin on Ethan's face.

Ethan Junior looked bewildered, that clearly wasn't the response he expected. "But it says you're my father. My mother said you're my father."

Ethan shook his head. "Not me."

"But . . ." Ethan Junior said. He looked at Ethan, then turned toward Stanley. Stanley held up his hands in a gesture of helplessness.

Constance wasn't buying any of this. "How could you have had a vasectomy and I didn't know about it?"

Ethan smiled. "Because I never told you."

Constance looked into Ethan's eyes, then shook her head. "I don't believe you."

He shrugged. "It's the truth. When you were pregnant with John, I was in St. Louis for an interview and I had it done there."

"Why?' she asked, still watching his face.

Ethan Miller rarely defended his actions and the question took him by surprise, he seemed at a loss for words. He glanced over at John. We all waited.

"This is a personal matter and I'd rather not discuss it in front of everyone." He looked around the room, his gaze settling again on John.

Stanley stood. "I understand. This is between you and your wi—uh, ex-wife. And, of course your, uh, Ethan Junior."

I don't know who was more relieved to be dismissed. John, who probably didn't want to hear the details of his father's vasectomy—or me, who didn't want to hear the details of my boss's vasectomy.

We were both out of our chairs and at the door when Ethan said, "Wait."

I groaned. John breathed a heavy sigh.

"I'd like Jessie to stay," Ethan said. "And, uh, this young man." Not one to be burdened by insignificant trivia, like other people's names, he waved a hand toward Stanley. "The rest of you can leave."

"But . . .," Ethan Jr. started.

Ethan Sr., nodded his head toward the door.

Junior looked at Stanley. Stanley shrugged.

Constance started to sputter. "I think this definitely concerns *me*." Ethan nodded toward the door again.

"Are you sure you don't need me here," Dan asked.

"No."

In addition to managing the business end of Ethan's writing career, Dan was used to cleaning up many of the loose ends of Ethan's personal life, which more often than not, involved a disgruntled woman. I think he was surprised at being dismissed. He opened his mouth, then closed it, turned and left the room.

The relief that swept over John's face was evident. He took his mother by the arm, pulling her to her feet. "Come on, Mom, and—you," he said to his maybe-brother.

John's relief turned to definite gloating as he looked at me and winked. "Have fun," he said, right before he pulled the door closed behind him.

Ethan, Stanley and I were the only ones left. I leaned up against the door, afraid that if I sat down, Ethan would take it as a sign that I wanted to engage in this conversation.

Stanley caught my eye and waved me toward an empty chair. Oh crap, I didn't want to be here.

I looked at Ethan. "I think this is something you should be sharing with your family," I said, "and not me. And certainly not Stanley. What's going on?"

"This is not something I wanted to admit in front of John," he said. "I'll explain it all to Constance once she calms down. I don't feel any obligation to explain myself to that young man. I don't know who he is or what he wants from me and I never met his mother—that I recall."

"Okay, it still doesn't concern Stanley or me."

"It does concern you, Jessie. Stanley is merely an unbiased outsider. I can use that right now."

I met Ethan a little over a year ago when I approached him for an exclusive interview. It was a longshot I knew. Ethan Miller hadn't given an interview in over a decade. To my surprise, he accepted my request and invited me from Omaha to his estate in Southern Missouri. It took a while to realize why I was really there.

In some strange backstory to my life that had culminated in me getting fired from my former job, Ethan had chosen me to help him investigate the death of the young woman who'd been murdered on his estate twenty years earlier—and in the process, he'd almost gotten me killed.

He was a master manipulator, I had no idea how much I could believe of whatever he was about to say.

I folded my arms in front of me. "Well?"

My defensive posture was not lost on him, he smiled. "It's not much of a story, but the ramifications are significant in light of the current accusation against me." He paused, and I could see that something about this bothered him. "This is the part I didn't want John to have to hear. I love my sons—my *real* sons—Matt and John, but I knew I wasn't a very good father. I tried to do right by them, but I probably never gave them what they needed."

I'm pretty sure John—and Matt—already knew what kind of a father he was. This revelation wouldn't have been much of a surprise to either one of them.

Ethan rubbed a hand across his forehead. "Matt," he turned toward Stanley, "that's my oldest son from my first marriage, had his stepfather to guide him—to be the role model that I never was. By the time Constance and I got married, I'd already realized that I wasn't cut out to be a parent. Her pregnancy was a surprise to both of us. She was elated, but all I could think about was, *oh great— here's another kid whose life I can screw up.*"

Ethan got up and walked to the window. He was a big man, handsome and rugged, with thick, wavy, silvery hair. But right now, he looked vulnerable. He was in his seventies, and from that generation, where men didn't share their feelings easily—but then, maybe no generation could lay claim to that part of the male DNA.

After a minute, I wasn't sure if Ethan was thinking or pausing again for dramatic affect. I looked at Stanley, he was watching Ethan.

"Are we supposed to fill in the blanks here, Ethan?" I asked. "You didn't think you were a good father. You had one son and another child on the way and you didn't want to make the same mistake again, so you went to St. Louis and had a vasectomy and neglected to tell your wife. Is that the gist of it?"

He turned. The look on his face was not a happy one. I'm not sure if it was because he was feeling a sense of guilt about being a crappy father or because, I'd cut his story short.

He raised an eyebrow. "Yes, that's the gist of it."

"Why didn't you tell Constance?"

He actually laughed. "If you think Constance has a temper, you should see her when she's pregnant. Constance and erratic hormones are not a good mix." He took the chair next to mine. "I was a coward. I didn't want to deal with her reactions. Even though pregnancy made her crazy, she wanted the baby, and was suddenly planning a family for us. Two or three more kids. That wasn't the road I wanted to take. I thought I'd tell her later, after the baby came. But there never seemed to be a good time. And then we got divorced."

"Twelve years later," I pointed out.

He nodded. "Yes. Twelve years later."

"So, you really are not Ethan Junior's father?"

"I am not."

Stanley cleared his throat. "Vasectomies don't always work, Mr. Miller."

"What are you saying?"

Stanley looked straight at Ethan. "He could still be your son."

Ethan set his jaw. "He is not my son, I'm absolutely certain of that. He doesn't even look like me." Which was true. The Miller men—all of them—were remarkably good looking. Ethan, Jr., was rather plain by comparison.

Stanley's gaze never wavered. "I think it would be in your best interest to have a DNA test—just to prove that you're right."

Ethan looked at me. "What do you think?"

"This one's a no-brainer, Ethan. Have the test, then there won't be any question."

Almost a full minute passed while he thought it over, and I wasn't sure what he was debating with himself. "Okay," he finally said.

CHAPTER THREE

Since we'd arrived at the college the day before, it felt as if Stanley had been avoiding me and I couldn't figure out why. After our initial OMG-it's-so-good-to-see-you!-how-have-you-been?, he'd side-stepped all my attempts to talk.

Yes, five years had passed since he'd left the *Omaha Tribune* where we'd both worked, but we'd parted on good terms. And even though our—my—love was never requited in the way I'd hoped, or any way for that matter, we'd been close. He'd been my best friend and I thought I was his. Now, there was this unsettling awkwardness between us.

After Ethan left Stanley's office, I planted myself in the chair across the desk from him. "I feel like you're avoiding me."

He looked toward me, but didn't directly return my gaze. "No, it's not that. I'm just swamped right now. It's a busy time of year."

"It's July."

When he finally realized that I wasn't going to leave, he agreed to meet in front of the Admin Building that night at seven. It sounded clandestine, but I figured it was merely another stalling tactic and he, very likely, wouldn't show.

The hallways of the Administration Building at St. Josephine's held over a hundred years of history, stories of thousands of young coeds echoing down the corridors like earthbound spirits. Victorian chairs with ornately scrolled arms and tapestry fabric, dotted the waiting areas outside almost every office.

The long, dark, halls with gleaming maple floors offered the first bit of respite from the heat that I'd felt since I left the air-conditioned RV that morning.

I took my time meandering down the corridor, thinking about Stanley, and Ethan, and how much my life had changed in the nine years since I started working at the *Trib*, as a naïve twenty-two-year old girl.

Stanley and I had started at the *Trib* a month apart. Eric Amundson, the former owner and publisher of the paper, had hired both of us right out of college.

Talk about opportunities landing in your lap. It couldn't have been a better start for two young hopeful reporters fresh out of school. Eric had been a friend, mentor, teacher and surrogate father until his death—well, to me anyway. He and Stanley had issues that were never quite clear to me. Stanley never developed that bond with Eric that meant so much to me and guided my career.

In those early days, when we were both still finding our way at the paper, Stanley and I formed a desperate bond. We were the new kids, in a sea of seasoned professionals, leaning on each other for support. That support turned to friendship and the friendship had turned to something deeper, or so I thought. It took me two years to realize what everyone else already knew—that Stanley was gay.

I'd envisioned a future together that was never going to happen and the grief that followed that realization was gut-wrenching. I didn't want to lose my friend, however, so I switched gears as best I could and what developed over the following year was an even closer friendship.

When Stanley left for San Francisco and the lure of a larger market, I had to grieve all over again, this time the loss of my friend.

We kept in touch for a while, and then life did its typical thing and got in the way.

I passed by the business offices on the main floor of the Administration Building and rounded a corner to see a pair of long, masculine legs stretching out from one of the alcoves.

Ethan reclined, head back, eyes closed, arms folded across his chest, on a velvet settee.

"I figured you'd want to talk," he said without opening his eyes.

I nudged him over a couple of inches and took a seat next to him. "You figured right."

We sat in silence for a few minutes, finally Ethan said, again without opening his eyes, "Well? Go ahead."

We'd had a rocky start, my boss and I. He'd unwittingly pulled me into that twenty-year old murder investigation. Bonnie, the young woman who'd been found murdered on his estate, was engaged to Ethan's oldest son, Matt, and was pregnant at the time of her death. The consensus had been that Ethan was the father of the young woman's unborn child. I'd jumped on that bandwagon with both feet, and it colored my opinion of Ethan Miller for a while. Now, the news of the vasectomy; it appeared we'd all been wrong.

"Everyone thought that you'd slept with Bonnie and fathered her child," I said, watching Ethan's face, more relaxed than I'd seen it since we started the book tour.

"Including you."

"Yes, including me."

I waited for him to say more. Apparently, I was supposed to carry the ball with this conversation.

"I wish we'd known this information earlier. It might have stopped all the speculation about Bonnie's baby. Why didn't you tell me, Ethan? Why didn't you tell Matt? He went through years—decades—of agony, thinking you'd slept with his fiancée."

Ethan finally opened his eyes and looked at me. "Would you have believed me?"

"Of course."

He grunted a reply and raised an eyebrow.

"Okay," I admitted, "probably not."

He cocked his head to one side.

"You're right. I wouldn't have believed you."

He pushed himself up into a sitting position. "Then what would have been the point?"

I didn't know what the point would have been, because, at the time, it wouldn't have changed my opinion. "At least you would have tried to set the record straight."

He watched my face. "I did try, Jessie. I tried twenty years before, when Bonnie was murdered, but no one wanted to hear it. People believe what they want to believe."

And, sadly, that was true.

He looked at me with an intensity I'd often seen in Matt's eyes when he was about to say something I probably needed to pay attention to. "You have to understand what that girl's death did to our family. I wasn't sure we'd survive. By the time, I realized that Matt suspected me of sleeping with his fiancé, it was too late. The rift between us was too big and I didn't know how to fix it. After a while I gave up trying. It seemed that every time I tried to defend myself, I was making things worse for Matt. I didn't want to cause him anymore pain, so, for once in my life, I stopped talking."

Sometimes Ethan surprised me. "Okay. I get it."

"I'm not sure you do."

"Meaning?"

He stretched and yawned. "There are two things about me that are very much a part of who I am."

After the vasectomy report, I wasn't sure I wanted to hear any more personal information about Ethan. Not only was he my boss, probably my friend. Someday, he might also be my father-in-law. Ethan's son, Matt, was a botanist who taught and did research at the University of Missouri at Columbia. Matt and I had been dating for the better part of a year and there were times when we were actually getting along, that we even talked about the future.

Ethan was still watching me—waiting.

I took my cue. "What is it that I don't know about you, Ethan?"

His gaze didn't waver. "I never expected to be voted Father of the Year. That isn't me, but I love my sons, I always have. I can't believe you—or anyone—could think that I would ever do that to Matt."

I knew that was true, whatever his faults, Ethan was not cruel. Family was important to him. Taking care of the people in his life was a responsibility he took seriously. And when I really looked at it, I knew he would never purposely hurt Matt.

"I'm sorry," I said. "I can't believe I jumped to that conclusion."

"Thank you."

I steeled myself for the next round. This honesty game was like standing on a steep cliff on a windy day. I wasn't sure which of Ethan's personal revelations was going to bring a gust strong enough to blow me off the side of the mountain. "And, what is your other secret?"

An enigmatic smile slipped into place. "I'm always faithful in relationships. I may not be easy to live with, but I am always faithful."

Ethan the womanizer? "Seriously?"

The smile stayed in place. "Yes. Seriously. Are you surprised?"

Ethan had probably never gone more than a month without a beautiful woman in his life. "I think anyone who's ever known or heard about you would be surprised."

"Perhaps."

"Does Constance know this side of you?"

"She does."

"Then why did she go ballistic about a potential love-child showing up in your life?"

He winced. "Not so crazy about the term love-child, but I know Constance and when she has time to think about it, she'll realize that it never happened while she and I were together. She's very reactionary, but she'll settle down soon."

"I hope you're right."

He stood up. "So, did you get everything straightened out with your young man?"

"You mean Stanley?"

"Sure."

"Well, he's not my young man, but we used to be very close. We're going to meet later and catch up." I looked at him. There was something in his eyes that I couldn't read. "What?"

"I don't have a good feeling about your young man."

"He's *not* my young man. And why don't you like him?"

"He seems a little slippery to me."

"Said the King of Slippery."

He raised his eyebrows. "I'm not slippery, just innovative."

"Call it what you like, the results are the same."

He shook his head. "I just know that Eric never thought much of him."

Ethan and Eric Amundson, my former boss, had been best friends since long before I'd made my earthly arrival until Eric's death a few years ago. I trusted and respected Eric and it concerned me that he had a negative opinion of Stanley. "What did he say?"

Ethan thought for a minute. "It was a long time ago, I can't remember much of it, just that Eric thought the young man was lazy and not entirely trustworthy. An opportunist."

"He's a hell of a writer."

"Uh huh."

Ethan left me and headed back to his RV for a drink and a siesta that may or may not have included Constance, depending on her present volatility.

I headed out to explore the campus and kill some time.

St. Josephine's College consisted of eight stand-alone buildings in the Spanish Revival style with white stucco walls, arched doorways, clay tile roofs, and a blue and green tiled fountain in the middle of the quad.

Earlier in the day, Sister Imelda had identified each building for me. Front and center, behind the fountain, was Administration, where Stanley had his office. To the right of that was the chapel, with stained glass windows with the Stations of the Cross and a spire housing the bell-tower.

The girls' dorm—well the only dorm since it was an all girls' school—and dining hall were in the first building visitors and students passed as they entered the campus grounds from the county road. Next to it was the cloister, nestled between the dorm and the chapel. On the other side of the Admin Building, a sidewalk crept up a small hump in the mostly-flat terrain to the library, and the Humanities and the Science Buildings. Science at St. Jo's was a big draw, I'd found, with one of the best nursing and physical therapy programs in the state.

Tucked away at the far end of the campus was an infirmary set-up like a mini private clinic, where the nursing students completed their preliminary practicums before their senior year rotations at nearby hospitals.

A small hill ran behind the buildings, sequestering the college from the remaining five hundred acres owned by the monastery. Up, over the top of the rise, was a fully-equipped gym with an indoor Olympic-sized pool, a nine-hole golf course, the arboretum and a cemetery with gravestones dating back over the past century.

The time alone cleared my head. I wanted to keep walking, but the heat wrapped around me like a shroud, I headed back down the hill toward the RV's and the only air conditioning on the campus. One more week, I kept telling myself, and we'd be home again.

For over a month, six of us had been crisscrossing the Midwest in an RV wagon train while Ethan promoted his latest novel.

Ethan and Constance and their rekindled love shared a motor home. Millie Gunderson, Ethan's housekeeper, and I shared another.

In her fifties, Millie was round and plump. She took care of us all, at home—back at Ethan's estate—and here on the road. She was the perfect roommate and I had the benefit of her cooking, wherever we were.

And Ethan and Constance's son, John, and Business Manager, Dan Ketner, occupied home-on-wheels number three. It was too much togetherness for any of us and we were all feeling the strain.

I was rounding the west side of the Admin Building when Ethan's voice broke through the heat. Things had gotten interesting again. Apparently, Ethan didn't know Constance as well as he thought.

"Constance!" Ethan bellowed from the sidewalk outside the door of his RV, "Can you keep your mouth shut for ten minutes?! Ten minutes! That's all I'm asking."

Constance stepped onto the pavement, her beautiful face, tighter than usual from her most recent face-lift. "Fine! I will not say another word to you. I promise!"

She stalked over to the RV that Millie and I occupied, and stomped up the three steps to the entrance.

Interesting was suddenly encroaching on my turf, I trotted toward our RV.

Millie stood in the doorway, a look of horror on her face. "This isn't good," she said, and followed Constance into the RV.

Constance was already taking over our home. She opened a closet and tossed some of my clothes on the bed. "We need to make more room in here." She opened another door.

I gathered up my flying clothes. "Why? What's going on?" She was pissing me off. I grabbed one of my blouses that never quite made it onto the bed. "Constance, you need to stop."

She opened a drawer under a built-in vanity where my underwear was hiding, reached in and pulled out a handful of cotton panties. I threw my clothes back on the bed and grabbed her arm, turning her around to face me. "Stop! *What* is going on?"

"Ethan Miller is a philandering pig," she said, as if she was the first woman to ever point that out. "And I will not spend one more night with him."

I turned to look at Millie. All the color had drained from her face. "What do we do?" she mouthed, running a hand through her short blonde hair.

There wasn't enough room for Constance in our living space and she refused to leave—even the threat of calling Ethan in, didn't budge her. Which meant *someone* else had to go in order make room for her and her extensive wardrobe. The *someone* was me of course. I was voted off the island, ousted to the hot, creepy girls' dorm a block away.

DAN KETNER CAME TO MY AID as I struggled across the hot pavement with an armful of clothes, pulling a red suitcase on wheels behind me, an overnight bag slung over my left shoulder.

"Let me help," he said, taking charge of the suitcase and overnight bag.

I didn't refuse the help.

I looked at Dan as we trudged along. "Did you know about

Ethan's vasectomy," I asked. Dan had worked for Ethan for over thirty years. I figured he knew everything.

He sort of looked my way, but Dan rarely made eye contact. "It was news to me."

"Do you believe him?"

This time he did make eye contact. "I have no reason not to. Don't you?"

"I actually do, although I'm not sure why."

"Ethan is a manipulator," Dan said. "No one can argue with that. But I've never known him to be a liar."

"And the difference is?"

Dan stopped walking. "Ethan will manipulate the hell out of events to get what he wants or what *he* thinks is best for others. But, outright lying? No. That's not him."

And he was right. That wasn't the Ethan I knew either.

Mother Abigail and her assistant, Sister Imelda, were waiting for me in the reception area of the girls' dorm.

Mother Abigail reached for my suitcase. "I'll take that from here, Mr. Ketner."

Dan held on. "I don't mind. I can take it upstairs."

She raised an eyebrow. "We have rules here, Mr. Ketner. No men are allowed past the front desk.

He started to protest, looked at me and surrendered the heavy suitcase to Mother Abigail.

Mother Abigail had to be somewhere in her sixties, but I was hard-pressed to guess which end of the decade she was on. Her clear, unlined skin refused to reveal her age. Thick, white hair escaped the edges of her modified veil. If she'd had to arm-wrestle Dan for the suitcase, I would have bet on her. Her stocky torso and thick arms would have given her the leverage advantage to knock him on his ass.

Sister Imelda was probably late thirties, early forties, tall and slim. She wore a gold chain around her slender neck that disappeared into her blouse and the illusion of cleavage—if nuns even had cleavage. I wasn't sure. A shy smile slipped into place whenever she was talking to someone.

I reluctantly waved good-bye to Dan. I felt like I might be the next victim in a B slasher movie. We boarded the elevator and rode to the fourth floor. Heat slapped us in the face as we stepped out into a long, dark hallway, a window at each end, offering only a stingy amount of light.

The lower floors housed the women who'd been at the reception in the Humanities Building earlier, and who would be attending Ethan's writer's workshop in a few days. It appeared that I was the only one on the top floor of the building.

Sr. Imelda led the way to my room, two doors down from the elevator. Mother Abigail followed, lugging my heavy bags.

Imelda walked over to the window and pulled open the curtains. "Oh look, you have a view."

I moved in behind her, looking down four stories to the parking lot below.

They left me alone to unpack. I felt like crying.

AT SEVEN THAT EVENING, I WAS SITTING ON A CONCRETE BENCH in front of the Administration Building, waiting for Stanley. Thunderclouds formed on the horizon, and I hoped a storm might bring a break in the heat.

Ten minutes later, I was beginning to think I'd been right earlier and that Stanley wasn't going to show up.

A blue Subaru Impreza made a sharp turn onto the campus from the county road, barely keeping all four wheels on the ground. It skidded to a stop at the curb fifteen feet away from me.

Ethan Jr. was behind the wheel, not looking particularly happy. Stanley, next to him in the passenger seat, gripped the dashboard. After a few seconds, Ethan Jr. told him to get out. He was so close I could read his lips.

Stanley threw a look his way, then opened the door and got out. Tires squealing, the Impreza lurched forward and headed toward the parking lot at the end of the quad behind the Science Building.

I walked up to Stanley. "Everything okay?"

He turned. "Not a good night for him."

"If he really thought Ethan was his father, then he's had a hard day. What happened?"

We moved over to the concrete bench and sat.

"I ran into him a couple of hours ago, coming out of Mother Abigail's office. You're right, he was upset about all that happened today, so I asked if he wanted to go out to dinner and talk about it. It didn't go well."

"Why not?"

Stanley ran a hand through his dark curls. "He really did believe Ethan Miller was his father. I told him they should both have DNA testing, but he should prepare himself for whatever the results might be. That wasn't what he wanted to hear. I think he wanted me to tell him things would turn out the way he'd hoped. He lost it then. It was a very uncomfortable dinner to say the least."

"I'm sorry."

"Yeah. Me too. I genuinely feel sorry for him."

Stanley looked at me with those deep blue eyes and a slow smile appeared. "I guess we've got some catching up to do."

He took my hand and we headed up over the hill toward the gym.

Like the other buildings, the gym's exterior was white stucco. Stanley bent down and flipped over a rock, an old-fashioned skeleton key lay in the dirt.

"Good security system," I said.

"Everyone knows it's here, I don't know why they even bother to lock the doors at all."

He let us inside and we walked the length of the pool to the deep end, slipped off our shoes and sat on the edge, dangling our feet in the water, a welcome cool contrast to the hot humid air outside. I'm not sure what had changed between us in the past several hours, but the old Stanley was back.

I looked at his handsome profile. "What brought you here from San Francisco? I thought you'd find what you were looking for out there."

In the fading sunlight filtering through the windows, I saw a half smile.

"So did I," he said. "But it didn't take long to realize, I'm not the big-city boy I thought I was. Don't get me wrong. San Francisco was great. So many opportunities, but it wasn't for me."

"But St. Josephine's College for Women? In the middle of Nowhere, Missouri?"

That brought a laugh. "Yeah, I know. Not exactly where I thought I'd end up."

"Yet here you are."

He wrapped his leg around mine, still dangling in the chlorine, a gesture of intimacy—a reminder of the friendship we'd once had. It brought tears to my eyes.

"It's hard to connect in a city that big. I never felt at home. I never had a friend like you. I missed that."

I pretended to push my hair back off my face and brushed away a tear.

"I know I hurt you, Jess. And I'm sorry. I wish I'd told you from the beginning that I was gay."

"It's okay. It was a long time ago."

"I know. But I am sorry."

I cleared my throat. "That still doesn't tell me how you got here."

"Right. I finally met someone. Someone that I was interested in."

I turned and watched his face, but there was no joy there. "I take it things didn't work out."

"Actually, they did."

He stopped talking and slipped into a silence that seemed to stretch all the way to the West Coast. I bumped my shoulder into his, prompting the information that was dribbling out. "Again, here you are in Nowhere, Missouri. Alone. What happened."

"I met this guy one night in a neighborhood bar. We hit it off. He was amazing. Good looking, kind, smart, funny. And we dated. And it was great." He stopped again.

This time I didn't interrupt the pause. I knew more was coming and probably not good.

His arm went around my waist and he scooted closer. This was the Stanley I remembered. This was the Stanley I missed.

He blew air out of his lungs. "The guy, his name was Peter, was a former priest."

"Oh?"

"It had only been a short time since he'd left the priesthood. It took him a long time to accept his sexuality—to accept that he was gay—but when he finally admitted it, at least to himself, he knew he needed to leave the priesthood. So, he quit his job and moved to the Bay area."

"And where is he now?" I was pretty sure I already knew the answer.

Seconds passed. The building grew darker. Finally, "He died. He jogged religiously every morning at six. One morning he was out running, he had a heart attack."

"I'm sorry, Stanley." My response came too quickly. The feeling was genuine, but it sounded lame. It sounded empty.

He nodded slowly. "Thank you."

"And St. Jo's?"

"Peter was the Chaplin here for about twenty years and taught Art History. He loved this place, and was sad to have to leave. He talked about it all the time. When he'd had too much to drink, he'd even get a little maudlin about what he'd left behind. I used to go to the website and look at pictures of the school. It's beautiful here. I could see why he loved it. Anyway, when the job opened up a few months ago, I applied. I wasn't happy in San Francisco, especially with Peter gone. I thought maybe coming here, I'd feel close to him again."

"And do you?"

He smiled. "Yes, most of the time I do."

It felt good to have my friend back. We finished filling in the details of the last five years. I told him about me getting fired from the *Trib* and how an interview with Ethan Miller had turned into a job as a researcher for a best-selling author.

We left the building at nine. Stanley locked the door behind us with the hidden-in-plain-sight skeleton key, and we started toward the path that led down the hillside.

Constance emerged from the cemetery. "I don't think Millie is happy to have me as a roommate. I thought I'd give her some space," she said.

The three of us wove our way down the hill and approached the Humanities Building. Ginny and Ethan Jr. sat on the cement bench, like a bizarre romantic interlude of a hugely mismatched couple, watching the sunset together.

I said goodnight to Stanley and Constance and hurried toward the hot, creepy dorm before Ginny could pull me into whatever details of her life, I'd missed the last time we'd talked.

CHAPTER FOUR

IT WAS SO DAMN HOT I COULDN'T BREATHE. The lumpy mattress on the narrow twin bed in my dorm room felt like some kind of ancient torture device. Things kept poking me in the back.

And I was so damn hot.

A car motor revved to life, the sound bolted through darkness and the open window. I got up and walked over, looking out at the compound below, lit by streetlights straight out of a Gothic novel.

The three over-sized RV's sat where they'd been since yesterday morning. Ethan Jr. parked his car next to the curb behind Dan and John's motor home, got out, slammed his door and plodded over to the cement bench in front of the Administration Building.

I wondered how long it would take him to come to terms with the fact that Ethan Miller wasn't his father, I wondered how long he'd believed that. Even from a distance, his frustration was obvious—the way he moved, the way he sat, his posture—a look that said, to anyone willing to pay attention, that life hat let him down.

The door of the RV I'd shared with Millie, opened. The streetlights illuminated the area in an eerie yellow glow. Even halfway across the quad, I could identify Constance's distinctive, seductive walk as she approached Ethan Jr. She said something and he slid over a few inches. Constance took the place next to him, her body half facing his. Ethan Jr. didn't even turn his head in her direction.

What was so important that she would get out of bed in the middle of the night to talk to him? She reached out and put her hand on his forearm. He pulled away. Without ever turning toward her, he got up and walked away.

Another form appeared from around the side of the building. Once under the security lights, I could see Ginny as she moved toward Constance, still seated on the bench.

Ethan Jr., didn't go back to his car, but made his way toward the county road. A light went on in John and Dan's RV, and seconds later, Dan opened the door and stepped out. He moved quickly down the accessway to catch up to Ethan Jr.

Ethan Jr. stopped and turned toward Dan. Whatever Dan said, it was enough to engage the young man in some kind of dialogue. The two of them continued the walk down the road.

I finally got bored and went back to bed, where I fell into a kind of half-sleep, dozing fitfully, drenched in sweat.

Sometime later, I jolted awake. Even in my half-sleep, I sensed I wasn't alone. I opened my eyes, waiting for them to adjust to the darkness, almost afraid to see whatever was there. A man loomed over my bed. I screamed.

A large rough hand clamped over my mouth. I brought my knee up and braced my foot against his stomach, pushing as hard as I could. Aiming for his head, I threw a punch, but he pulled back before it landed, his hand still covering my mouth. I bit down hard on the fleshy part of his hand.

He yelped and jumped back, banging against the wall in the small room. "What the hell did you do that for?"

"Matt?"

"That really hurt! Why did you bite me?"

I sat up in bed and turned on the bedside lamp. Matt—my boyfriend and the oldest son of Ethan Miller—slid to the floor, his back against the wall.

I put my hand on my chest, willing my heart to return to a normal rhythm. "You scared the shit out of me! What are you doing here?"

He sucked on his hand. "I think I'm bleeding."

I got up and went to look at his hand. "Don't be a baby. Why didn't you tell me you were coming?"

"I wanted to surprise you."

"Good job. I almost had a heart attack. Next time could you call or text me please?"

He looked at me like I was an idiot. "Well, then it wouldn't have been a surprise, would it?"

"And then you almost smothered me."

He rubbed his hand. "I didn't want you to scream and wake up the whole building."

My heart rate was finally returning to normal, I moved back over to the bed. "How did you find me?"

Matt Wheaton, who had been raised with his stepfather's surname, had the good fortune to be teaching summer classes in bio-chemistry at the University of Missouri at Columbia. The commitment of his real job had been enough to get him off the hook with Ethan and lucky enough to be released from the book tour with his father and his traveling band of merry idiots.

Matt wasn't happy about me being gone for five weeks, but Ethan was my boss. How could I say *no*?

Matt sat on the side of the bed, sucking on his hand. "I went to the camper first and woke up Millie and then Constance. What's she doing in your RV anyway? Why isn't she with Ethan?"

"Long story. Well, actually not so long. They had a big fight and she moved in with Millie and me. Since there wasn't enough room in the camper for three people and all of Constance's clothes, I was exiled to this lovely building."

"Yeah. Millie sent me here."

"How did you get in here? Isn't there like a sentry nun downstairs, guarding this bastion of virtue of the young women of Southern Missouri?"

He shrugged. "No one on duty tonight." He leaned in to kiss me. "And, by the way, I missed you."

"I missed you too."

He stood up. Within seconds, his clothes were in a pile on the floor next to the bed. He crawled under the sheet next to me.

"Yeah? Show me how much you missed me."

So, for the next two hours—in the heat, on the lumpy bed—I did.

MATT WAS SNORING. I looked at the clock on the nightstand—five. I knew I couldn't get back to sleep, so I gathered some clean clothes, shampoo and toothbrush and headed toward the communal bathroom.

The cold shower washed away the sweat and restored my hope that I might survive another day.

I dried my hair, got dressed and headed outside, just as the nuns, led by Mother Abigail, walked single-file, from the cloister to the chapel, like a mother duck and her ducklings. Sister Imelda, hurried out the door of the monastery and joined the ranks moving down the sidewalk. She looked at me, a sheepish smile on her face, and shrugged.

If Millie was up, breakfast would be in the works and I was starving, but there didn't seem to be anyone stirring in any of the motorhomes, so I headed up over the hill, to finish exploring the grounds.

I passed the gym, where Stanley and I had finally reconnected the night before. The cemetery gates were maybe fifty yards away and I headed in that direction.

The wrought-iron archway was easily wide enough to drive a hearse through. I moved among the old grave markers and monuments that told their own sad stories of the history of the college.

I was maybe eighty feet inside the sacred grounds when a scream tore through the early morning silence. A second agonizing scream followed. I hit the dirt path in a full-on run, weaving my way through the maze of gravestones, which cluttered the ground.

On the other side of a large maple, a pair of legs sprawled on the grass. I rounded the tree, Ethan Jr., lay on his back, his eyes staring, unblinking toward the leaves and the heavens above him. Kneeling over the body, blood covering the front of her tailored blouse, Constance looked up at me, a long silver knife with an engraved handle in her left hand.

"I didn't mean to hurt him," she said, so softly I could barely hear her.

CHAPTER FIVE

"**W**HAT HAPPENED?" I ASKED.
"I don't know. I just found him here. Help me. Please help," she said, her voice coming out in a breathless whisper as if she'd just run all the way up the hill. She looked at the knife as if it had mysteriously appeared in her hand and threw it on the ground. "We have to stop the bleeding. Do you know CPR?"

I looked at Ethan Jr's face again, the unblinking, unfocused eyes—the death stare.

A year's time did little to obliterate the memory of that look. People who deal with death on a regular basis somehow learn to put it in a box, somewhere in their minds for their own sanity. But for the rest of us, it's one sad, massive jolt of reality.

As a reporter, I'd been on police calls where, invariably, a dead body was found. But it all changes shape when it becomes personal. I'd met Ethan Jr. and had seen his anguish and confusion, trying to come to terms with the fact that Ethan Miller might not be his father. *This* felt very personal.

"Jessica," Constance said sharply, when I hadn't moved. "Help me!" She pulled his shirt tail out from the belt of his jeans, and pressed it against the bloody wound in his chest.

There was no hope, from what I could see. I stepped over the body and knelt beside him, feeling for a pulse—anywhere, his wrist, his neck.

I bent over, listening for the whisper of a breath, then looked at Constance. "It's too late."

"No. Please, God."

Her body deflated like a balloon. Her hand relaxed its pressure against his chest. She closed her eyes and bit her lip. Then, some low mournful sound escaped from the depths of her soul. "I didn't mean to hurt him," she repeated. Again, so softly, I wasn't sure I heard her.

I put a hand on her shoulder, then stood and walked away. On my I-phone, I dialed 9-1-1 and tried to give directions on how to find us. I wanted them to find us. I needed them to find us—fast. The dispatcher fired questions at me. I couldn't focus. Adrenaline crept up my spine.

I hung up and called Matt, waking him from sleep. "Something's happened. I need you up here at the cemetery right away. Find Ethan and tell him I need him too." I told him how to get here.

His concern was mixed with confusion. "Are you okay? What's going on?"

"Just get up here. Now."

"Jess—"

I hung up on him and called Ethan.

"I'm on my way," he said, when I explained the circumstances. "Take pictures."

"What? Why?" But he was gone.

When I finally realized what he was saying, it made sense. Pictures wouldn't lie like our memories could, once we'd had too much time to think about what we'd seen. And pictures would always be there—to go back and study, when we needed to figure out what really happened here.

I'm not sure that I would have thought of it on my own, as shock has a way of dulling your thinking.

The distraction helped center me in the moment as I aimed the lens of my camera at the body and started clicking. I got shots of the ground around Ethan Jr., and Constance still distraught, kneeling beside him, rubbing her perfectly manicured fingers across the back of his hand, as if to reassure him, and, of course, the knife now laying on the ground next to the lifeless form.

The pockets of Ethan Jr.'s pants had been turned inside out, as if it were a mugging gone terribly wrong. His phone lay on the ground three feet from his right hand. I took some tissues out of my pocket, and bent to pick up the phone, covering the screen with the tissues I held.

Ethan Jr. wasn't there by accident. He was there for a reason, and I wanted to know what that reason was. An early morning mugging at St. Jo's College would have been an astronomically random act. I wanted to see if there was anything on his phone to tell us *why* he was there, and even though things probably weren't looking good for Constance right then, I wanted to make sure they weren't going to look worse once the sheriff arrived.

Constance looked up. "What are you doing?"

"I want to see what's on here."

"You're not supposed to do that. Put it down."

"I will. Just give me a minute."

It was a little difficult to scroll the screen using tissues instead of a naked finger, but not impossible. I pulled up the main screen and glanced quickly at the apps that came to life. Nothing appeared out of the ordinary.

"What do you see?" Constance asked from her kneeling position. I shook my head. "Nothing."

I went to his texts. The last one he received came in at midnight the night before. There was no name tied to the text, just the number. *Meet me at the place at five a.m. You really screwed everything up,* was all it said.

There hadn't been much of a dialogue with this person prior to that; an accusatory argument the previous afternoon, and Ethan Jr. accusing the other of using him. But the texts were brief and only went back a few days.

Prior texts to and from other callers were bland, typical everyday stuff that we all have. And every other conversation was tied to a person's name. So, who was this other one who needed to remain anonymous?

If I forwarded the text to my phone, the police would see that immediately. "Do you have a pen? And paper?" I asked Constance.

"What?" She was rubbing his hand again, in a futile gesture of comfort.

"Paper and a pen. I need to write something down."

She was lost somewhere else. I scoured the ground. A blue pen lay on the ground next to the body, that looked like it might have fallen from Ethan Jr.'s pocket when someone was turning the pockets inside out, looking for . . . whatever. A few feet away was a lined, blue post-it note, blood spatters already soaked into the paper. I pulled up the mysterious text on his phone and copied the phone number, then gently replaced the phone where I'd found it. I started to toss the pen back in the general vicinity of where it had been next to the body, then realized my fingerprints were all over it. I shoved the pen and the post-it note into my pocket, hoping I wouldn't get searched. The bloody paper had much to tell.

Sirens blared. An ambulance carrying Mother Abigail, sitting in the passenger seat, pointing out directions and potholes, raced up the hill. Ethan and Matt arrived in the back of the sheriff's car. A deputy sheriff aimed his car at the wrought-iron fence and skidded to a stop.

The Cavalry had arrived, only too late to save any of us.

The sheriff jumped from his car, yanked open the door for Ethan, then barked orders at his staff as they cordoned off the area. The first thing he did was to separate Constance and me.

A deputy appeared and took extensive pictures of Constance's blood-stained hands, and mine, getting closeups of our palms and the backs of our hands with special attention to our fingernails. He did crime scene mugshots of both of us, making us turn around to get the backs of our clothing, then aimed the camera at our shoes.

When he was finished, the sheriff led Constance to his car. Her eyes vacant, she slipped into the backseat. Dried blood covered her hands and face. Someone handed her a towel, before the sheriff closed the door and turned away.

Ethan moved in, but the sheriff blocked him. "I want to talk to my wife."

"Later," the sheriff told him.

Sheriff Allen wasn't tall, maybe five eight, but he was solid and muscular. He reached for my arm and as I moved, I bumped up against Ethan. He looked down at me, and I palmed him my phone. It took a beat for him to realize what I was doing, then he took it and slid it into the pocket of his jeans.

The sheriff handed me off to a baby-faced deputy, who walked me to his vehicle and motioned me into the rear of the car.

I looked over and met Matt's gaze. Tall, dark haired, handsome, he was standing next to Ethan, a forty-something version of his father. I don't know if Ethan had brought him up to speed on the events of the day before, but it was obvious that, not for the first time, his family was in the middle of an ugly murder investigation. And, at the moment, his girlfriend and former stepmother were likely the primary suspects.

Once the emergency vehicles were at the scene, it didn't take long for the rest of the campus to arrive, to see what all the commotion was.

Sister Imelda came traipsing over the rise, followed by a gaggle of nuns, Dan, John, and finally the contingent of women who were there to attend Ethan's workshop the following week.

A lone female deputy in her twenties was in charge of keeping the onlookers away from the crime scene. Dan Ketner slid away from the group of women, inching his way toward the body. No one seemed to notice. He moved in behind the Coroner, a fifty-ish woman with thick auburn hair, who was studying Ethan Jr's face.

I wondered if Dan might remember Lois Westenfeld, the young man's mother and if she really was one of the women from Ethan's past that he had conveniently forgotten?

John pulled Matt off to the side near a stand of Cottonwood trees. He whispered in his brother's ear and pointed to the body in the center of the action. I assumed that he was telling him about their possible younger brother.

Sweat trickled down my back. The deputy had cracked the car windows for me, but it offered little comfort in the rising morning humidity. I glanced around, hoping someone from the sheriff's office might take pity on my and let me out of the car.

Ginny broke through the crowd, carefully making her way across the minefield of evidence markers that lay on the ground. The deputy who had escorted me to the car stepped in front of her, motioning her back. She said something to him, he nodded several times and pointed her in the direction of the sheriff who was talking to the Coroner.

Sheriff Allen looked up as Ginny approached, a dark look on his face. He pointed to the group of onlookers, but she didn't take the hint. She leaned in and said something in his ear, and then they moved toward the edge of the graveyard, away from everyone.

He listened, nodded, and turned his back on the crime scene. They moved farther away. I wondered what she could be telling him that would elicit so much interest in the middle of his investigation and I hoped, for his sake, that it entailed more than her days as homecoming queen.

The sheriff, was back. The stress that had been etched on his face since he arrived had turned to something that I couldn't read.

Ginny walked toward the sheriff's idle squad car that housed Constance, looked around, then put her head through the open window and said something in Constance's ear.

Constance turned her head to look at Ginny, who nodded and walked away.

Half an hour later, Constance and I were moved separately to the Administration Building. They took Constance to the Office of the Registrar, according to what the sign on the door said. Deputy O'Malley, the only female deputy, stood guard outside.

The young baby-faced deputy, Einwach, according to his name tag, deposited me in the Mother Superior's office. It was twice the size of Stanley's office, with beautiful dark paneled walls, plush overstuffed chairs, and a window that looked out over the fountain. I think I got the better part of the deal. Einwach stepped out into the hall and, right before the door closed behind him, I saw Ethan being led by yet another deputy into the Human Resources office.

I paced, and waited for over two hours, wondering what was going on with Constance and Ethan.

Finally, Sheriff Allen opened the door and walked in, followed
by his two underlings, Deputies O'Malley and baby-face Einwach.

Sheriff Allen took a seat behind Mother's Abigail's expansive walnut desk and waved me into the chair across from him. The deputies
flanked me on both sides. Allen, O'Malley and Einwach each had a
legal pad and almost simultaneously flipped to a fresh page.

The sheriff ran his forearm across his brow. "Miss Kallan," he
said, "this is an informal interview. You are not currently under
arrest. We are trying to gather as much information as possible in
order to aid our investigation."

I wasn't *currently* under arrest, which meant, I was definitely a
person of interest.

"What about Constance?" I asked. "Is she under arrest?"

He looked me in the eye. "No. Not at this time."

Hedged answers—I knew that's how it worked, but I'd never
been on this end of an investigation before.

"And Ethan?" I asked. "Why was he being questioned?"

He raised his eyebrows. "I'm pretty sure you can guess. He had
motive and no alibi."

"I don't think a potentially unknown child is motive."

He looked exasperated. "We will sort this all out as we go along."

Einwach read me my rights. The sheriff asked if I wanted coun-
sel. When I told him no, he nodded his head at Deputy O'Malley.
She stepped forward, did a few taps and finger swipes on her
I-phone and laid it on the desk in front of the sheriff.

"Let's get started," he said. "For the record, please state your full
name and address."

"Jessica Marie Kallan." I gave the address of Ethan's estate outside of Sedgewick, Missouri, because that's where I lived most of
the time—when I wasn't at Matt's house in Columbia.

The sheriff opened his mouth with what I assumed was
his next question, but I jumped in before he could speak. "Is
Constance okay?"

He looked at O'Malley, she met his gaze and turned toward me.
"Mrs. Miller is understandably shaken, but has been cooperating
with us on our investigation."

Police-speak, which is a language all its own. I could only speculate as to what condition Constance was in at that moment.

"We need to move forward, Miss Kallan," the sheriff said. "Time is of the essence in a murder investigation."

I nodded. "Yes. Okay."

"Please tell us your version of the events that led you to the cemetery this morning. What you saw. What you heard. Anything you remember, even if you think it's trivial, please tell us. We can sort it all out later, but the more we have to go on, the better." He stopped talking and looked at me.

Most days, I was on auto-pilot, moving through a routine so mindless, I couldn't even tell you what I ate for breakfast. But the events of that morning would be forever seared into my brain. "I woke up about five."

"Is that typical for you?" the sheriff asked.

"No. I'm not a morning person per se, but I was sleeping in the dorm and it was so damn hot, I couldn't get comfortable."

"Why were you sleeping in the dorm? I thought your group was traveling in those pimped out RV's out front." He waved his hand toward the window behind him, in front of which sat three very expensive motor homes. "I'm sure they're air conditioned."

"Well, yes, they are. I was sleeping in the dorm because," I paused. This could get sticky. Constance and I had nothing in common. We were from two very different worlds and two different generations, but I genuinely liked her. She could fly off the handle at the drop of a hat, but she was also smart, interesting, funny and surprisingly generous. I didn't know what happened in the cemetery, but I didn't want to implicate her in any way until I knew— until I had a chance to talk to her. The deck was not stacked in her favor, I didn't want to make things worse.

"Miss Kallan?"

"Constance moved into the RV I'd been traveling in. The three of us, Constance, Millie Gunderson and I thought it might be tight quarters with three people there, so I, uh, volunteered to move out to give them more space."

I could tell by the look in his eyes, that the sheriff wasn't buying it. "Wasn't she traveling with Mr. Miller? Why did she suddenly decide to move in with you?"

Okay, here's where it could get sticky. I had to tread lightly. "We've been together as a group for five weeks, in very tight quarters. I think Constance just needed some time away from Ethan for a while."

Sounded good to me. The sheriff raised an eyebrow. "Did she and Mr. Miller have a fight?"

"A disagreement of sorts."

"Was it physical?"

"No. Not that I'm aware of."

"Tell me about the incident yesterday with the deceased."

I filled him in on the events of the previous day with Ethan Jr. at the afternoon social and our group encounter in Stanley's office.

"And you'd never seen him before yesterday?" Sheriff Allen asked.

"I think he was at one of Ethan's functions at the Ritz Carlton in St. Louis three nights ago."

The sheriff cocked his head. "Why hasn't anyone else I talked to mentioned this?"

"I don't know. He stayed to himself, kind of in the background. Maybe they didn't notice him."

He focused first on Deputy O'Malley and then on Einwach. "Did anyone tell you this information?"

Einwach shook his head. He was well over six feet tall, but his round baby face, made him look like an overgrown preschooler.

"No, sir," O'Malley said.

The sheriff wrote something in his notes, then settled his gaze back on me. "Let's move on. Were you in the dorm all night?"

"Yes."

"Can anyone corroborate that for you?"

"Matt Wheaton showed up sometime between ten and midnight. I'm not sure exactly when. I wasn't paying attention."

"And he is Ethan Miller's son." It wasn't a question.

"Yes. His oldest son."

The sheriff did another swipe at the sweat on his forehead, this time with his hand. "How long did he stay."

He wasn't my mother or one of the nuns, but I was still a bit uncomfortable. "All night," I told him.

He scribbled something on his pad. "Tell me what happened after you woke up at five."

I recounted every detail I could think of—minus a few. I didn't tell him about the photos I'd taken on my phone, that I'd handed the phone off to Ethan, or about the bloodied knife Constance was holding in her hand, or what she'd said in the cemetery. *I didn't mean to hurt him.*

They had their own photos of the crime scene, Constance's fingerprints on the bloody knife were Forensics 101 and would soon be discovered. And, in all honesty, I couldn't be sure I'd heard her correctly, which could be another potentially sticky little minefield.

And I didn't tell him about Constance's covert meeting with Ethan Jr. in the middle of the night.

CHAPTER SIX

I WASN'T AS CLEVER AS I THOUGHT.

"Is there something on your cell phone, which you don't want us to see, Miss Kallan?" Sheriff Allen asked.

"No."

"Then why did you give it to Mr. Miller?"

"I didn't want it to get lost."

"I hope that's true. If there's evidence on your phone that pertains to this investigation, I need to know about it."

There was nothing on my phone that the police couldn't have observed on their own. "No, there isn't."

He stood up. "I hope that's true," he said again. "Withholding evidence is a crime."

"What happens now?" I asked.

"You and Mr. and Mrs. Miller are material witnesses to this investigation. I expect you to stay on the campus until further notice."

"And the rest of the people here for the weekend? Are they free to leave?"

"They are, but I understand there's a workshop starting on Monday and we're requesting that you move forward with the workshop and that any participants who can will also be on campus and available to us should we need more information."

There was a knock on the door, another deputy opened it and slipped inside. He was older than the sheriff and a little paunchy.

He made his way behind the desk and handed the sheriff a piece of paper.

The sheriff read it and looked up at the deputy. "Son of a bitch," he said.

The older deputy handed him a cell phone. "Sheriff Allen," the sheriff barked into the phone.

Then he was quiet as he listened to whoever was on the other end, his jaw muscles tightening. He wasn't stressed, he was pissed.

"But, sir," he finally said. More talking on the other end. Finally, he said, "Yes, sir. We will do everything we can to assist." And hung up the phone.

He looked at his team. "We're out," he said, 'let's pack it in."

I didn't understand what was going on. "What should I do if I need to get in touch with you?" I asked.

"Not my case anymore," he said. "Contact Sergeant Andrews, Violent Crime Support Unit with the State Highway Patrol."

Sheriff Allen and his deputies left me alone in Mother Abigail's office.

ON MY WAY OUT OF THE ADMIN BUILDING, I passed the open door to the Human Resources Department and glanced in. A deputy was swabbing the inside of Ethan's cheek. When he finished, he dropped the cotton swab into a glass vial and screwed on the lid. The DNA test, which Ethan had been reluctant to take, had just been taken for him.

I made my way back to the motorhome to see if Millie had anything I could eat, which, of course, she did. That's what Mille does. She cooks. When she's happy, sad, stressed or any other emotion, her caretaking gene kicks in and she cooks. The fallout for the rest of us is, we are always well-fed.

John and Matt were finishing lunch when I walked in.

I'd totally missed breakfast. Millie sat me down at the table in the big-ass RV and handed me a bag of chips, then started frying a hamburger with onion slices and her homemade barbecue sauce.

A glass of iced tea appeared in front of me and she slid into the seat next to John, on the other side of the table.

The guys had already told her the basics of what had happened. "I don't like this," she said. "I don't like this at all. Where's Constance?"

I shoved some potato chips into my mouth. "I don't know."

John pushed his plate away and brushed invisible crumbs off the table and into his hand. He looked unsettled. This, for him, was personal. His mother was implicated in the murder of his alleged half-brother.

"You okay?" I asked him.

His eyes met mine and I saw something I'd never seen before: Was it fear, compassion, concern? "I don't know."

John was a walking cliché— pushing forty and he'd never held a job as far as I knew. A man-child. The rich, playboy son of a millionaire he was tall, handsome, had thick blonde hair and deep blue eyes. His life was one big drunken party, full of beautiful women, fast cars, tropical vacations. Outwardly, there wasn't much he took seriously.

He passed a hand over his face. "Tell me what happened up there this morning, Jess."

There was something therapeutic about reliving those horrible moments again, like I could somehow distance myself from what I saw.

I told him, almost word for word, what I'd told Sheriff Allen— an edited version of the real event. As with the sheriff, I didn't tell him about the photos of the crime scene on my phone. I didn't think he was ready to see his mother kneeling over a dead body, covered in the victim's blood, the knife that had probably killed him not far from her hands. I'd leave that for Ethan.

And, I couldn't bring myself to tell him what his mother had said in the cemetery. *I didn't mean to hurt him.*

But, unlike the sheriff, I did share the fact that I'd seen his mother talking to Ethan Jr. outside the Administration Building hours before he was murdered.

That got his attention, and Matt's.

"What were they talking about?" Matt asked.

I gave him my best *I-can't-believe-you-asked-that* look. "How would I know?"

He raised his eyebrows. "Okay. Fair enough. How long did they talk?"

"Just a few minutes."

He rolled his hand at me to speed things up, an annoying gesture. "And then?"

"Ethan Jr. got up. Looked like he stormed away. Or was annoyed about something. He headed down the access road and Dan came out of the RV and caught up with him. They seemed to have a conversation going and kept walking toward the edge of the campus."

"Dan?" John asked.

"Yes, Dan."

"Didn't you find that odd?" Matt asked.

"I'm finding all of this odd. For some reason, that Ginny woman was out wandering around and approached Constance after Ethan Jr. took off. She's starting to creep me out. She's everywhere."

"I noticed her up at the cemetery this morning, talking to the sheriff," John said.

Matt looked at me. "Which one's Ginny?"

"Matronly, spiky orange hair, a little on the frumpy side. About Constance's age maybe."

He nodded. "Oh yeah, I saw her too."

John was pinned up against the wall in the booth seats at the kitchen table. "I think I need some air I'm going for a walk." He started to inch Millie off the bench so he could get out.

She stood up and rubbed his shoulder. "I can come with you, if you want some company." Millie had worked for Ethan for over thirty years. In some ways she was as much a mother to Matt and John as their own mothers. Her concern was obvious.

John stood then bent down and kissed her cheek. "Thanks. I think I need to be alone."

"I'm worried about him," Millie said, when the door closed behind him.

Matt was inching me out from our side of the booth, much like his brother had displaced Millie. "He'll be all right. Just give him some time."

I stood and Matt stood next to me. I looked up into his gray eyes. "Where's Satan?"

Matt's dog, a black lab named Satan, was almost always with him. Satan had saved my life once and I adored him. He was a big, dumb, happy dog and was a grounding force in Matt's life.

"He's not liking this heat wave," Matt said. "I left him with the neighbors, they have air conditioning, he may never come home."

"Do you want to go for a walk?" I needed time alone with Matt. I would never admit it to him, but he was *my* grounding force—the voice of reason, when things got crazy, which they often did for anyone living in Ethan Miller's shadow. But more than that, I wanted to tell him about Ethan's vasectomy—that what everyone had accused Ethan of for over twenty years, sleeping with Matt's fiancé, wasn't true.

He smiled. "Nope. I'm taking a nap. After that torture rack you made me sleep on last night in the blasted heat, I need my beauty rest. Millie has kindly offered me her bed. It's soft and comfortable and air conditioned here."

"But—"

He bent down and brushed his lips across mine. "Good night."

"But—"

"Shoo. Go away now." He turned and walked down the short hallway to Millie's room.

Millie started to gather up plates. "You can go lie down with him in my bed if you want," she said. "But no hanky panky."

"I wouldn't. But—"

She gave me a stern look. Or as stern as Millie can be. "I mean it. No hanky panky."

Well, I wasn't really in the mood for hanky panky. A nap sounded nice, but I was too keyed up, so I headed out the door.

Sr. Imelda sat on the cement bench where I'd been the night before waiting for Stanley, her blonde bangs poking out from her veil, plastered to her forehead.

She looked up as I approached, but her shy smile was gone.

"Mind if join you?"

"Please." She patted the bench next to her.

"Are you okay?" I asked.

"I will be. It's been an unsettling turn of events." A tear slid down her cheek. "I lost someone not that long ago, and you know those feelings just bubble to the surface."

She looked at me. "Not that this isn't tragic enough in its own right."

"I know the feelings and I know they can blindside you when you least expect it."

She nodded. "Most of the police left, except the ones up at the cemetery, so I'm guessing Mrs. Miller isn't a suspect?"

"I think she and Ethan and I are all primary suspects right now, and maybe everyone who was on campus last night, but they need more evidence."

She looked out at the county road.

"Who was it you lost?" I asked.

"A friend. A very dear, dear friend."

"When?"

"Last spring."

As with Stanley, the other night at the pool, I was at a loss. There was never anything to say to ease their pain. Everything that came to mind sounded empty. "I'm sorry. That wasn't very long ago," I finally said. "How old was he?"

"Fifty-three."

"Was he ill? I mean was it expected?"

She took a breath as if to steady herself. "No, he wasn't ill. He was murdered."

I'm sorry wouldn't cut it now. I couldn't even begin to imagine her anguish. I reached for her hand and gave it a quick squeeze. "Did they catch the person who did it."

She turned to look at me and her eyes were filled with more than loss and pain. "Not yet."

We sat quietly for a few minutes, looking out over the grounds and the meadow across the road. Wild flowers filled the field.

"It's beautiful here," I said. And in spite of the record-breaking heat, it was.

She nodded.

"How long have you been at St. Jo's?"

"Only a few months. I miss my old convent where my friends are. I could use them now"

A champagne colored Toyota Camry pulled onto the access road. Thirty seconds later, Stanley came to a stop behind Dan and John's RV and got out.

He walked over to us.

"What are you doing here on a Saturday?" I asked.

"Mother Abigail called and told me what happened. She wanted to meet with me. Is everyone okay?" He looked at Imelda, but she looked away.

"I think so," I said.

Stanley headed off to Mother Abigail's office.

I got the feeling that Imelda wasn't in the mood to talk. I made my way to Ethan's RV and knocked on the door.

I could hear him pounding across the floor and seconds later the door opened.

"Where the hell have you been?" he asked as I stepped up into the motorhome.

"Well, I sat cooling my heels for quite a while in Mother Abigail's office this morning, then had a nice long chat with the sheriff."

He grunted something to show his exasperation. "That was almost two hours ago. I've texted you at least ten times to get your ass over here."

I plopped down on the plush blue sofa. "Sorry, I had to take care of a few personal items first. Like food. I hadn't eaten since dinner last night. And . . ."

He raised his bushy gray eyebrows, waiting for me to finish.

"I don't have my phone," I reminded him. "I gave it to you."

He reached into an overhead compartment, pulled out my phone and handed it to me. "I finally realized that after about my tenth text. Every time I hit 'send', I'd hear a beep somewhere and couldn't figure out what was going on. Then I remembered I still had your phone."

Most people would have thought it was funny. But Ethan Miller wasn't most people. It clearly perturbed him that the phone wasn't in my hands when he texted me, and, once again, the universe wasn't responding to his needs at that particular moment.

"Did you save the pictures somewhere?" I asked.

Ethan sat down in a captain's chair across from me. "I downloaded them to my computer."

"Have you had a chance to look at them?"

"I was going over them when Constance came in to get cleaned up from . . ."

He didn't need to finish. Constance had been covered in blood when I came upon her and Ethan Jr.

"Did you see anything in the pictures that looked out of place?" I asked.

"No. Constance looked at them too."

"That must have been disturbing for her."

"It was. But she's stronger than people give her credit for."

"Did she have any comments on the pictures?"

"Not really. She recognized the knife from the chapel, but that was all."

"The chapel isn't locked. Anyone could have taken it from there."

"Tell me what went down with the sheriff."

So, I told my story, again. Except this time, I repeated what Constance had said, *I didn't mean to hurt him.*

To Ethan's credit, he didn't interrupt me once, but I could tell it took a great deal of restraint. When I got to the part about Constance's revelation, he held up his hand. "What? Say that again."

"She said, *I didn't mean to hurt him.*"

"Was she talking to you?"

"I don't think so."

Ethan got up and walked over to the window, pulling back the curtain he looked out. He stood there for almost two full minutes. Just when I wasn't sure if he'd left me, he turned. "Something's going on here."

"Well, a man got killed."

He looked at me like I was kind of stupid. "Something more. Something bigger."

"What are you talking about, Ethan?"

He sat down in the Captain's chair again and leaned forward with his elbows on his knees. In the enclosed space we weren't very far apart. "Did you wonder why Constance was so hell-bent on this fund-raiser and writer's workshop here?"

"I assumed she wanted to raise money for the college. Why? What do you think is going on?"

"I'm not sure." He stood up again. I think if we'd been in a bigger space, he would have started pacing. "When she brought it up the first time, I thought it was a nice idea and if we could fit it into the schedule, why not. But, as this book tour started to take shape, it seemed like a lot to tack on at the end when we'd all be exhausted and ready to head home."

"Constance is used to getting her way."

"Yes, she is. And sometimes, she'll dig in her heels just to make a point. But I know her very well, and this seemed different, like there was something else driving it."

"Like what?"

He looked at me. "I don't know."

I couldn't even imagine where this was going or what he thought was behind it. "You could be wrong."

He smiled. In Ethan's mind, he was never wrong. "No, there's something going on that we're not aware of."

"Aside from the dead guy who claimed to be your son?"

He cocked his head. "Yes. Aside from all that. Constance is into something deeper than we know and I think she needs our help."

"She's also suspect number one in an active murder investigation. Do you think she's guilty?"

There was no hesitation. "No."

"What about you?"

He looked surprised. "Do you mean am I guilty?"

"No. I mean, you're a suspect here too, Ethan. The sheriff thinks an illegitimate son coming out of the woodwork is a darn good motive and the fact that you were sleeping alone last night . . ."

"Don't worry about me, I can take care of myself. It's Constance's welfare I'm concerned about. Help me with this, Jessie. Help me find out what's going on."

Ethan was a proud man. He rarely asked for favors, so this must have been important to him. And as much as I hated to admit it, he was rarely wrong.

"Okay."

CHAPTER SEVEN

"WHERE'S CONSTANCE NOW?" I ASKED.

"She said she wanted to be alone and left about forty-five minutes ago. I saw her heading toward the library." Ethan looked a little lost. "Find her, Jessie. Find out what's going on with her. She likes you."

"She likes *me*?"

Ethan appeared to be as surprised by my question as I'd been by his statement. "Yes. She likes you a lot. I think she'd like to be friends with you."

Really? I didn't dislike Constance. I even liked her. She was one of those people who made life interesting, but I'd never gotten any BFF vibes from her—like *ever*.

So, once again, I headed out into the sweltering heat and made my way to the library. The door was unlocked and a nun was on duty behind the circulation desk, although I wasn't sure why. There were no students on campus—just our little traveling side-show, the nuns who lived in the monastery and the ladies in residence waiting for an audience with the great Ethan Miller.

The nun behind the desk looked to be pushing ninety. She glanced up from her magazine, smiled at me from behind her thick-lensed glasses, then put a finger to her lips to remind me of library etiquette.

I waved a greeting then moved into the dark, cool building, as far from the heat as I could get.

Three white-marbled steps led down from the entryway and the circulation desk, into the bowels of the library and thousands of reference books filling aisles of floor-to-ceiling wooden bookshelves.

Polished oak woodwork ran the perimeter of the room and the outside shelves. The beautiful oak slithered up the walls to frame the long-paned windows. Even though the windows looked new—circa this century—the old wooden rods with the metal tips, used a hundred years ago to open the top sash of the original windows, still hung on the walls.

I ventured down an aisle and continued until I'd covered the entire first floor. Constance was nowhere to be found. A marble stairwell at the back of the large room led me to the second-floor stacks and computer lab. Ethan's missing ex-wife wasn't among them.

I continued to the third floor, which appeared to house the entire history of the college with memorabilia from by-gone days. At the back of the room, Constance sat cross-legged on the floor, a stack of old yearbooks in front of her. White cotton shorts and a hot pink tank top showed off her tanned and toned body. She absently pushed her hair behind her ears.

Constance was a beautiful woman. Even the surgical nips and tucks over the years didn't diminish the fact that her smooth skin and delicate features were gifts of nature and genetics. She and her son, John, had the same blue eyes and captivating smile. She was a softened version of his handsome features. Her hair was blonde like his, and even in the midst of an emotional thunderstorm, there was always a glint of mischief in her eyes.

She didn't even look up. "What took you so long?"

At first I thought she was expecting someone else. "Were you waiting for me?" I slid to the floor across from her and leaned up against the metal shelving. The marble slab a cool relief to my backside.

She finally met my gaze and smiled. "Of course."

I raised an eyebrow.

"I'm pretty good at reading people, Jessica. I know your background and I knew, eventually, you'd need to find out what happened. Leaving the answers to someone else, like the police, isn't in your makeup. And, I know Ethan. This is driving him crazy to have something touch our lives that's out of his control. I knew he'd send you to find me."

"I'm impressed."

"You needn't be. I didn't get where I am in life without paying attention to other people's signals."

"And where are you in life?"

"I'm the ex-wife of Ethan Miller."

She smiled again and we left it at that. I think we both understood what she was saying. As much as Ethan liked to think he could maneuver people like human chess pieces to get his own way, someone else had called the shots at one time in his life, and he was the pawn for a change. It had its own poetic justice that Ethan Miller, master manipulator, had been played.

"What are you doing up here, Constance? A little jaunt down memory lane?"

She looked me in the eye, but all the joy had slipped away. "Something like that. I couldn't get Lois Westenfeld's name out of my mind. I knew it from somewhere. Look."

She took the yearbook she had in her lap and turned it around so I could see. There was a freshman picture of a rather plain young woman, smiling at the camera. She wasn't terribly attractive. Maybe average, maybe a little less, but there was a sweetness to her smile and her young face seemed full of hope and promise. She looked like someone I would like to know more about.

"She went to school with you?"

Constance reached out and took the book, tracing the edges of Lois's picture. "No, she was six years behind me."

"Then how could you remember her?"

"Her older sister, Judy, was in my class. Lois used to come on weekends to visit her. She was a nice, quiet girl. Nice family."

"I wonder where she is now?"

"Easy enough to find out."

I took out my phone and went to a Google search, typed in Lois' name and state and voila! Five Lois Westenfelds in Missouri appeared. It probably wouldn't take much time or effort to figure out which one was Ethan Jr.'s mother.

"Did you know this is where Ethan and I met?" she asked.

"Here in the library? Or here at St. Jo's?"

She rolled her eyes. "St. Jo's, silly."

"Tell me about it."

"I think he'd just had his first best-seller, young and handsome and still making a name for himself. This was before Dan came along and Ethan's agent was booking him all over the place for book signings and speaking engagements."

Forty years ago, Ethan, with his rugged good looks, would have been a popular celebrity among the coeds.

Constance put down the yearbook she was holding, picked up another one and thumbed through the pages. "Look."

She handed it to me. There he was, surrounded by adoring young women. That would be Ethan's version of heaven on earth.

"So, did you actually meet him then?" I asked.

Constance took the book and stared at the picture. She nodded. "I went to hear him speak, mostly because my friends had read his book and wanted to go, but when I was sitting there in the audience, I knew I had to find a way to meet him."

"And?"

She looked at me and smiled. "The other girls flocked the stage when he was finished talking, asking for autographs and if he would pose for a picture with them. I think he had a book signing afterwards. While everyone was busy giggling, trying to get his attention, I went outside and found his car and climbed into the driver's seat and waited."

"How long?"

"About an hour. I didn't mind. Look how things turned out."

I could picture the whole thing. "Didn't the other girls follow him out to the car?"

She laughed. "St. Josephine's College for Women? Forty years ago? The nuns watched us like hawks—or tried to. They'd opened a Pandora's box just letting Ethan come and talk, but they thought they had control of the situation. After the book signing, all the girls were herded back to the dorm."

"Except Constance."

"Except little Connie Zahowski."

"Yikes. Zahowski?"

"Right? Miller was a welcome change. I would have married him just for that."

Constance stretched. I was starting to enjoy this alone time with her. If a young man hadn't been murdered only hours ago and she and I weren't the primary suspects, this would have been great fun.

I reached for the book again, looking at the black and white photo of Ethan. "Okay, so all the girls are shooed back to the dorm, what happened when Ethan got to the car?"

A self-satisfied smile lit up her face. "All the nuns were gone. I waited, and then Ethan appeared . . ."

She stopped. The story was just getting good and she stopped. She and Ethan were great for dramatic pauses, but it left the rest of us hanging, which was the whole point, I guess.

"Dammit, Constance! What happened next."

She leaned her head back and closed her eyes, a dreamy look on her face. "When Ethan realized there was a wayward college girl waiting for him, who took the initiative to do something different from the other girls, he was flattered. He scooted me over, so he could get in and drive, invited me to dinner and we drove off into the sunset."

"Wait a minute. If the nuns were so Gestapo-like in their surveillance tactics, didn't they do bed checks or something?"

She opened her eyes. "My roommate was used to covering for me if I didn't make it back to the dorm by curfew. We all covered for each other. The sisters would have gone berserk if they knew what we were doing half the time."

I did the rolling hand-gesture, like Matt had done to me, to get us back into the story. "So, you left the campus with Ethan . . ."

"Oh right. Ethan was staying at a motel about twenty minutes from here. We headed back there. There was an all-night café across the highway and Ethan and I went there and talked all night—or, most of the night. We talked until three or four in the morning. And then we went back to his room." She paused and smiled again. "And six months after I graduated, we were married."

I liked the story. It was kind of sweet, in its own sordid way. And it was a nice picture to have of Ethan and Constance when they were young.

She had about five yearbooks on the floor next to her. I picked up the top one and looked at the date, it would have been from Constance's sophomore year, if my math was correct.

I thumbed toward the back, and found her picture. Pretty girl, but more wholesome than she was today, with less glamour to hide behind. It was fun looking at the hairstyles and clothes from a generation I hadn't been a part of.

I scanned the girls on the opposite page, then stopped. I looked up, Constance was watching me, but there was no mischief in her eyes, as there had been moments before. Our gaze met and her face confirmed what I'd just discovered.

I looked down again at the girl on the opposite page. The face of a former Homecoming Queen, smiling up at me: Virginia Clude—Ginny.

"I didn't know you two had gone to school together," I said.

She nodded. Her gaze held mine for a moment. "She was actually a sophomore when I started college. She was a year ahead of me, but took a year off and then came back to school, so we graduated together."

I looked down at Ginny. Something made me turn the page back toward the front. Another familiar face, then another page and another girl whose aged face was stuck in my recent memory.

Twenty. That's how many I counted by the time I'd gone through the whole class, that's how many women were signed up to take Ethan's writing class on Monday, that's how many had been at the social hour the day before—twenty.

And then there was Mother Abigail, or Abby Vargas back then, wearing the nursing cap of the school in honor of her chosen profession. Almost half the girls in the class were nurses.

I looked at Constance. "Mother Abigail?"

"Abby was probably the best student in our class. She took college very seriously, unlike the rest of us. She came from a very poor but devout family, and got in on a full-scholarship. I think she was the first in her family to go to college."

"Impressive."

"She is impressive. I think St. Jo's is still here because of her and her fundraising efforts to keep the school going. She has single-handedly brought in hundreds of thousands of dollars over the years. St. Jo's would have died out long ago if not for her."

"What do you mean?"

She glanced up at me. "An all-girls Catholic college isn't the first choice for young people these days. Even their parents aren't interested in such a parochial setting anymore."

"How do you know all of this?"

"I was on the Board of Trustees for several years."

Interesting, but it was hardly relevant. We had more pressing matters than the fate of this institution of higher learning. "Why are all of you here this weekend? Is it some kind of reunion for your graduating class?"

She shrugged. "Unofficially perhaps."

"Meaning the college is unaware of the reason for the gathering?"

"Perhaps."

Our moment of closeness had vanished. Her vague answers were pissing me off. "I don't want to play cat and mouse with you. Whatever's going on, does Ethan know?"

"No, he doesn't, and don't tell him." But it wasn't an entreaty, it was a command.

"Why?"

"Because he'd try to stop us."

A chill ran up my spine. "I don't even know what I'm not supposed to tell him. Constance, what the hell is going on?"

She took the yearbook and placed on top of the pile on the floor next to her and stood up, so gracefully, you wouldn't have guessed that she was carrying around more than six decades on her small frame. She reached for my hand and pulled me up.

"Let's take a walk," she said.

CHAPTER EIGHT

W E RETRACED MY STEPS DOWN THE STAIRWELL, past the circulation desk, the old nun and out again into the oppressive humidity.

Constance nodded toward the hill that ran behind the buildings and I followed a few feet behind her. At the top of the rise was a dirt path, heading off to our left, and she took it.

The path flanked the perimeter of the cemetery, a rusty, wrought-iron fence separating us from the gravesites a few feet away. From where we were, I couldn't see any Sheriff's deputies, but I had no doubt that law enforcement was nearby, combing the crime scene for anything they could find to aid in their investigation.

On one side was the cemetery, on the other a wall of Pin Oak and Silver Maple trees, which provided much needed shade. The fact that I could identify one tree from the other and most of the wildflowers was the price I paid for dating a man with a doctorate in Biochemistry and Plant Pathology— Matt.

Constance and I hadn't said a word to each other since we left the third floor of the library. I was curious to see where she was taking me, and equally curious to find out if we would get caught— two murder suspects returning to the scene of the crime.

After about three hundred yards of variegated rusted spikes, integrated with occasional black posts of wrought-iron fencing, we came to an opening, an archway, complete with seraphim hovering overhead, guarding the entrance—either welcoming us in or keeping evil at bay.

Once inside the gate, an old brick road half-appeared, the other half buried by decades of neglect.

"Where are we?" I asked.

"The back of the cemetery." Constance kept moving.

"How far are we from the crime scene."

She stopped and pointed off to her right, as the crow flew, I assumed. I couldn't see anything that resembled where Ethan Jr.'s body had been. "We're pretty far away. It's a big cemetery. We can talk, they won't hear us."

She started walking again, but I stayed put. When she realized I wasn't with her anymore, she stopped and turned toward me. "What?"

"I want to know what's going on and where we're headed. And why."

She walked back and took my hand, pulling me into movement. "Trust me."

"Trust might not be the issue, here," I said. "It's more about keeping my ass out of jail."

"You're *fine*, just trust me."

She wound an unidentifiable path off the brick road, over and around and through gravestones. If I had to run for my life, I wouldn't have a clue which way to go.

She came to a grouping of markers that were relatively new, compared to the ones dating back over a hundred years, then moving down the row to the one second to the end, stopping in front of a large black granite monument.

"This is where I was this morning. This is where I was coming from last night when I ran into you and Stanley."

I moved in beside her. The front of the monument had flowers engraved on both sides. The name etched between the strands of roses was *Barbara J. Baker*. It meant nothing to me, until I saw the year Barbara died. It was on April fifth, the same year Constance graduated from college. I looked to see when she was born. They would have been the same age.

"A classmate of yours?" I asked.

She ran her hand over the smooth, polished granite. "More than a classmate. My best friend."

"I'm sorry. She was so young. What happened?"

"You want the long or short version?"

"Whichever one you need to tell."

She planted her bottom on the monument and looked at me. "Barb was my best friend. You would have liked her. She was smart and had a wicked sense of humor. We were always getting into trouble. One night, during our freshman year, we got drunk and sneaked into the priory and stole the nuns' underwear from the laundry room."

I have to admit that was pretty funny. "Barb's idea?"

"Yes. She was laughing so hard she woke up some of the nuns. We almost got caught, but got out of there just in time."

I moved over to one of the other monuments and sat down. I was coming to understand that Constance had to tell a story in her own way and in her own time. I waited for her to go on.

"I was from St. Louis. Barbie was from Kansas City. In the summers, we only got together a couple of times, when one of us could talk our dads into letting us take the car for a road trip. But it was okay. When we came back to school in August, we would talk for weeks, trying to catch up."

I watched her face. I could see the story take place right before my eyes. Every emotion Constance felt was right there for the world to see.

"When we came back for our senior year, we were all so excited. We'd made it. This was our last hurrah and then out into the world, but not Barbie. She didn't share in our joy. I was worried about her. She was sick all the time. She had no appetite, couldn't keep food down, kind of moody, but not in a PMS-y sort of way. I wanted her to see a doctor, but she refused. Every time I pushed her, she'd start to cry. Which scared me more."

I had an inkling where this was going.

"Finally, I told her if she wouldn't go to the infirmary, that I was going to call her mother to come and get her and take her to a doctor back home."

Constance swatted at the gnats that were swarming around her face. "Well, my threat worked. She agreed to go see someone, but she didn't want to go to the infirmary on campus, so we found a doctor a couple of towns over . . ."

She looked at me. "You guessed it, right?"

"She was pregnant."

"Yup. She had a boyfriend back home. They broke up right before she came back to school, but, you know . . ."

"It was too late."

"Jessica, I don't know if you can understand this, but when it came to unwed mothers, it was a whole different world back then."

"I thought you guys were part of the sexual revolution."

She snorted. "Yeah right. We were all having sex, but that's as far as the revolution had gotten."

The gnats had found me and seemed to have brought in reinforcements. They were buzzing in my eyes, my ears, my nose. I couldn't swat them away fast enough.

"I don't follow," I said.

"We were still nice girls from good Catholic families and expected to be virgins on our wedding nights. We had the pill, we had sex, but the expectations hadn't changed. It was okay to have sex until you got pregnant. Then we were right back in Victorian England. The shame was too much. And no one—absolutely *no one*—wanted their parents to know."

"So, what did Barb do?"

"She was terrified to tell her parents. The jerk who got her pregnant was useless. She couldn't tell the nuns and she was less than a year away from graduating. She didn't want to quit school. All she had was us, her equally naïve friends."

"Who was that? The women who are here for Ethan's workshop?"

"Most of them were part of our circle. We had a meeting in our dorm one night and Barb told everyone what was going on. We all cried for her, but we knew it could have been any one of us."

Constance looked down at her hands. "I wanted to help her. We all wanted to help her. So, we came up with a plan. She would keep going to class and hide the pregnancy."

"You really were naïve. How do you hide a pregnancy? And what were you going to do when the baby came?"

She rubbed her forehead. "It was a stupid plan, but we were determined to try. Barbie was going to keep going to classes and started wearing baggy clothes. She was tall, so we were hoping that she wouldn't show. Much. And by the time the baby came, we'd only have about a month until graduation, we decided that we would take turns watching the baby in the dorm and hide it whenever the Dorm Mother was around."

It sounded like a plan concocted by a bunch of ten-year olds, instead of a group of intelligent, well-educated young women.

"And what did you plan to do when she went into labor?" I asked, but I already knew the answer.

"This is a nursing school. Half the girls in our class were going to be RN's. How hard would it be to deliver a baby?"

"Right. Complications during delivery never come up."

Constance made a face. "We were twenty-two effing years old, trying to protect our friend. It's not like we were thinking it through beyond the obvious."

I'd once been a twenty-two-year old girl myself not that long ago, in love—for two years, I might add—with my obviously gay coworker. "Okay. I understand. So, what happened to Barb?"

"We thought we had it. We thought we were going to make it. It got a little dicey at times, but we worked it out. When Barb went home for Christmas, she still wasn't showing much, and she told her parents that she was recovering from mono, so needed a lot of rest before coming back for her final semester. That was a good cover because they didn't expect much of her."

A squirrel ran full-speed from out behind a grave marker. I screamed, he stopped to look at me, then turned and ran the other way.

Constance's eyes got big and she put a finger to her lips, exactly like the library nun. We listened, waiting to see if deputies would come crashing through the cemetery, guns drawn.

Five minutes later Constance took a breath. "I think we're okay. Where was I?"

"Barb went home for Christmas and told her parents she had mono."

"Right. So, we made it to our last semester and I have to say we really were pulling together to help Barbie through this thing. None of the usual pettiness or backbiting that happens when a bunch of girls live together."

"Wait a minute, what was Barb going to do after the baby came?"

"We'd thought of that. She had an aunt in Springfield. A pretty cool aunt who she thought would keep her secret. She was going to go live with her and get a job there. Later, when the baby was older, she'd tell her parents she adopted the baby, or it was a friend's baby and her friend had died so she was raising it." She saw the look on my face. "I know. We didn't have a clue what we were doing. There wasn't a lot of planning down the road."

I swatted more gnats and shifted on the hard granite surface beneath me. "Did Barb ever think of giving the baby up for adoption?"

"At first, that was her plan. But when she got to the point where she could feel the baby kick and move, it all became real to her and she didn't think she could give it away."

Constance was somewhere back forty years ago. I could see it in her eyes. Through much of the story, there was a wistful melancholy, for a part of her life and the lives of her friends that was gone forever. But now, as we approached the end of the story, the melancholy slipped into sadness.

She got up and walked over to the adjoining plot. There was no monument there, only a small gravestone. She bent down and brushed the dirt away, although it was obvious someone had done that very recently, and I was pretty sure it was her.

I stood up and moved in behind her. In the corner of the small gray stone was a lamb, in the center, Rosalee Baker, who died with her mother on that day in April forty years ago.

Tears came to my eyes. Not one piece of this story was a surprise. I think I knew when we started where it would take us. And sadly, it was not unique. But seeing that small reminder that a baby had come into this world and then left so quickly, filled me with an unexpected sorrow.

I pulled myself together. "What happened to Barb?"

Constance looked over her shoulder. "I don't know."

She stood and walked back to sit on Barb's monument. I followed and ended up back at my perch.

"Barbie went into labor one night after dinner. Oh my God, this is how stupid I was—I thought, good, she'll have the baby tonight and I can still make my eight o'clock English Lit class the next morning."

"Where was she when she was in labor?"

"In the dorm. There was a vacant room down the hall from us and we put her there. We didn't think anyone could hear her at the end of the building. We took turns sitting with her, holding her hand, trying to encourage her. We all pulled together. Even Abby Vargas—Mother Abigail—jumped in. Early on, she didn't want any part of it, because the baby had been conceived out of wedlock. It was a sin and she couldn't condone it. She was going to enter the convent the next fall and didn't get involved in a lot of the wild stuff the rest of us did. But she was a trained nurse, and she stepped up to the plate and took over."

"Were you surprised?"

"Yes and no. She had higher moral standards than the rest of us, I guess. But she was also a nurse and a soon-to-be nun, two professions that require a great deal of compassion. And, no matter what she thought of us or our life choices, we were all relieved to have her take over. She was at the top of her class and was going to be a kick-ass nurse."

I wondered if Mother Abigail would be flattered by that description of her.

"Barb's in labor. At some point this took an unexpected turn."

She looked down at her feet, her three hundred-dollar sandals and her painted toenails. "It took a very bad turn. About midnight, Abby came running down the hall and pounded on my door. I was sleeping, getting ready to take the two a.m. shift with Barbie. I opened the door, and by that time, half the floor was awake and in the hallway. Abby told me we had to do something quick. We had to get Barb to the hospital."

Constance hugged herself and continued to study her toes. I wondered if she'd ever shared this story with anyone and whether or not it was a good idea right now. She took a breath. "I ran down the hall and when I got to the room," her voice faltered. "Oh my God. There was blood *everywhere*. It looked like a crime scene—worse than anything we saw this morning."

She finally looked up at me. "Barb was unconscious. We couldn't revive her. Abby said we *had* to get her to a hospital. Somehow, I couldn't even tell you how we did it, we got her down the elevator and into someone's car."

"You didn't call 9-1-1?"

"We didn't think of it. That's how stupid we all were. I'm not sure there was 9-1-1 back then, but we didn't even think of it."

"How far away is the nearest hospital?"

"About twenty-five miles. But Abby said there was a retired doctor about two miles from here who could help us. So, we took her there. The doctor had a makeshift clinic attached to his house from when he was in practice. We got her inside and he shooed us all out, except for Abby. It was the longest night of my life, Jessica."

And I knew how the story ended. We were sitting at the finale.

"About six in the morning, he came out and told us that Barbie didn't make it."

"And the baby?"

"She lived for about an hour, but then she was gone too. I guess, in a way, that was a small blessing. That, after all they'd been through that they were together. I didn't even get to hold her."

We were both quiet, then Constance said, "We were a bunch of spoiled, sheltered girls. None of us had been touched yet, by life's cruelties. That was the night we all had to grow up."

"Why are they buried here? Why not Kansas City near Barb's family?"

It felt like the temperature had dropped some since we'd been in the cemetery.

Constance ran a hand through her hair. "Her parents were unforgiving about the pregnancy. Well, her father was. I think her mother would have come to terms with it – but they didn't want her in the family plot back home. They came for the funeral, but left right afterwards. Two closed caskets. That was all they saw of their daughter and granddaughter."

CHAPTER NINE

CLOUDS WERE MOVING IN FROM THE WEST. The temperature had dropped to something slightly above bearable, but sill an improvement.

"I'm so sorry, Constance. I'm sorry for all of this. Is this why so many of your classmates are here this week?"

She glanced up at the sky then back at me. "Sort of. I ran into Ginny and when she found out Ethan was coming here, we emailed our old group to see if anyone else wanted to come. It's been ages since we've all been together. And Ginny and I thought it might be a good memorial gathering to remember our friend that we lost."

I watched her face. I wasn't sure that's all there was to it. It seemed, with Constance, there was always something smoldering just below the surface. Maybe that was her great appeal to Ethan—he liked living on the edge."

We both stood.

"Did you believe Ethan about the vasectomy?" I asked.

"After I thought about it, yes. I know Ethan pretty well. I know he would never have done that to me."

"Then why the theatrics?"

She shrugged. "It caught me off guard."

This was stuff Matt needed to know. He'd worked hard over the years to rebuild a relationship with his father in spite of what he thought had happened with his former fiancé. But the healing wasn't complete. Matt needed to know about Ethan's vasectomy—that Ethan was innocent.

"How do you feel about the vasectomy?" I asked. "About him not even consulting you?" On some level I respected Ethan's decision not to bring more children into the world, knowing he wasn't a very good father, but, it was also typical Ethan Miller behavior, thinking he knew what was in everyone's best interest—like his wife at the time, who clearly wanted to have more children. I know I would have been very angry that he had taken the choice away from me without even discussing it or asking for my input.

She thought about it. "I don't know how to answer that. If I'd known at the time, our marriage probably would have ended years before it actually did. I truly thought I wanted more children. Ethan had no right to make that decision on his own, but thinking about it for the past twenty-four hours, I realize that it really was the best for all of us."

"All of whom?"

"Ethan, John and me. Ethan admitted he wasn't a very good father. The truth is, I probably wasn't a very good mother. I love John more than I've ever loved another human being, but . . ."

I waited. And waited. I swore that the Millers were in cahoots to drive me insane with all the dramatic pauses. Finally, before insanity took hold, "But *what*?"

A hint of sadness was in her eyes, then it was gone. "I'm not any better than Ethan. My son was raised by two self-absorbed people, and that's putting it mildly. I don't think I would have truly wanted the burden of another child. And, believe me, John was more than enough to handle."

"If you know Ethan didn't cheat on you, does that mean you're moving back into his RV?" I tried to keep the hopefulness out of my voice. I'm not sure I was successful.

Constance laughed. "No, no, no. I'll let him stew for a while."

Whatever their dysfunctional dynamic, it was taking its toll on my life. I didn't think I'd survive another night in the dorm, and I was pretty sure I wouldn't be able to talk Matt into suffering with me.

"When I found you this morning next to Ethan Jr.'s body, you said, *I didn't mean to hurt him*."

Her eyes suddenly filled with tears and she brushed them away.

"Constance?"

She took her time regaining her composure, but I hoped it wasn't a stall to come up with a believable story. I seriously did like her, and I wanted to know that she was innocent.

"I couldn't sleep last night," she said, "so I got up. Those damn tin cans Ethan has us living in are so small, I didn't want to wake Millie, so I went outside. That young man was there."

I don't think I'd heard her say his name. Some form of denial that he really might be tied to her former husband?

She leaned her backside against Barb's tombstone again. "He was sitting on that bench outside the Admin Building when I went outside. Scared me to death, I didn't expect to see anyone. Anyway, we started talking and I wasn't very nice to him—even though I don't believe Ethan cheated on me, I didn't like what that young man was doing to us."

"I'm not sure he was doing anything. He was raised believing Ethan really was his father."

She bit her lip. "I know," she said softly. "I thought about that after I went to bed. I'd even planned on apologizing to him if I saw him again. I just hadn't planned on seeing him the way I did."

Her voice broke at the end. I gave her a minute. "So, you didn't mean to hurt him, meant that you didn't mean to treat him the way you did?"

"Yes."

It was plausible I guess, but I didn't want to be stupid. Stupid was never a good operating platform when you were in the middle of a murder investigation with a possible suspect. I wasn't afraid of Constance. I didn't think she was a murderer. But, stuff happens and I needed to pay attention.

"Did you know him from before?" I asked.

"No." It came out harshly. She softened it. "No," she repeated.

"He was in St. Louis when we were there."

She shrugged, then pushed off from the marker she was leaning against. "I didn't know that."

She turned toward the back entrance we'd come through when we arrived and I put out a hand to stop her. "Do you know how to get over to where we found the body, going the back way?"

She nodded. "I know every inch of this cemetery. Why?"

"I want to see what's going on, but I don't want to get close enough for them to see us. Can you get us over there?"

"Absolutely."

It was another circuitous route, that I never would have found on my own. Seven or eight minutes later, and a ton of new scratches on my legs as we made our way through the unkempt sections of the cemetery, we moved in behind a mausoleum.

Constance bobbed her head to the right. "Over there," she mouthed.

I crouched down and poked my head around the corner of the mausoleum. The sheriff was right, it wasn't his case anymore. Men with vests that said CIB—Violent Crimes Support Unit—were combing the scene, taking pictures and samples in evidence bags. Other than the fact that Ethan Jr. was gone, not much had changed since earlier in the day—except the actors.

I didn't know enough about Missouri murder investigations to know if this was a typical turn of events or who had jurisdiction. I only knew that the sheriff had been pissed to be booted off the case.

There wasn't anything we could do or look at as long as the troopers were here, and I guess this scene told me what I needed to know right now. I signaled to Constance to head out and she led the way to Barb's grave and out the back way of the cemetery. We followed the path around the perimeter and zigzagged our way down the hill.

Ginny sat on the cement bench where she'd found Constance the night before, thumbing through a bunch of computer printouts on her lap. She looked up and smiled at us when we approached.

"Have a nice walk," she asked. The print-outs—reports and emails from what I could see—disappeared into an oversized leather satchel.

"Therapeutic," Constance said.

A local television news crew was packing up their van, another station already heading off-campus. Stanley's car was still parked in front of the Admin Building. I nodded at Ginny and headed toward the front entrance.

The Director of Communications was sitting behind his desk when I opened the door. Feet up on the windowsill, he faced the windows.

He glanced over his shoulder when I walked in. His feet fell to the floor with a thud and he swiveled around in his chair until he was facing me. "Where were you? I could have used you about an hour ago."

I took the chair across from him. "Press releases?"

"Yup. It feels different when you're on this side of them. I figured once I came to St. Jo's, my days of hard news were behind me. All I'd have to be concerned about from here on out would be Lacrosse scores, swim tournaments and introducing new staff to the community and alumni."

"It never ends, I guess. Is that why Mother Abigail called you in?"

"Damage control. She wanted to make sure that whatever was put out there would in no way reflect negatively on the reputation of the college. Enrollment has been down in the past few years. She didn't want to lose any prospective parents, afraid to send their daughters here. Tough to put a neutral spin on a murder story that happened on the campus and doesn't implicate us or scare people away."

He was keyed up. I could see it on his face. Whether from the murder itself or being responsible for the future of the college, in how he presented his facts, I wasn't sure. But the truth was, we were all keyed up. It just came out in different ways.

I looked into his blue eyes. "I'm sure you did fine. That's what you're good at."

"Let's hope I still have the magic touch."

"Who all was here?"

"A couple of area papers and television channels. CNN out of St. Louis."

"CNN?"

"Ethan Miller is a big draw."

I wondered about our old paper. "Anyone from the *Trib* in Omaha?"

"I called it in this morning. Got Bob Elliot's replacement, Doug somebody."

"Doug Reynolds," I said automatically. Bob Elliot was our former editor, now retired.

"Yeah him. Now that Eric's gone, I figured I was safe. I asked for an exclusive." He winked at me.

The wink felt a little creepy. Ethan Jr. was dead. Eric Amundson, our former publisher, had died a couple of years ago, and Stanley was capitalizing on this recent tragedy. He wasn't a reporter anymore—he didn't need to compete in that arena. But, I knew from experience that old habits die hard, and an exclusive was an exclusive.

"So, what was the deal between you and Eric?" I asked.

He shrugged. "Personally? I think he was a homo-phobe."

"That doesn't sound like Eric at all."

He looked at me. "Maybe you didn't see it because you're not gay. Or," he paused for a beat, "maybe you didn't want to."

"What does that mean?"

He smiled, but it was forced. "Come on, Jess, you were Eric Amundson's golden girl. He doted on you. If you saw the darker side of him, it might not have been quite so easy to enjoy the ride, would it?"

This was a side of Stanley I'd never seen and I wasn't liking it. I stood. "I think I'll go find a place to cool off. And for the record, I worked my ass off at the *Trib*. Maybe that's what Eric saw in me."

On his desk was a Mizpah necklace, or half of one. The Mizpah is a piece of jewelry usually shared by two people who have a strong emotional bond, sometimes they're separated by distance, sometimes by death. It's based on the Old Testament verse in Genesis, "The Lord watch between me and thee, when we are absent one from another." The pendant for the necklace often looks like a coin split down the middle with a jagged line, the words from the Scripture split down the middle as well. One person has half of the pendant, the other person wears the other half.

I picked up the Mizpah on Stanley's desk. It was not like the others I'd seen. The chain and background of the medallion were silver, two golden hearts in the middle, broken by the jagged line. Most are not expensive, they're worn for the emotional connection to the person the necklace is shared with, rather than the cost of the medallion. I wasn't an expert, but I guessed the gold used might be eighteen to twenty-four karats, more high-end than most.

I turned it over in my hand. "This is beautiful."

Stanley reached for it. "It was Peter's."

"I'm sorry."

I think Stanley was done with me for the time-being, I turned and left. Too many ghosts were haunting us today. I needed a break.

CHAPTER TEN

I WAS BARELY OUT THE DOOR AND back into the heat, when my cell phone rang. A deep, gravelly voice greeted me. At least, I think it was a greeting. I couldn't tell.

"Speak of the devil," I said.

"I'm guessing my name came up somewhere and I can guess with whom."

"I'm sure you can," I told Bob Elliot, my former editor at the *Omaha Tribune*.

"What the hell have you gotten yourself into now, Jess?"

Bob had probably mentored me at the *Trib*, as much as Eric Amundson had. After Eric passed away, and the paper fell into the hands of his idiot son, Hank, Bob couldn't get to retirement fast enough. He was a total stereotype—a tough, gruff old newspaper man. A throwback to when newspapers were still a major source of news. He'd taught me a lot. I respected him and trusted his judgement and considered him my friend.

"What have you heard?" I found myself seated on the uncomfortable cement bench, hoping our conversation might be brief and I could sneak into the RV and cool off and get some of Millie's food before I was sent into exile again.

"A young man, Ethan Miller, Jr., who claimed to be the son of best-selling author, Ethan Miller, was murdered this morning. His body found in the cemetery on the grounds of St. Josephine's

College for Women in Missouri. Ethan Miller is currently in-residence, preparing for a writer's workshop next week. The body was discovered by Ethan Miller's ex-wife, Constance, and a former staff writer for the *Omaha Tribune*, Jessica Kallan." He sounded like he was reading a press release.

"Well, see. You know as much as I do. Who told you? Doug Reynolds, your protégé?"

"Yes, he did. Called me this morning after he talked to Stanley. Woke me up. Eight effing o'clock in the morning. Doesn't he know I'm retired? So, what's the deal with Stanley? How'd the two of you end up in the same place at the same time? Was that planned?"

Sweat ran down my back. "Pure coincidence. Stanley is the Director of Communications for the college now. Constance is the one who spearheaded the workshop. This is her alma mater."

Bob was quiet. I hated when he did that. It meant he was thinking, mulling things over. And he was always two steps ahead of me, even though I was the one in the middle of a murder investigation and he was more than three hundred miles away.

"I thought Stanley was going to make a name for himself in San Francisco," Bob said.

"That was his plan after he left the *Trib*."

Bob grunted. "He didn't *leave* the *Trib*, Jess."

"What are you saying?"

"He was fired. Eric fired him."

Now I was quiet. That was news to me. "Are you sure?"

"I was there when Eric let him go."

"Stanley's a hell of a writer," I said. "Why would Eric fire him?"

"Because he was a bum, and a liar, and a cheat."

"That didn't take long to come up with those attributes. What happened?"

"You're right. Stanley's a good writer. He could have gone far. But, he's lazy. Most of what he turned in was fluff, because he wasn't willing to go out and do the hard news. And toward the end, well . . ."

"Well, what?"

"Remember Joan Segley?"

"She got hired right before Stanley . . . left."

My pause was not lost on him. He grunted again. "Joan Segley, turned in a piece about the City Councilor who got a DUI. Not his first, I might add. A well-written and well-researched piece. At least we think it was Joan's story. Somehow it got submitted under Stanley's byline and that's how it was printed. Joan went to Eric to tell him it was her story."

This whole thing was making me uncomfortable. Even after all these years, I still felt a sense of loyalty to Stanley. "And how do you know it wasn't Stanley's story?"

"Joan had a list of all her data research and contacts. The writing didn't sound like anything Stanley had ever submitted."

"But you couldn't prove it?"

"We couldn't prove it."

"So, how would that be grounds for dismissal?" It was a dumb question, really. I trusted Bob. I trusted Eric Amundson. But I still couldn't let go of what I'd once felt for Stanley. I didn't want to believe he would do something so slimy.

"Eric had been documenting Stanley's transgressions for over a year. There was enough to let him go even without Joan's accusations"

I was a trained investigative reporter, how could I have been so blind to who Stanley was? But I was in love, and love and stupidity seem to go hand in hand.

"Bob, do you still have connections at the paper?"

"Of course."

"Could you run some background checks for me? I'd do it myself, but yours would be quicker and more thorough."

"Send me the names and whatever else you have." You'd never know it by the sound of his gravelly voice that always seemed to hover right on the edge of *why are you bothering me with this*, but I knew him well enough to know that he was grateful to be involved in this thing.

We talked for awhile longer, until I knew I needed to hit the air-conditioned RV or pass out where I sat. "I'll send you the names of the people I need you to run checks on."

"Okay. And, Jess, watch your back."

"I will."

"That's what you said last time and you ended up getting shot. Not a fan of Ethan Miller's if you recall."

"So, I've heard—several times. I promise I'll be careful."

He grumbled something I suppose was good-bye.

What Bob had told me about Stanley was disturbing on so many levels. Not the least of which was my own stupidity. For whatever reason, I'd chosen to not see who he really was. Or maybe he was that good at hiding it—a borderline sociopath. Which moved beyond disturbing into the realm of frightening.

I was hot and tired and stressed. All I wanted to do was eat and go to bed, but first I wanted to find Matt.

I was getting up from the bench when Dan Ketner stepped out of the RV he was sharing with Ethan's son, John. He walked over and sat down beside me.

Just like with Ethan, Dan and I had gotten off to a rocky start in our relationship. When I'd shown up on Ethan's doorstep over a year ago, hell-bent on doing an exclusive interview with him, Dan had been reluctant to let me inside the inner circle that surrounded his boss. More than reluctant, on several occasions, he'd told me flat-out to go home. I later realized that his abrasive manner, had more to do with protecting Ethan, from whatever came along. I just happened to be what came along.

Dan's social skills were limited, but I'd come to realize he was trustworthy and reliable and, as with Ethan, I'd grown very fond of him.

"How are you holding up?" he asked.

"I'm sinking fast. Have you seen Matt?"

"Not for a while. Last I saw, that Ginny-woman was leading him off to the dorm."

I was so tired I wasn't sure if I found that annoying that she had somehow lassoed my boyfriend—or incredibly funny that Matt had been pulled into her clutches.

Dan was watching me.

"What?" I said.

"How deep are you going into this investigation?"

I raised an eyebrow. "Whatever do you mean?"

A noise came out of him that was probably a laugh. Hard to tell with Dan. "I've seen you jump head first into a murder investigation before. Just wondering if we're wandering down that same path?"

I took my time answering. "Probably," I finally said. "This time the stakes are higher."

"How so?"

"Constance is a primary suspect. And I'm right behind her, followed by Ethan. And all of a sudden, the sheriff's investigation has taken a surprising turn and he was pulled off the case. If we can't find who did this, soon, then this could get uglier than we ever imagined for Constance and me."

"And Ethan."

I nodded. "And Ethan."

"And?"

"And what?"

"I think there's more."

I looked over his shoulder then back at him. "Everything about what happened to Ethan Jr. makes me sad. I think he honestly believed Ethan was his father. So, he finally confronts him, only to find out that was a lie and less than twenty-four hours later, he's dead. That's a hell of an ending to a young man's life."

Making eye contact was not Dan's thing, so when his gaze settled somewhere near my forehead, I felt that whatever he was about to say was serious.

"I remember her," he said.

"Who?"

"Lois Westenfeld."

I reached out and touched his face until he really was looking me in the eyes. "What are you saying?"

"Because of Constance's connection to the college and the fact that she and Ethan met here, there was some emotional draw, so in the early years, Ethan spoke here often."

He paused. I waited. And waited. Before he made me go berserk, I said, "Dan, finish the story before I hurt you."

He knew I was kidding—sort of—but he raised his eyebrows in mock surprise. "Ethan was here on a speaking engagement after one of his books came out. I don't remember which one, although, I'm sure I could find it. It's probably in my files back home—"

"I don't care."

"What?"

"I don't care which one of Ethan's books the tour was about. I want to know about Lois."

"Well, I was getting to that."

Again, he paused, but the look on my face, must have been enough of a prompt to jumpstart him again.

He scratched his nose. "It was not uncommon for the coeds to flock around Ethan when he was done talking. He always spent a fair amount of time with them. Some of them were flirting with him. Well, most of them were flirting with him. Some were definitely groupie-like, if you know what I mean." He paused to look at me to see if I understood. "And then there were the needy ones, who just wanted some attention. Lois was one of them."

"It's hard to believe you'd remember one girl out of all those others, from so long ago."

"Well, she's not the only one I remember, but whatever group we were with, there was always one or two that stood out. She was one of them."

"Because she was needy?"

He shrugged. "Maybe. She hung around a lot. We were here for an entire weekend and she was around a lot. Maybe Constance took pity on her, I'm not sure."

"So, Constance was with you?"

"It was after they'd been married a few years. I wasn't here when she and Ethan met, but when I finally came on board, St. Jo's was a routine stop for Ethan back then."

"Do you think Ethan slept with Lois?"

"I couldn't say for sure, but I doubt it. She wasn't his type and Constance kept him on a short leash."

"Then why would she name her son after Ethan?"

Dan shrugged again. "Maybe Ethan was her idol. Maybe he was nice to her and she construed it as something more. I couldn't say."

I pictured Ethan Jr., and studied Dan's face—the glasses, the straight brown hair and round face, their builds almost identical—the possibility was there. "Did *you* sleep with her?"

I thought he was going to swallow his tongue. "What? No. Absolutely not. No."

"Okay, okay, calm down. I had to ask."

That turned out to be the end of our conversation.

FOR THE FIRST TIME IN HOURS, I was back in the airconditioned RV and didn't want to ever leave. John was seated at the kitchen table, not looking all that great, Millie sat me down, brought me iced tea and started to heat up some lasagna in the microwave. She slid a chilled salad in front of me.

"You okay?" I asked John.

"A trooper from the Violent Crimes Support Unit showed up while you were gone, looking for my mother."

"She was with me. What did he want?"

"He said he had a few more questions for her. I don't like this, Jess."

I finished my salad. "I don't either." We could pretend all we wanted, but Constance was currently topping the list of suspects. Her fingerprints were all over the bloody knife and a roomful of people had seen her go ballistic when Ethan Jr. accused her ex-husband of being his father.

John looked up to make sure Millie wasn't listening in the small, enclosed area. She was busy putting dishes in the sink. He leaned across the table and took my hand. "We have to do something," he said, his voice a low whisper. "I can't let my mother go to prison. She didn't do this, Jess. You know that."

I did know that. "What do you want me to do?"

He raised his eyebrows. "You found a murderer before, you have to do it again, before they come to arrest her."

"John—"

"Please."

Millie was still busy over by the sink. I thought about it. "We need to find out more about Ethan Jr."

"How?"

I pulled my hand away from his and reached for my phone. A Google search for Ethan Jr. showed that lived less than an hour away. "I need to search his apartment."

"Don't you think the sheriff or somebody already did that?"

"I'm sure they did, but it would give me some feel for who he was and maybe there's something they missed or they left behind." I'd seen first-hand how a small-town local investigation could easily get bungled. For Constance's sake, I was hoping I'd see it again.

John thought about it. "Okay. We should probably go tonight. Wait until it gets dark—"

I held up my hand. "Whoa. I go alone." I didn't need one more chance of getting caught. John was a loose cannon. I couldn't risk it.

His face had a look I'd never seen there before. Determination maybe. "I'm going with you whether you like it or not. This is my mother's life we're talking about, I need to help her. And if you leave without me, then I'll go on my own."

Letting John loose to do whatever he thought an investigation entailed was far riskier than taking him with me, where I could keep an eye on him.

"Fine," I said. "But I'm in charge."

He smiled his charming John-smile. "Of course."

And then I was sure we were in trouble.

Seconds later, the door to the RV banged open. Millie jumped. Constance stormed in and looked at her son. "Your father is an ass," she told him. "Do not become him or I swear, I will disown you." She moved quickly down the small hallway to my former bedroom and closed the accordion door. Had there been any way of slamming it, I'm sure she would have.

There went my hopes of sleeping in comfort. After dinner, I reluctantly headed back to the dorm to get a few hours sleep before John and I sneaked off into the night and our nefarious escapades.

CHAPTER ELEVEN

STANLEY'S CAR WAS STILL PARKED IN front of the Admin Building, but I had no desire to talk to him at the moment.

He'd never led me on, or even pretended to be anything other than what he was, I guess. Most of who I thought he was, I'd made up to fit my own needs. Still, there was a part of me that felt betrayed.

I paused in front of the fountain and pulled up my email account on my phone. The names of all the workshop participants were on a document in my email and I wanted to send it off to Bob Elliot for background checks before I forgot. I scrolled through my inbox until I found the list of names, added a few of the nuns, just to round things out then forwarded it all to Bob.

In my pocket was the blood-spattered post-it note that held the phone number of the last person who had texted Ethan Jr. I fished it out, dialed the number and waited.

It started to ring. Off in the distance another phone rang—two out-of-sync tones a second apart. It wasn't long before my call went to the generic automated recording, telling me the person had not set up a voicemail box. I hung up. I hadn't expected an answer.

Ginny came up behind me. "I haven't seen you all day. How'd it go with the sheriff?"

"Fine," I said. I started to move in the direction of Ethan's RV.

I was almost ten feet away when she said, "That's not what Connie said."

I turned to meet her gaze. "What did she say?"

"She said he was very accusatory, like he was playing the *good cop-bad cop* routine without the good cop." She smiled at her own joke.

"He was just doing his job." I moved in closer. "You and Constance have quite a history together."

She raised her eyebrows. "I wouldn't say that."

"You went to college together, were in the same graduating class, kept in touch all these years."

She smiled again. The thing I didn't like about Ginny was that I couldn't read her. She seemed pretty straight-forward, almost simple. But when I looked into her eyes, there was an intelligence there, as if she was observing and weighing everything that went on around her.

"We were never really close," she said. "We were a small class, at a small school, so everyone knew everyone else, but we haven't exactly been exchanging Christmas cards over the years or anything."

"Then what brought you here this weekend."

"I thought it would be fun. We ran into each other earlier this summer and she mentioned it."

"When was that?"

She looked away, then back at me. "Gee, I don't remember exactly. Early June, maybe late May."

"Aren't you from the area?"

The fake smile seemed permanently in place. "Mossberg. About forty-five minutes from here. We own a dairy farm."

Constance lived most of the time at one of her homes in Miami or Barbados, with infrequent trips to Sedgewick Missouri to visit her son. She hated the mundane pace of life in Sedgewick and usually preferred John to visit her. "Where did you run into Constance?"

"Miami."

Randomly running into someone in Miami that you hadn't kept in touch with for years, seemed to defy the odds, but who knew. "Quite a few from your class have signed up for the workshop next week, almost like a reunion."

"Almost," she said. "I've got to get back to the dorm. By the way, that young man of yours is a doll. He's been entertaining us all afternoon."

I could only imagine what Matt had been doing to entertain the ladies. Ginny took off and I made my way to Ethan's RV. He opened the door and I climbed up the steps to the living area.

He sat down on the sofa and waved me into a recliner across from him. "Where were you all afternoon?"

I knew I needed sleep. Everyone was starting to annoy me. "You sent me on a mission, remember?"

"Yes, but I didn't expect you to be gone all day."

"I wasn't gone all day. Just the afternoon. And if you want to do this yourself, then go ahead."

"Why are you being so snarky?"

"Because I'm hot and I'm tired and my boyfriend has defected to the other side."

"What other side?"

"Apparently there's a gaggle of middle-aged women who want to adopt him."

"The Miller charm," Ethan said, as if it were a scientific phenomenon.

"Which is a myth made up and endorsed by all the Miller men."

Ethan raised his eyebrows. "Okay, now you're just tilting at windmills."

"Uh huh." I closed my eyes and leaned my head back against the chair. I may have even dozed off for a few seconds.

"Jessie," Ethan said loudly.

I jumped. "What?"

He looked exasperated. "Tell me what you learned today."

I told him about finding Constance in the library and her connection to Lois Westenfeld.

"That doesn't sound good," Ethan said.

I also told him about our trip to the cemetery and her friend, Barb Baker, who died in childbirth and baby Rosalee, buried next to her young mother.

Ethan nodded. "I've heard the story," he said. "It impacted Constance profoundly. I don't think she ever got over it completely."

"It would be difficult at that age to lose your best friend in such a tragic way. I wonder if she ever told her parents about it or got any other kind of support."

"Probably not. I think all the babies that came along with the four-year degree from St. Jo's were well-kept secrets, almost like an underground baby factory."

"You make it sound like everyone who graduated from here walked away with a baby."

He shrugged. "Constance's friend wasn't the first or the last to get pregnant here. Back then it was still a taboo for an unmarried woman to have a baby. Parents sent their naïve daughters to this Puritanical college, thinking they'd be protected from the sins of the world, not realizing that they were at that age and set loose for the first time in their lives. Of course, they were going to try the forbidden fruit. It's only natural."

"I can't believe all of them were virgins when they came to college and I can't believe that most of them got pregnant."

"I don't have a clue about the percentages, I know, and you do too, that it's an active time in a young person's life."

Talking about sex with Ethan, even in abstract terms, made me uncomfortable.

"Have you had time to study the pictures I took this morning?" I asked.

"No. You?"

"I've been busy, remember?"

I took my phone out of my pocket and scrolled through them. To me, they were just pictures of a dead body lying on the ground.

Ethan reached for the phone. "Anything?"

I handed it to him. "Not that I can see."

He swiped his finger across the screen, paused on one photo, enlarged it and moved the phone closer to his face. "Look at this," he said and handed it back to me.

The picture of the ground next to the body had been enlarged, showing a shoe print in the dusty ground. I rubbed my forehead. "I'm sure the police will look into that, but that doesn't tell us anything."

"It looks like a man's footprint."

I looked at Ethan. "How would you even know? And even if it is, it could be Ethan Jr.'s. Or a groundskeeper. Or any number of people. It could be mine or Constance's for all we know."

"I know. I'm just desperate for anything right now."

"That isn't the kind of evidence that's going to help a bunch of amateurs. The cops will check it out, I'm sure."

He wasn't giving up. "What about that pen next to the body?"

"Uh, yeah. That's not there anymore."

"Evidence?"

"No. It's in my pocket."

He rolled his eyes. "I won't even ask. What's next on the agenda?"

"How much do you want to know? The less you know, the safer you are."

He glanced out the window. "This is my family we're talking about. Constance. You. I'm involved no matter what."

I was touched that he thought of me as family, but not surprised. In his own bumbling way, Ethan was a protector. He took care of the people who shared his life—again, in his own bumbling way.

"It's not just Constance and me, Ethan. You're on the list as well."

"I told you before, I can take care of myself. So? Your plans?"

"John and I are doing a reconnaissance mission tonight."

"Where?"

"Ethan Jr.'s apartment."

"And the police?"

"We'll be careful."

"See that you are. I'm not looking to break any records on how many family members I can bail out of jail in a twenty-four-hour period."

CHAPTER TWELVE

M Y PHONE DINGED WITH AN INCOMING TEXT and I startled awake. It was dark out and I couldn't remember where I was. A fleece blanket covered my body, but I wasn't in bed. I was in a chair—a recliner, with my feet up, the motor from an air conditioner whirring somewhere in the background. All I wanted was to snuggle down with the cozy blanket and go back to sleep. My phone dinged again.

It took a minute to get my bearings. My eyes slowly adjusted to the darkness and I looked around. The living room of Ethan's RV came into view. I was still sitting in the same chair, but he must have raised the footrest to recline the plush blue chair. The blanket that covered me, his contribution before he headed off to bed. I wasn't even aware of when I'd fallen asleep.

Ethan's muffled snores pulsed gently through the bedroom door.

I pulled my phone out of my pocket, the screen much too bright in the darkened room. I had to blink a few times before I could focus on the words.

A text from John, *Where are you?*

A second text, *Where the hell are you?*

The final text, *Get your ass out here now! Let's go!*

Whatever sleep I'd gotten, it wasn't enough. I walked into the small bathroom, and splashed cold water on my face, then reluctantly left the safe, inviting comfort of Ethan's RV.

We had a green Toyota RAV4 that Millie and I had taken turns driving, following the RV's as we crisscrossed the Midwest on Ethan's how-can-I-punish-my-family book tour. It was our wheels when we didn't want to drive the big honking motorhomes every time we went to dinner or to the grocery store. It was currently parked behind John and Dan's RV and John was sitting behind the wheel when I climbed in.

He glared at me. "Where the hell were you? I went to the dorm, but couldn't find you. Matt said he hadn't seen you since lunch."

"I fell asleep in your dad's place."

He started to say something, which I knew would set the mood for the hours ahead and we'd spend the rest of the night snarling at each other. I held up my hand before he could speak. "Let's just go."

He started to speak again, stopped himself, put the car in gear and made a tight U-turn to head down the access road to the county highway. A black, unmarked sedan sat parked across from the entrance to the college, a patrol car, keeping track of the comings and goings on campus. I wondered if we warranted enough interest to be followed.

I pulled up directions to Ethan Jr.'s place on my phone. "It says it should take us about forty minutes to get there," I told him. I looked out the window and at the darkness that swallowed up the car. The only lights were the dashboard, our headlights and a few lonely stars. I felt like we were driving into a horror movie, never to be seen again.

The patrol car stayed put.

We'd been on the road for about ten minutes when John said, "I think we're being followed. The car behind us is quite a ways back but it's been there almost since we left the college."

I turned around in my seat to see the distant headlights. "It doesn't mean they're following us."

"They've made every turn we've made."

"Is it the sedan parked in front of the campus when we left?"

"I don't think so. They didn't pull out when we left."

I'd been in a position before where I'd been followed. It's a frightening feeling. And here we were, late at night, in an area that was unfamiliar to us.

"What do you think we should do?" I asked.

"When's our next turn?"

I looked at my phone. "About four miles up this road, we take a right."

"Hold on." He hit the accelerator with a force that threw my head against the back of my seat.

I turned around. The headlights grew fainter and I felt a sense of relief. Then they moved into view again, closing the gap on us. My relief blew right out the window.

John glanced a look in the rearview mirror. "Crap!" he said when he realized that we weren't losing them.

He gunned the gas pedal harder. I looked out the windshield, praying there would be no stray cows on the loose or wild animals. We'd be dead in the ditch before he could even slow us down.

The sign for our next turn flew into view. "Turn!" I yelled, which may not have been the right thing to say.

He pulled the steering wheel hard to the right and we skidded around the corner. I could have sworn we were on two wheels as the car listed to the side. We righted ourselves and kept going.

We were a mile down the road when I looked back again. Another brief moment of relief, before the other car turned the corner and headlights came into view.

John looked in the mirror, I could feel the tension radiating from his body.

"What now?" I asked.

Without a word he lifted his foot from the gas and slowly applied the brake. A farmhouse came into view and he swung the car onto their dirt driveway, cutting the lights. About a hundred and fifty feet in, he pulled off the drive into the cornfield.

The other car whizzed by out on the highway.

I didn't realize I'd been holding my breath. My hands ached from bracing myself against the dashboard. I let go and leaned back in the seat.

We sat for the longest time, neither of us speaking. The only sound, the crickets in their nighttime litany.

"Was that necessary?" I finally asked.

John looked over at me. "What was the alternative?"

"I don't know. Maybe we're being paranoid. Maybe they weren't even following us."

"Or maybe they were." His voice was tight. "Some dude that we just met got murdered this morning for who-know-what-reason. You and my parents are all prime suspects in his murder. We're living on some creepy campus from a gothic novel, out in the middle of nowhere. And while we're on our way to visit the dead guy's apartment in the middle of the night, a car comes out of nowhere and follows our every turn—even breaking the speed limit to keep up with us. So, yeah, I'm guessing we were being followed."

"So, what do we do now?"

John started the car. "We finish what we started."

"We're still going to Ethan Jr.'s apartment."

"Hell yes. We just made someone very nervous. I think that says we're on the right track. If you want out, I'll take you back."

"Not on your life. Drive."

It took us another twenty minutes to get to Ethan Jr.'s apartment. It was in one of those generic, two-story brick buildings that were commonly built around the mid nineteen-sixties, situated on the edge of a small town, across the street from a grocery store. The only light on in the building was in the entryway and shining in the parking lot, right next to a side entrance.

John parked in the supermarket lot. We looked around for our friend from St. Jo's. Neither of us had gotten a good look at the car, so it was hard to tell. Hard to tell if they'd followed us or not or if they had somehow figured out where we were headed and beat us here.

We got out of the car, crossed the quiet street and made our way around the apartment complex, checking entrances, looking for security cameras. When we were satisfied that we were alone and had a feel for the layout of the building, we approached the front entryway.

The mailboxes were located in a small foyer. A locked glass door barred our entrance into the building.

I was going to head back to the RAV4 to see if there were any tools to circumvent the lock, but I didn't have to worry. Many would have called John precocious when he was younger, but from the stories I'd heard, precocious was a cover word for delinquent. I'm sure if it hadn't been for Ethan's money or influence, John might have spent some of his adolescence in a juvenile detention center.

He jiggled the door and smiled at me, a look that said this wasn't even a challenge. There was a small storage cupboard off to the side of the mailboxes. He pulled the door open, revealing sleeves of replacement lightbulbs for the foyer and cleaning supplies to wipe the fingerprints off the glass doors. He rummaged around, until he found a key resting under a spray bottle of Windex. He unlocked the main door and I held it open, while he replaced the key to its hiding place.

"Misspent youth?" I asked.

"Among other things."

Ethan Jr.'s apartment was at the end of the first-floor hallway, conveniently located next to a fire door—in case we needed to make a hasty exit.

The apartment door was about as challenging as the outside door. John used a credit card to unlock it.

We stepped inside and closed the door behind us, waiting in the darkness, listening for any sounds before we turned on the hallway light.

It was a small apartment with a typical layout: kitchen on our left, coat closet on the right. Straight ahead was a small living room and eating area with a hallway off of that leading to the bathroom, a linen closet and a bedroom facing the front of the building.

All the drapes were open and we used our phones and the light from the front hall to close them before we turned on any lamps.

"Whoa," John said when I flipped on a living room light. "This dude was a pig. Or do you think the cops did this?"

I looked around. Papers were strewn everywhere. Drawers from his computer desk had been pulled out, the contents dumped in piles on the floor. "I don't think this was the cops."

"What are you saying?"

"I think someone else has been here."

"Maybe our friend who was following us?"

"I doubt it. They couldn't have been here long before us to create this kind of a mess and still look for whatever they were looking for."

John picked up a stack of papers. "What do you think they were looking for?"

"Beats me." I walked over to the coffee table and picked up a pile of unopened mail.

"What are *we* looking for?"

"I don't know what to tell you. We need to get a feel for who this guy was, why he confronted your father the way he did. See if anything looks out of the ordinary."

I could tell by the look on his face that he was hoping for something more specific but that was the best I could do. I didn't really know what we were looking for.

"Don't you think the cops would have taken anything important already?" he asked.

I pointed to the empty desktop. "They took his computer. Not sure what else they would have taken. But all these papers, they probably took pictures of what seemed important to them. Remember, we're not in St. Louis. These guys don't deal with a lot of murder investigations, so I'm hoping they missed something that could help us." I shooed John with my fingers. "Just start looking."

He headed for the bedroom and I tackled the volumes of paper Ethan Jr. had in his living room office space.

All his bills—rent, electricity, car payments and credit cards— were meticulously dated, with the check number written on each invoice. So, Ethan Jr. was anal. I'd suspected as much, which underscored the fact that someone had been through his apartment long before we'd arrived. Someone who had documentation of old bills, dating back two years, was someone who would file everything away so it could be easily retrieved when needed. This led me to the four-drawer metal filing cabinet nestled in the corner of the living room.

The two top drawers were open and empty. It must have been where he'd kept the files for his bills, that had already been displayed all over the living room floor.

The next drawer held college papers and ten years-worth of tax returns.

I opened the bottom drawer and sat down next to the filing cabinet taking out files one at a time. Toward the back were two file folders, one labeled *Mom,* the other labeled *Project*.

I opened the *Mom* folder. Decades older, I still recognized Lois Westenfeld. She'd kept the same sweet smile she'd had as a girl. I was looking at the picture from her obituary a year ago, when she'd lost her battle with cancer.

Ethan Jr. was her only child, which made his situation seem even sadder. He'd lost his entire family in his mother's death, and then the humiliation to find out, so publicly, that Ethan Miller wasn't his real father as he'd been led to believe.

I thumbed through the folder. More pictures, some of Lois with her young son, her death certificate, even her college diploma—more reminders of his loss.

I opened the *Project* folder, not surprised that the police hadn't confiscated this material. They had his computer, the hard copy printouts were of no consequence.

The emails dated back to May, the first somewhat tentative, saying they had pertinent family information about Ethan Jr., hoping to set up a meeting time, the wording like a marketing ploy from a floundering ancestry website. I couldn't find a response to it.

The second contact sounded a little more insistent. Ethan Jr. finally responded to the third email, saying he wasn't interested.

The emails continued. There was a dialogue between Ethan Jr. and the sender, but wording was often vague. I wondered if this was the spark that started the confrontation yesterday with my boss, and if it was the beginning of an extortion scheme.

The email didn't originate from any known email provider or institution of which I was aware. I had to assume that the sender was savvy enough to not be easily traced.

Ethan Jr. hadn't initiated any of this, he merely wanted to meet his father.

My guess was that Ethan Jr. had gone rogue and not followed the blackmail plan when he confronted Ethan the day before, and the person who originated the emails was the same one who'd texted him for a meeting shortly before he was killed.

I looked again at the obituary for Lois Westenfeld. Her sister still lived in the area. I wanted to talk to her. With Lois dead, I hoped that Ethan Jr.'s aunt would be able to fill in some of the missing information about her nephew.

John came out of the bedroom. "Nothing," he said.

I showed him what I'd found. "We need to talk to his aunt."

"Let's go." He started for the door.

I caught him by the arm and pointed out the window. "It's two in the morning. I don't think we'd be well received."

"Oh. Right."

We made one more sweep through the apartment. When John closed the door behind us, I had both folders under my arm.

It was easier getting out than in and we crossed the street to the RAV4.

"I need coffee," I said.

"I think we passed a twenty-four-hour diner about a mile out of town."

John found the diner, parked and went inside to get us both some coffee. He returned carrying a bag with warm cinnamon rolls and hot coffee.

I took the lid off my cup. "You are officially my favorite Miller."

"If I'd known all it took was two a.m. coffee and gooey, sugary carbs, I would have done this months ago."

I almost had the cup to my lips when John bumped his elbow into my arm.

"What the hell?" I said, looking at him.

He nodded his head toward a dark sedan parked under the fluorescent light at the end of the parking lot—I could tell it wasn't the same one that had been parked across the road from the campus entrance when we left. I looked at the person sitting in the driver's seat, half expecting to see one of the deputies who worked with Sheriff Allen.

Ginny made eye contact with me and smiled.

CHAPTER THIRTEEN

WE WERE IN MOSSBERG, THE TOWN GINNY WAS FROM. The obvious question at that moment was why would she have traveled home in the middle of the night? My gut told me she hadn't, that her trip back to Mossberg had everything to do with John and me and Ethan Jr. and nothing to do with her husband or the dairy farm.

I told John my suspicions.

"You're right," he said. "Too much coincidence and then for us to see her at the diner. It's like she wanted us to know she was there. I don't like this. But then she didn't impress me when I met her in Miami."

"Wait. What?"

"Last month. When I was in Miami visiting my mom. She stopped by the apartment."

"So, they didn't just run into each other?"

"What are you talking about."

"Ginny said she ran into your mother in Miami."

He snorted a laugh. "You don't just run into people in Miami."

I was glad for the coffee. The monotony of the road was making me sleepy and I wanted to hear this story. "Tell me what happened. Did your mother know she was coming? Or did Ginny show up uninvited?"

I watched his profile in the dark car. He kept his eyes on the road, but seemed to be thinking. "I'm pretty sure their meeting was planned. I'd been out the night before and slept late." He turned toward me and smiled, which meant his late night involved a beautiful woman. "When I finally got up that morning, my mom had the table set for company. Mimosas, iced tea, a lobster salad with crudités and toast points. Looked good to me. When I started picking at the food, she slapped my hand, gave me some money and sent me away."

John, the man-child; both of his parents gave him money, cars, plane tickets. No wonder he never grew up. He didn't have to. Matt's mother and stepfather had been more traditional in their parenting and expected him to earn his way in the world. He could easily have gotten on Ethan's parental-guilt-train and taken the free ride, but that wasn't who he was and I was proud of him for not taking the easy road.

I downed the last of my coffee. "How do you know her luncheon date was Ginny?"

"I came back about three, and they were still lingering over coffee at the table. My mom introduced Ginny as an old friend from college, although, I'd never heard her mention Ginny before."

"What was she like?"

"You've met her. She was the same as she is now." He kept his eyes on the road, illumed only by our headlights and an occasional farm. "I mean she's pleasant enough. Pretends to be interested in whoever she's talking to—but I think she's more, nosy than interested. Anyway, I talked to them for a while and left."

Nosy was the best way to describe Ginny. But something about the story—hers and now John's—felt off. "Ginny isn't the sort of person I'd picture as one of Constance's friends."

"My mom's friends might surprise you."

"What do you mean?"

"I know my mother comes across as flighty and superficial—probably self-absorbed—but, she really is interested in other people and has a caring heart. She doesn't just root for the underdog, she's in there, helping them get where they need to be."

"But Ginny's not an underdog. I think she takes care of herself very well."

"I'm just saying that my mother has friends everywhere. She accepts people for who they are. Except for Ethan."

I had to admit, I didn't really know Constance very well. As I said before, I liked her. She was intelligent and interesting. But, even traveling with her these past weeks, she'd spent more time with Ethan and John than she had with me, so I may not have been getting the whole picture of who she was.

Almost as if John read my thoughts, he said, "You've mostly seen my mother with Ethan. Those two are like oil and water. No, they're more like two meteors colliding in space, creating an explosion that echoes through the universe."

He looked at me again and smiled at his analogy. "Yet," he continued, "oddly enough they love each other. But my mother has an entirely different focus when Ethan's not around. She's involved in a lot of non-profits, dealing with the homeless and drug rehab and after-school programs for disadvantaged kids. Stuff like that."

I could see that part of Constance too. Especially this bizarre day we'd spent together. Her compassion for Ethan Jr., the impact of the loss of her friend, Barb and the baby decades ago, there was something deep and kind about John's mother.

I moved John back to the condo in Miami. "Okay, so you came home early, met Ginny, chit-chatted politely and left, right?"

"Right."

"Was there anything about the scene when you came home that seemed unusual to you?"

He was quiet. Finally, he said, "Now that you mention it, they were still at the table when I came home, four hours later. They hadn't moved to the living room or the balcony."

"And that's not typical?"

"My mother loves to entertain in her living room. And the balcony has a million-dollar view of the ocean."

"Anything else?"

"The table had been cleared, except for the coffee pot and a bowl of fruit, but they were both sitting there with pads of paper in front of them."

"Were they playing cards?"

"There weren't any cards. And they both had a pad of paper and a pen."

He paused and I wondered if there really was any significance to that.

"Oh wait, now I remember, I went over to kiss my mother on the cheek and she turned her paper over—face down. When I went around the table to shake Ginny's hand, she moved her left arm on the table to cover up her pad. I just remembered that. Weird. Do you think it means anything?"

I thought for a minute. "Probably. I guess. Although I can't imagine what. It's one of those things that seems like nothing, except in the light of what happened today. And tonight."

"Right."

"When did you meet Ginny?" I asked.

"A little over a month ago."

"How long?"

"You want an exact date?"

"Yes."

"Why?"

"I'm not sure."

He let out a sigh, took his phone out of his pocket and handed it to me. "Pull up my calendar, you can see when I went to my mom's. I'm pretty sure it was the first week in June. I know it was after Memorial Day."

I found his calendar. There were more women's names there than I cared to know about. I scrolled back to June. He was right, he'd been in Miami the first week in June. I handed his phone back and he slid it in his pocket.

He glanced over at me. "So? What did that tell you?"

"I'm not sure. Your mother and father started their, uh, rekindling the following week, right?"

"Yeah, she flew home with me and Ethan picked us up in St. Louis. By the time we made it to Sedgewick, the *rekindling* was already in full swing."

"Have they ever rekindled before?"

"A couple of times over the years. I've never seen it start with such intensity, though."

"Who initiated it?"

"My mother. No question. She started flirting with him the minute we were off the plane. But, I'm not sure what any of this means."

"Unfortunately, neither do I."

WE WERE ONLY ABOUT HALFWAY BACK to the college when I conked out again. John shook me awake. "We're here."

I opened my eyes to see we were parked, exactly where we'd started, behind John and Dan's RV.

"Can I spend the night here?"

"No. Get out."

"Drive me to the dorm."

"No. The walk will do you good."

I opened the door. "Aren't you going to walk me home?"

"I'm going to go to bed."

"Nice of you to be so concerned for my welfare. There are murderers roaming around out there."

"I know. And trust me, if one of them offs you tonight, I'll feel like a real jerk. Good night."

He walked to his RV and left me standing alone in the dark.

I made my way to the fourth floor of the dorm, feeling the heat rise with me as I rode up in the elevator. I was hoping to see Matt asleep in my bed, but the room was empty. I wondered if he'd left for home without saying good-bye.

It didn't take long to wash my face and strip out of my sweat-soaked clothes. I fell into a deep dreamless sleep.

Someone bent over me and whispered in my ear, but the words were confusing. A rough hand on my shoulder, shook me fully awake.

When I opened my eyes, Matt was looking down at me. "Scoot over," he said.

I scooted and he slipped under the sheet with me. I put my head on his shoulder against his cool skin, then sat up quickly and turned on the light, I ran my hand up and down his arm.

I glared at him. "*Where* have you been?"

His eyes rounded in surprise. "Waiting for you."

"Why is your skin so cool?"

"Hey. What can I say? I'm a cool guy."

"You found an air conditioner somewhere. Were you sleeping at Ethan's?"

He rolled his eyes. "No. I wasn't at Ethan's."

"Then where were you just now?"

"Aren't you just happy to see me?"

"Where were you?"

"Okay. The ladies—"

"The workshop ladies?"

"Yes. The entire second floor has air conditioning. And there was an empty room and they insisted that I sleep in there."

I punched him as hard as I could in the bicep.

"Ow!" He rubbed his arm. "What did you do that for?"

"I'm hot and tired and miserable and you're here less than twenty-four hours and *the ladies* offer you an air-conditioned room to sleep in. It's not even close to fair."

He sat up and tried to kiss me. I pulled away. "It's not my fault they like me and wanted me to be comfortable."

I punched him again.

He rubbed his arm. "Would you quit doing that."

"Show me where the room is. I want to sleep there."

"Well, here's the thing about that, the ladies made it very clear that it's my room and that the nuns wouldn't like it if I had a woman in there with me."

I got out of bed and started putting on my clothes.

"Where are you going?" he asked.

"I'm sleeping in your special room tonight. If you want to join me, feel free."

He reached for my hand. "Okay, okay. We'll sneak down there in a minute. Tell me what happened today. I haven't seen you since lunch time."

I sat down on the edge of the bed, temporarily mollified that I would get to sleep in comfort tonight. I told him everything that had happened, starting with Constance in the library, the trip to the cemetery and my midnight journey with John to Mossberg, Missouri. It didn't take as long as I thought it would. In fact, it didn't take long at all, which reinforced the fact that I didn't know anything about what happened to Ethan Jr.

Matt was silent the entire time. He didn't interrupt me once, which was unusual.

When I was finished, he shook his head. "I don't like this. Once again, Ethan has pulled you into an ugly, dangerous mess."

"Ethan hasn't done anything."

"Really? I thought you said he asked you to look into it for Constance's sake."

"Well, yes, but I would have done it anyway. And except for Ginny following us, nothing really bad has happened."

"Yet."

"Okay—yet."

"Why do you think Ginny was following you? Doesn't that worry you at all?"

"I don't know why she'd follow us. I know she's a busybody."

Matt got out of bed. "Don't be stupid, Jess. I don't care how nosy someone is, they don't go off in the middle of the night just to find out where someone might be going."

I knew that, and I couldn't even guess what Ginny's motive might be, but she didn't feel like a threat.

Matt took his phone off of the nightstand. "I did a little investigating on my own today and look what I found."

He opened his pictures and handed me the phone. I'm not an expert on guns, so I had no idea what make or caliber it was, but the handgun in the photo was strapped into a black leather holster, buried in the bottom of a drawer somewhere.

I looked up at Matt. "Whose is it?"

"Ginny's."

I looked at the picture again, then up at Matt. "What?"

"I searched a few rooms this afternoon, when everyone was out having group pictures taken. This is what I found in the bottom drawer of the desk in her dorm room. So, when I say that

Ethan has pulled you into another nasty mess of his, I have proof to back it up."

Matt's face was painted with an anger, I had seen once before when I was looking for a murderer.

"She's not the only person who carries a concealed weapon," I said.

"She's the only person at the writing workshop who has one."

"That we know of. She lives on a farm. Guns may, very likely, be a part of her life."

"Are you telling me this doesn't concern you?"

"It worries me a lot. I don't like her, but lots of people have guns. More people than we know about, so we can't automatically assume that the gun makes her a threat."

"Well, it makes her more of a threat than if she didn't have one."

"I know. I can't think anymore. I need to get some sleep. Show me where the room is."

He raised an eyebrow. "I'll take you there, but I hope you realize that my credibility with the ladies will be in great peril because of you."

"Take me there before I hurt you again."

I FELT THE COOL AIR as soon as the elevator doors opened onto the second floor. Matt stepped into the empty hallway and put a finger to his lips and smiled.

As much as he was annoying me, our tryst on the second floor brought back that wonderfully illicit feeling of college escapades.

The room was at the end of the corridor, the same drab décor as I enjoyed two floors up, but with a temperature difference of almost twenty degrees. I lay down on the bed, closed my eyes and didn't wake up until eight the next morning.

CHAPTER FOURTEEN

MATT KISSED ME AWAKE. I opened my eyes to sunlight and the smell of morning coffee.

He handed me a cup. "When you're ready to leave, let me know so I can check the hallway. I want you to slip out of here without getting caught."

I sipped the coffee. "I may never leave. I like it here. Especially the service. If you bring me breakfast in bed, I may hire you full time."

"Sorry. I already have a job. I teach Plant Pathology at the University in case you hadn't heard."

"Impressive." I slid my hand up his thigh.

He stopped its progress mid-thigh. "And, should I decide to leave my present position, I have already received several offers from the ladies on this floor."

I raised my eyebrows. "I can only imagine what those offers might be."

"All very proper, I assure you."

"I'm sure." I kissed him and swung my legs over the side of the bed.

"Where do you think you're going?"

"Well, first, I'm going to the bathroom. Then, I'm going to take a shower. Is there a problem, Professor Wheaton?"

"No one can see you leave here."

"You're kidding, right?"

"No, I'm not kidding."

"By the way, where do you pee?"

"Excuse me?"

"This is a women's dorm. I haven't seen a men's room."

"There's one on the first floor, for gentlemen callers."

I slipped on my clothes. "Gentlemen callers? Where do you shower?"

"At Ethan's."

I moved toward the door, but he stepped in front of me and opened it slowly, looked up and down the hall, then shooed me out of the room. "Head for the elevator. Hurry."

MATT WAS SITTING ON THE BED in my room on the fourth floor when I got out of the shower.

"What's on the agenda for today?" he asked.

I pulled a clean cotton blouse out of the closet. "I'd rather not say."

He narrowed his eyes. "That makes me think you're going to do something stupid. Or dangerous. Or both."

"It is neither stupid nor dangerous, but I'm pretty sure you won't approve."

He stood and walked over to where I was standing, buttoning my blouse. "Tell me."

"John and I are going to visit Ethan Jr's aunt today."

"You're right, I don't like it."

I slipped on my shorts. "It's not dangerous."

"You don't know that yet, do you? And even if it's not dangerous, it's intrusive. The woman just lost her nephew."

He was right, but as a former journalist, I also knew, that it's easier to get information out of people when they're vulnerable. Clearly opportunistic, but true. Under the worst conditions, most people are almost desperate to talk—to tell their story—and it's amazing the information they will share at that time. Under normal circumstances, people are usually more guarded and suspicious.

"This isn't just about Ethan Jr. and you know it," I said. "Constance could be arrested, if we don't find out what happened. Or your father."

He set his jaw. "And that's what the police are for. Let them do their jobs."

We'd had these conversations before, he didn't like what I was doing in a previous investigation and I had no reason to believe that his feelings would be any different now.

I looked him in the eye. "You, of all people, should know how that works. You knew a man who was sent to prison for a crime he didn't commit. Twenty years of his life were taken from him, Matt. You saw it first-hand." He knew exactly who I was referring to and the investigation Ethan had gotten me into before.

"And that didn't end well, did it?"

No, it hadn't. I got shot. I didn't say anything.

"I can't change your mind, can I?" he asked.

"No."

"Then I'm going with you."

"That's not necessary. John and I can handle it."

"I'm going with you. I have to go back to work tomorrow. It might be the only time I get to spend with you. Where does this woman live?"

I showed him on my phone. A small town, maybe half an hour away, in the opposite direction of Mossberg, where Ethan Jr. had lived.

Matt headed for the door. "We'll take my truck. You can ride with me and John can follow in the RAV4 and drive you back here when we're done. I'll head home from there. Be out front in twenty minutes."

He slammed the door behind him. This was not going to be a fun day on any level.

I texted John and told him the plan. Then I grabbed my purse and headed downstairs, hoping there was a McDonald's on the way, where I could get some breakfast. I was starving.

JOHN AND CONSTANCE WERE CLIMBING INTO THE RAV4 when I got outside. I made a *what's-she-doing-here?* gesture when I caught John's eye. He shrugged, shook his head and climbed into the driver's seat.

Seconds later, Matt pulled up in his truck and I climbed inside, he made a U-turn in the middle of the road and motioned for John to follow him.

Matt wasn't talking. Whenever he was mad at me, I got the silent treatment.

I let him stew for about fifteen minutes before I asked, "Did John tell you about the vasectomy?"

He looked over at me. "What the hell are you talking about?"

So, I was the one who had the pleasure of telling him about Ethan's vasectomy.

When I was finished with the story, he looked over at me. "And I needed to know that why?"

"You needed to know that because of Bonnie." Bonnie, his former fiancée, who was murdered over two decades ago, was pregnant with a child that wasn't his. Matt had spent too much of his life believing that his father had slept with the young woman.

He watched the road. I knew how this worked—he had to process the information in his own way before he would talk about it. The frustrating part was, I never knew how long the processing would take. All I could do was wait until he was ready.

Five minutes later, he looked at me again. "And do you believe him?"

"Yes."

He grunted.

"What does that mean?"

"Just because Ethan says something, doesn't mean it's the truth. We've both learned that the hard way."

I reached over and put my hand on his arm. "Matt, I believe Ethan on this one. He had no reason to lie. If he was merely trying to side-step the accusation of being Ethan Jr.'s father, a DNA test would have proven that. He didn't have to tell us about the vasectomy. I think he wanted us to know. I think he wanted you to know. Whatever you do with that information is up to you. But don't you think it's time that you and Ethan found some healing? He's carried your accusations around for a very long time. Maybe it's time to start fresh."

We would talk about this later, but it would be on Matt's terms in Matt's time, and that was fine with me. The information was out there, he was the one who had to figure out what it meant to him.

We didn't pass a McDonald's on the way to Ethan Jr.'s aunt house in Dallum, Missouri, but Matt stopped at a small café and bought me doughnuts and coffee. All the carbs were making me sluggish, but at least I had something in my stomach to get me through the morning.

Judy Grossman, formerly Westenfeld, lived in a Craftsman bungalow, probably built in the nineteen twenties, on F Street in Dallum, Missouri. F Street, being six blocks east of Central Street, that ran through the middle of downtown.

As I climbed out of the cab of Matt's truck, I remembered it was Sunday morning, and hoped Judy Grossman wasn't at church.

Matt and I reached the front porch, just as John brought the RAV4 to a stop behind the truck

I knocked on the front door. A minute later, a tall thin woman with brown hair and glasses opened the door. She was dressed in white linen slacks and a bright green cotton blouse.

"Mrs. Grossman?"

"Yes?"

"I'm Jessica Kallan—"

She looked over my shoulder and saw Constance coming up the sidewalk. "Connie Zahowski?"

She bolted out the door and down the steps and threw her arms around Constance's neck. "Oh, my goodness. I can't believe it's you."

When the hugging stopped, Constance pulled away. "It's so good to see you, Judy. I'm so sorry about your nephew."

"Thank you." Judy cleared her throat. "It was a shock. I heard you found him. I'm so confused about what happened."

"Can we go inside?" Constance asked.

"Yes, yes. Of course." She took Constance by the hand and led her into the living room, with its pale-yellow walls and furniture that looked new.

Constance introduced all of us and we sat down while Judy went into the kitchen to get coffee. She returned with a coffee carafe and blueberry scones. More carbs. But they looked fresh and I took one anyway.

Judy sat next to Constance on the large sectional, telling us that her husband had just left for his office as a computer programmer for the county to get caught up on some work.

Constance patted her classmate's knee. "How are you holding up?"

Judy's eyes filled with tears. "Lois passed away only a year ago, I was barely used to her being gone and now this. It's been a hard year for all of us, but especially Ethan. He and his mother were very close and he'd been floundering a lot this past year. When the sheriff told me, I felt like I'd been kicked in the gut. It was a shock, but I guess not a total surprise."

"Why do you say that, Mrs. Grossman?" I asked.

She took a tissue from her pocket and wiped her eyes. "Like I said, he was floundering without his mother. I knew her death would hit him hard I just had no idea how hard. My husband, Ron, and I tried to be there for him as much as we could, but we lived over an hour away and we all had jobs and other obligations, so we didn't see him as much as we'd like. I texted him almost every day—but it's not the same as being there with someone."

"I'm still confused why you weren't surprised by his mur—." Matt elbowed me in the arm. "By his death."

She looked out the window. "Sometimes you just sense things are going to end a certain way, but you don't realize it at the time. And then when they do, you look back and see that all the signs were there, you just couldn't put them together. Does that make sense?" She looked at me.

"I'm not sure. What were you seeing that led to your nephew's murder?"

It took a while for her to gather her thoughts. "I don't know that I knew Ethan would be murdered, or even that he would die or have a horrible accident. But I sensed that something bad was coming and there was nothing we could do to stop it."

"Like what?"

She picked up a photograph of Ethan Jr. that was sitting on the end table next to the couch. "Someone contacted him last spring about Ethan Miller." She looked at me. "The *real* Ethan Miller."

"Who contacted him?"

"I don't know. He wouldn't say. I'm surprised he told us as much as he did. I'm pretty sure he knew what our response would be. We'd want him to go to the police."

I scooted forward on the love seat. "So, this person contacted your nephew about Ethan Miller? What was the purpose of that?"

"He—she—whoever it was, was encouraging my nephew to try to extort money from Ethan Miller, or make it public that Mr. Miller had never acknowledged his son or supported my nephew or his mother in any way over the years. Ron and I told him, that it was illegal and unethical and he should contact the authorities, so this person—this instigator—could be dealt with."

"But your nephew didn't want to do that? Was he planning on getting involved in the extortion scheme?"

Judy looked embarrassed. She turned toward Constance. "I'm so sorry about all of this."

Constance patted her knee. "Don't worry about it."

Judy said to me, "I don't think my nephew wanted to get involved at all. But, with his mother gone, and the fact that he'd struggled with his identity his whole life, I think he just wanted some kind of contact with the man he thought was his father. I think he needed that connection."

"So, you don't know who was behind this?" I asked.

"Not a clue," Judy said.

I reached out and took the picture of her nephew that she'd been holding. There was no resemblance to my boss or his two sons sitting in that room with us. "Do you believe Ethan Miller was your nephew's father?"

"Oh, God no," she said.

"Excuse me?"

Judy looked at me and then turned again to Constance. "My nephew's father wasn't Ethan Miller, the author."

"You're sure about that?" Constance asked.

Judy nodded then looked around the room at each of us. "Absolutely. My nephew's father was a custodian at St. Jo's that my sister was dating."

I'd believed Ethan yesterday when he said that Ethan Jr. couldn't possibly be his son, so I don't know why this new bit of information took me by surprise. Maybe what surprised me was that Judy knew. And Lois knew. And still, Ethan's name had been on the birth certificate. No one said anything for a minute.

I handed the photo back to Judy. "How did Ethan Miller's name end up on your nephew's birth certificate as the boy's father?"

The question brought her to tears. "Please don't judge my sister. She was such a good-hearted person." She stopped talking and cried harder.

Constance put an arm around Judy's back and pulled her closer, letting her cry on the shoulder of Constance's three-hundred-dollar silk blouse.

Finally, Judy pulled away. She wiped her eyes and smiled weakly at Constance, then turned her attention back to me. "My sister was dating the custodian. He was a nice young man, but really had no ambition and wasn't ready to settle down. I think by the time Lois found out she was pregnant they'd already broken up. She was fine with that, she saw no future with him. Abby Vargas—Mother Abby—had just taken her final vows. She was Sister Abigail then. Anyway, she'd helped a couple of the girls from St. Jo's who'd gotten pregnant. She tried to talk Lois into putting her baby up for adoption. She even knew a doctor who would help her with the arrangements, but Lois wouldn't hear of it. She wanted her baby. She knew it would be tough being a single mother, but she was willing to do whatever it took."

"Mother Abigail seems to have a calling to help pregnant young women."

I hadn't meant that to be sarcastic, but Matt frowned at me. My second faus pax if anyone was keeping track—which he probably was.

Judy didn't seem offended by my statement. "Abby grew up dirt poor, I think she was the first in her family to go to college. She came from a super religious family, who believed that we were all here to help others. She took it to heart."

"That was very brave of your sister to make the decision she did, she sounds like a remarkable person," I said.

Judy smiled. "Yes, she was."

"That still doesn't explain how Ethan ended up listed as the father."

She turned again to Constance, "I am sorry about this. Maybe I should have stopped her. We were all so young, I guess we never realized what the ramifications might be."

"It's okay," Constance said softly. "Tell us what happened."

"Lois was determined to keep her baby. The farther she got into her pregnancy, the more she realized that the baby's father was kind of a loser and she didn't want him to ever have any claim on her baby. She admired Ethan Miller so much. Remember how he used to come to the campus every year?"

Constance nodded. "I remember."

"She met Ethan once on one of his speaking engagements. He was very kind to her. She wanted her baby to feel special. To have a father he, or she, could look up to, so she decided to put Ethan's name on the birth certificate. In the beginning, we all thought it was kind of funny. But, after the baby came and she started to make up stories about how his father and she met, it wasn't funny anymore. I tried to tell her that she needed to tone it down. That, at some point, it was going to backfire on her, when her son found out she'd lied to him. But, she was in too deep and she didn't know how to stop what she'd started. I think she hoped it would never become an issue."

John shifted in his chair. "Didn't he ever wonder why his father never came to visit?"

"Lois had an answer for everything. She told her son that she and his father had parted ways years ago and he had another family now and they didn't want to cause problems for the new family. Ethan was a gullible child. He took what his mother said at face value. But you could tell, he really didn't understand. He wanted a father."

"And he never learned the truth," I said. "So, when Ethan showed up at the college to confront Ethan Miller, he really thought he was meeting his father for the first time."

Judy nodded. "Yes. When he found out a couple of weeks ago, that Ethan Miller was going to be at St. Jo's, he didn't' want to miss out on something he'd dreamed about his whole life. I'd been wanting to tell him the truth ever since that person contacted him last spring, but I never got the chance. I didn't want to do it in a text or over the phone, and this all happened before I had the opportunity. I wonder now if he even would have believed me, he was going to meet his father and nothing would stop him."

She put her face in her hands and cried.

We waited. Finally, she wiped her eyes and drew herself up, steeling herself against another loss that had come all too soon on the heels of her sister's death.

Constance rubbed her shoulder. "When is the funeral?"

"We haven't made arrangements yet. Some family will be coming from out of state and we're trying to coordinate that. Please tell Ethan we're so grateful for all he's done."

Constance looked at her friend. "What has Ethan done?"

"I thought you knew," Judy said. "He's offered to pay for the funeral and interment and to fly in our relatives that will be coming."

Constance nodded. "I'll tell him," she said.

CHAPTER FIFTEEN

THE TIME APART FROM MATT since we'd started the book tour had been way too long and the weekend had been sidetracked by a tragedy no one could foresee. Now he had to leave and I didn't want to say good-bye.

He hugged me harder than usual then bent down to kiss me. "Please be careful," he said in my ear.

"I will be."

"Why do I always find that so hard to believe?" He kissed me again, and climbed into the cab of his truck and then he was gone.

I opened the door and got into the backseat of the RAV4 behind John and we headed toward the highway.

"When was the last time you saw Judy?" I asked Constance.

"Probably graduation." She turned around to look at me. "So, are you and Matt going to get married?"

I wasn't sure what to say. "I don't know. The subject has come up. But not for a while."

She smiled. "You make a cute couple. It will come up again."

"How can you be so sure?"

"I've never seen Matt so . . ." She turned to John. "What's the word I'm looking for?"

"Horny?"

She rolled her eyes. "Invested. Maybe that's it. He likes you. A lot. I can tell."

I hoped she was right. We rode in silence and I replayed the conversation with Judy over and over again in my head, trying to find that spot, that didn't gel with what I knew.

"Judy didn't want Ethan Jr. to meet Ethan," I said to no one in particular.

Constance glanced over at John, then turned around again in her seat. "No, I don't think she did."

My gaze met hers. "How did Ethan Jr. know Ethan was going to be at St. Jo's? There was no press release about this part of the tour. You said you would handle getting the word out yourself. What did that entail?"

"It was mostly email to our graduating class. The weekend and workshop were by invitation only."

"Facebook?"

"No social media. Direct email only."

"Then how did he know?"

I could see that she was thinking, but I couldn't even guess where her thoughts were going. "I don't know. Maybe he heard it from someone else."

"Seriously? How many women in your graduating class, do you think he's in touch with on a regular basis besides his aunt?"

She didn't look away. "Probably none."

"Then, again, how did he know?"

"Jessica, I don't know what you want me to say. He obviously found out—somehow—and decided to show up. Maybe Judy did tell him after all."

"No, I don't think she'd do that. It would just be a set-up for the eventual fallout when he found out Ethan wasn't his father. She was trying to protect him from a scene like that. When was the decision made to pull this weekend together?"

"I don't remember exactly. You were there when we talked about it." This time, her eyes told me what she didn't want me to see—that she was lying. She turned around in her seat and fixed her gaze on the acres of cornfields that were flying by.

JOHN PARKED THE TOYOTA AND HEADED for the comfort of his RV.

Constance headed for mine. The only one left was Ethan's.

I knocked on his door and he yelled for me to come in.

He was seated in one of the recliners, his tablet and papers on a tv tray in front of him. "Where have you been?"

"Trying to keep your ex-wife out of jail. And me too."

"And?"

"And I don't know anything yet." I told him about our trip to Ethan Jr.'s apartment and to his aunt's house today and told him how his name ended up on the young man's birth certificate. "Ethan, were you involved at all in setting up this workshop at the college?"

He grunted. "No. We wouldn't be here if I'd had anything to say about it."

"So, it was all Constance?"

"You were there when she came up with the idea. You saw how excited she was and how insistent she was when I realized, it would be too much to add to the schedule we already had planned."

She had been both of those things, six short weeks ago. Six weeks would have been mid-June. Nothing had been arranged as far as I knew, prior to Constance's insistence that Ethan end his tour at St. Jo's. Ginny told me that when she ran into Constance in Miami in late May or early June, that Constance had told her this is where we'd end up. At that point, Constance hadn't even *rekindled* with Ethan yet.

Where were people getting their information on a workshop that wasn't open to the public and hadn't even been planned yet?

"Jessie," Ethan said, rather loudly, and tore me away from my thoughts.

"What?"

"I was saying that today is Sunday."

"So?"

"The workshop starts tomorrow. Is everything set up?"

"Well no. We've all been a little distracted these past twenty-four hours."

He looked exasperated. Ethan was never happy when events, such as murder, infringed on his life. "Don't you think you'd better make sure we're ready for people to show up tomorrow morning?"

Sure. Constance finagled this writing conference, for whatever reason, and sent out a bunch of emails to her pals. The real work now was left to me.

TWO HOURS LATER, SISTER IMELDA AND I were in a classroom in the Humanities Building, moving desks, hauling fans from the janitor's storage room, and sweating our asses off. We moved through the humidity like jogging in a pool, everything in slow motion. I hoped the large window fans would be enough to keep our audience from passing out from the heat.

A desk for Ethan was dragged in front of the whiteboard, although, I had my doubts that he would be able to master the whiteboard before the workshop ended on Friday. A circle of student desks surrounded Ethan's.

Imelda had traded her modified habit for a pair of linen capris and a sleeveless cotton blouse. Her shoulder-length black veil was the only piece of her wardrobe left to identify her vocation.

I stopped and wiped the sweat off my forehead with the back of my hand. "I need a break."

She finished wiping off one of the desks with an anti-bacterial wipe. "But we're almost finished."

"I need to stop." I took a bottle of water from the small handheld cooler I'd brought from Ethan's RV. "You want one?"

She stood up and arched her back, stretching tight muscles. "Yes."

I sat behind Ethan's desk, directly in front of one of the window fans, she took the desk next to it, but appeared to be doing everything she could not to make eye contact.

After I left Ethan's RV, I'd tracked down Mother Abigail to see what arrangements had been made for the workshop. Except for the designated room, there were none. So, I asked if she could send some help my way and headed off to the Humanities Building. Sr. Imelda showed up shortly after that.

The minute she walked in the classroom she'd been subdued. This was not like the woman I'd met three days ago.

"Where are you from?" I asked.

She looked up and met my gaze. "Originally?"

"Yes. And recently. You told me you missed your friends at your other convent."

She smiled, but it seemed sad. "I grew up in a little town about an hour east of here. I've had a few different assignments, mostly in the Midwest. I did some missionary work in Ecuador, but I came here from Redwood City, California."

"Where's that?"

"Northern California."

"How long were you there?"

She thought about it. "Five years, I think. It was a great group of sisters. A very close community."

Talking seemed to pull her out of whatever funk she was in. "What brought you back to Missouri?"

The light that had been coming back into her eyes disappeared again behind a curtain of sadness. "It was a necessary move. I had some work to do back here."

And that was the end of the conversation. We sat in silence, drinking our cold water and letting the fans blow across our faces.

Imelda looked at me. "I've heard you solve murders," she said.

"Not really. Where did you hear that?"

"Mrs. Miller."

"I helped solve a cold case once, but there was a lot of research that had already been done on it. I just picked up where someone else left off."

"Are you looking into that young man's murder?"

"You mean Ethan Jr.'s?" A dumb question, but I was stalling for an answer.

"Yes."

I wasn't sure how much I wanted people to know regarding my involvement in the current investigation. "I'm somewhat involved, but I'm not working with law enforcement if that's what you mean."

She made a face—her expression filled with contempt. "I don't put a lot of stock in what the police have to say. When my friend was murdered, they didn't do a very good job. Have you found out anything?"

"Such as?"

"Suspects."

"No." I stood. "Maybe we should finish up here, so we can both go cool off somewhere."

I'd cut her off abruptly and she retreated back into her silence.

We finished cleaning the desks, put out some supplies that Ethan and the attendees might need in the morning. The only thing left to do was drag a long table down the hall where we could put out a coffee urn, bottled water, pastries and fruit the next day.

There was a six-foot conference table in one of the other classrooms that we placed up against the wall outside the room Ethan would be using, only to find that it wobbled precariously.

Imelda bent over to check the legs of the table. "I think I can fix this."

She found a small piece of cardboard on a windowsill, folded it and pushed it under the bottom of the too-short leg. When she stood up, a Mizpah medallion fell out of the top of her blouse.

I reached for it and turned it over with my fingers. The chain and background were silver, the one heart on the necklace a rich gold—the other half to the Mizpah I'd seen on Stanley's desk. I looked at the nun. "This is beautiful," I said. "Stanley has half of one that looks identical to this."

She looked at me blankly, took it from my fingers and tucked it back into her blouse. "They're not that unique," she said, then left the room.

CHAPTER SIXTEEN

I WANTED TO MAKE SURE SISTER IMELDA WAS OKAY. I glanced around the room to make sure everything was set for Ethan the next day, then headed for the door. Mother Abigail stopped my progress.

I took the room key from my pocket. "I was just leaving."

She walked in and moved to the middle of the classroom. "This should work for Mr. Miller, don't you think?"

"Yes, I think we have everything we need here. Did you pass Sister Imelda on your way in?"

"She hurried by me on the walkway. She seemed upset. Did something happen?"

"I don't know. She's been rather subdued since the murder yesterday."

"I noticed that too. There's too much death surrounding us." She studied my face for a moment. "Our Chaplin passed away recently while on sabbatical."

"Father Peter?"

She looked surprised. "You've heard of him?"

"Stanley met him in San Francisco. From what I understand, Father Peter is the reason Stanley came to St. Josephine's."

There was a small, tight smile on her lips. "Yes, I'd heard that too. Father was also an instructor and a well-loved teacher. The girls sought him out, not only for academic guidance, but also personal and spiritual counsel. He was a kind and wise man, a part of our community for almost twenty years. He will be greatly missed."

"I'm sorry for your loss."

"Thank you."

"You said he was on sabbatical when he died?"

"Yes, he'd taken time off during second semester."

According to Stanley, Father Peter had quit his job. "So, he was coming back to St. Jo's?"

"His sabbatical was almost over."

As far as I knew, it was mostly academics who offered sabbaticals, but there was usually research or professional development tied to the time away from the job. I asked Mother Abigail, "Was he doing research?"

"Yes."

"For what?"

"I don't know. I wasn't on the committee that granted his time off. I know that when he left, he told me I would find his research project of particular interest. I was looking forward to it."

"What did he teach again?"

"Art History. He was fascinated with the history of Missouri and spent many summers on archeological digs looking for artifacts. He was convinced the area was full of buried treasure, that many valuable pieces of art were stolen and hidden during the Civil War."

"He sounds like someone who would have been interesting to talk to."

"He was. He was always so animated when he got on the subject, you almost couldn't stop him from talking. He even wrote a book about the area. Self-published, but I'm sure you can order it online. It's called *Buried in Missouri* by Father Peter Greene. We have a copy in the library if you'd like to look at it."

"Thanks. I might do that this week." The afternoon heat was taking over the room. I walked out into the cool dark hallway. She followed and I locked the door behind us.

Mother Abigail and I made our way to the convent, passing a Missouri State Patrol car parked in the quad on our way. This was our new normal. Whether we saw them or not, they were present. They were part of the background now, until Ethan Jr.'s killer was found. Every once in a while, I'd notice an unfamiliar face hovering in the vicinity of Constance. Most of the troopers were women, so they blended in well with the workshop ladies.

In the reception area where the sisters lived, an older nun sat in an upholstered tapestry chair.

"Have you seen Sr. Imelda?" I asked her.

"She left about five minutes ago for a walk."

"Did she say where she was going?"

"No, dear. I'm sorry, she didn't."

The college sat on a tract of land that covered hundreds of acres. There was no point even trying to find her, so I headed back to the RV where Millie, and now Constance, lived.

I was almost in front of the Administration Building when my phone rang. I looked at the caller ID: Bob Elliott, my former editor at the *Omaha Tribune*.

"Miss me?" he said when I answered.

"More than you'll ever know. What's up?"

"I have the background checks you asked for. I just sent them to your email."

"Anything noteworthy?" I sat down on the cement bench that was becoming all-too familiar, unfortunately not anymore comfortable to my backside.

"Not much. The Mother Superior has lived in the area all her life from a poor rural farm family. She went from home to college, to the convent and never left. That Sister Imelda, was born in the area, adopted when she was three days old, attended St. Jo's. Worked at schools in the Midwest, did a stint in South America—Ecuador, I think—and ended up in northern California five years ago. Returned to Missouri rather abruptly a few months ago. Most of the women at the workshop have led uneventful lives, minus a few DUI's and divorces. One lost her job when she was accused of embezzlement, but it was never proven. There are two lawyers, one doctor and a state senator in your midst, all graduates of St. Josephine's College."

"Well, that doesn't help much does it?"

"Not yet," he said. There was a long pause and I knew Bob well enough to know that the rusty old wheels in his brain were churning.

"I think there's a *but* coming."

"No *but,* I just want to check out two more people."

"Who?"

"The trail of Stanley to San Francisco grew cold at one point and I want to find out what he's been doing the past couple of years."

"You're kind of fixated on Stanley. I know you don't like him, but that isn't necessarily cause for suspicion."

"Uh huh. Sorry. I don't trust the dude. Let me finish what I started before you dismiss my suspicions."

"Fine. Who else do you need to look into?"

"Virginia Andrews, formerly Clude. I haven't been able to find out much about her at all. I have an address in—"

"Mossberg, Missouri."

"You've heard of it?"

"I've been there, very recently."

"I'm not sure why the information on her is so sparse, almost nonexistent."

"Maybe her life was even more uneventful than the others."

"Maybe, but there's always something out there on the internet, lurking around in your past. Even a blue ribbon at the county fair bake-off. It concerns me that she's almost invisible."

I remembered the gun Matt had found and told Bob. "She'd have to have a license and a permit to carry it, wouldn't she?"

"That should have popped up. I'll keep looking."

"While you're at it, could you also check on a Peter Greene? Father Peter Greene." I gave him what I knew about the priest and he added it to his list.

"Stay safe," he said before he hung up. What, for most people, would have been simple words for the state of my welfare, came out as a low growl. I knew his intent was well-meant, but only because I knew him.

MILLIE TOOK ME IN AGAIN, AND fed me. She sat down across from me while I was finishing a cold tuna and pasta salad and an iced tea. She looked as weary as I felt.

"You okay?" I asked.

"Just tired."

"Constance?"

She looked around the motorhome even though we were the only two there and nodded. "She's a lot of work and I don't mean picking up after her. Just her presence is overwhelming."

"She's a whirlwind wherever she goes."

"Do you think she and Ethan will be making up soon?" There was a look of desperation in her eyes.

I wanted to move back into the motorhome more than Millie wanted to be rid of Constance, but I had my doubts that our wishes would come true. I reached over and rubbed her arm. "We can only hope."

She looked at me with concern. "You don't look so great yourself. Why don't you stay here tonight? You can sleep on the couch."

The couch was about as comfortable as the torture chamber bed in the dorm, but at least I'd have air conditioning if I stayed with Millie, although, I'd be giving up precious privacy.

"I'll try it," I told her. If I was too uncomfortable, I'd sneak into Matt's special dorm room in the middle of the night.

By ten Constance had made her way back home. We were all exhausted and settled into our beds and couches with the lights out. Within minutes, I was off into dreamland.

My cell phone dinged with an incoming text and I jolted awake, a glance at the clock told me it was two a.m.

It took a few seconds for my eyes to adjust to the backlight on my phone screen. Finally, I opened a text from Matt.

I miss you. It said.

I miss you too. I wish you were here.

I'd rather you were here in my bed with me.

I smiled. *Much better choice. Don't you have to teach in the morning.*

Yup.

Then go to sleep.

I love you.

I love you too.

It was worth waking up for. Moonlight flooded the RV, I lay on the couch missing Matt more than ever, and wondering what had become of my life that led me into these murderous situations. Oh yeah, it was Ethan.

My phone dinged again, I expected to see another text from Matt, but this one was from Bob Elliot. *Check your email.*

That's about as warm and friendly as I would get from Bob, especially at two in the morning.

I opened my email and saw one from him with an attachment from late last April from the *San Francisco Chronicle.*

The link took me to a story about the death of a jogger in Presidio National Park. The body of an unidentified white male was found Saturday morning, violently murdered in a wooded area off of a popular jogging path. The middle-aged man, later identified from a discarded wallet found in the area, is believed to be Father Peter Greene of Missouri. Suspected motive was a mugging turned violent.

I lay on the couch, staring at my phone until the backlight turned off.

It wasn't likely I'd get back to sleep anytime soon. I got up off the couch and reached for my clothes.

I wanted to do some further digging into the old news story, and it would be easier to do on a real computer than on my phone. Ethan had laptops in his RV, but I didn't want to wake him in the middle of the night for several reasons, not the least of which was that he'd be in a foul mood for the rest of the day. I wasn't really sure yet what I made of the article I'd just read and I didn't want to talk to him about it either.

The good thing about being stuck on a college campus, was there were computers everywhere, right? All I had to do was break into one of the buildings without getting caught.

I slipped outside and headed toward the Admin Building, watching closely for any police presence, hoping security down here was as lax as it had been over the hill when Stanley and I got into the gym the other night.

The shadow of the building offered good cover in the dead of night and I stayed close to the outside walls as I walked the perimeter, jiggling every door handle until I finally found an unlocked fire exit in the back.

The light from the full moon streamed through the windows as I headed for the front offices. Human Resources might have paper files on Father Greene—and Stanley.

I was halfway down the dark, empty corridor when I heard a footstep behind me. My heart missed a beat. I pressed my body into an alcove.

The footsteps moved closer, within seconds Constance rounded the corner, the moonlight dancing off the shining barrel of the gun in her hand.

CHAPTER SEVENTEEN

THE LIGHT FROM CONSTANCE'S FLASHLIGHT BLINDED ME. I pushed her hand to the side. "What the hell do you think you're doing here? What's the deal with the gun?"

She lowered the revolver and clicked on the safety. "A guy just got murdered here, remember?"

"Put that damn thing away."

She slid the weapon into a small holster on the belt of her slacks. Even in the middle of the night she was dressed to the nines.

With my back still against the wall, I slid to the floor. I wondered if everyone on campus had a gun—except me. It had been less than eighteen months since I'd been shot. The memory was still too vivid. "You scared the shit out of me."

"Sorry." She waited a full half a minute. "Are you okay now?"

I put my head between my knees and took a few deep breaths, then looked up at her. "I think so. What are you doing here?" I stood and she pulled me out of the alcove and into the hallway.

"I heard you leave and figured you must be up to something, I wanted to find out what."

"And you followed me with a gun?"

"Just being careful. It's really for my protection. And yours."

"Seriously? You're going to protect me?"

She took a step toward me. "If I have to."

"You are suspect number one in a murder investigation. Do you think it's wise to be roaming the campus armed?"

"I'm not roaming. I was following you."

"Okay. And now it's time to leave. All I'm doing is looking for a computer."

"I don't believe you. You know something."

"I don't know anything, I want to get some background info on a couple of people who work for the college."

"Who?"

"God, you're stubborn."

"I've heard the same about you."

"You're not leaving, are you?"

"No."

"Fine. Let's get out of the hallway. I was headed to Human Resources."

She walked beside me as we moved toward the front of the building and the HR office.

I looked at her. "You weren't followed, were you?"

"Everyone's asleep. Who would follow me?"

"Haven't you noticed the State Troopers hovering around? They've taken a particular interest in you."

She sounded offended. "Yes, I've noticed them and no, I wasn't followed. I'm not stupid."

"I'm just saying—"

She stopped and took hold of my arm, forcing me to a halt. "I told you, I wasn't followed. I checked. We're safe. Quit worrying. Now tell me who we're investigating."

"Stanley Groveland—"

"The gay guy?"

"How did you know he was gay?"

"Just a hunch. Who else?"

"Father Peter Greene. He was the Chaplin here for twenty years and was murdered last spring while he was on sabbatical in San Francisco."

"I remember that from the alumni newsletter. Do you think it was related to the murder here on campus?"

"I don't know. Could be coincidence."

"I'd met him a few times. He was a nice man."

"So I've heard."

We moved down the hall to the Human Resources office only to find the door was locked.

"Wait," Constance said and ran down the hall, her heeled sandals clicking on the maple floor. A door opened and closed. She came back with a ring of keys. "The janitor's closet. We used to wander around here at night. There was a time I knew every inch of these buildings."

She tried a few keys and eventually found the one that opened the office. Like mother, like son—now I knew where John learned his nefarious ways.

The reception area of the HR department had no windows opening onto the quad, hence no visibility from the outside. I found a switch and flipped on the overhead lights.

Constance walked over to a desk with a nameplate that read Lucy Brown. Lucy's in-basket was overflowing. "What are we looking for?"

She obviously wasn't leaving. I might as well make the most of her presence. After all, she'd gotten us into the office. "Personnel files on Stanley and Father Peter. Hopefully they have hard copies. Anything you can find."

"Do you think that's going to help? What could there possibly be in their files that will tell us who murdered Eth . . . that young man?"

"You don't want to call him Ethan Jr., do you?"

She hesitated. "No. I can't."

"Because?"

She glanced over my shoulder then back at me. "It's too personal. I mean, not because that was his name, but because of the implication that he was Ethan's child."

"But we know that he wasn't."

"I can't do it right now." She pushed back her hair. "What exactly are we looking for that will help us find his murderer?"

"I wish I could tell you. But I don't know. Maybe nothing. Somehow all these threads come back to a center and that's what we need to find."

She walked over to a wall of black four-drawer filing cabinets, almost as tall as she was, and started opening drawers. I attacked the stack of papers on Lucy's desk.

Constance quickly went through the manila folders in the first three filing cabinets. The fourth filing cabinet was locked.

"Aha," she said.

"Did you find something?"

"Locked drawers. All the good stuff is in the locked drawers." She rifled through Lucy's desk until she found keys, then turned back to the last filing cabinet.

She unlocked the drawers and returned the keys to Lucy's desk. John would have been proud.

The in-basket was full of insurance changes, reimbursement forms, requests for professional workshops, nothing that would help us.

Constance pulled Stanley's personnel file out of a drawer and handed it to me.

"Father Peter's should be in that drawer too."

She pulled out another folder and gave it to me.

I elbowed her out of the way and opened another drawer, thumbing through the manila folders from front to back, looking for familiar names. Two drawers down, I found St. Imelda Rolf's file and handed it over my shoulder to Constance. In the drawer below, was Mother Abigail Vargas's file. I took that too, for good measure.

Constance was jazzed. "What next?"

"Let's find the copy machine."

There was a small copy room off the reception area, directly across from Lucy's desk. We made copies of the files we'd pulled from the filing cabinet, then returned the originals to their rightful places. I found a large manila envelope stuffed all our papers in it.

Constance pushed the lock buttons on the filing cabinets. "Okay. Where to now?"

I looked at her. "We haven't really had a chance to talk about what happened. Are you concerned?"

She pursed her lips and thought about the question. "About?"

"This case? Someone getting murdered? The fact that the murderer might not be done yet? About how this might play out for you? Or Ethan?"

She was quiet for several seconds. "Yes. I'm worried about all those things. I don't want to go to jail. I don't want Ethan to go to jail. That's one of the reasons I'm here with you now."

"And the other reason?"

Her eyes filled with tears. "I can't stop thinking about that young man. What happened to him shouldn't happen to anyone. He was almost the same age as John. I don't know what I'd do if something happened to my son. That young man had his whole life ahead of him and someone was hateful enough to take that away."

This was the Constance John had told me about, showing her depth and commitment to those she loved and her compassion for those in pain. And not unlike Ethan, who could drive you to the brink, but would always, always, have your back.

"I think there's more going on here than we realize," she said, her voice low.

"Like what?"

She seemed to be struggling with something, it took a while for her to answer. "I can't say exactly."

"You can't say because you don't know or because you can't tell me."

She paused way too long for my comfort. "Both, I guess."

"Constance, if you know something that will affect the outcome of this case, I need to know what it is. I don't want to be running around on a wild goose chase if I don't have to. And I sure as hell don't want to get shot—again."

She grasped my forearm tightly and I was surprised by her strength. "I would never let that happen to you, Jessica. Ever."

"Good intentions are nice, but they don't offer a whole lot of protection when someone is pointing a gun at you."

"I've probably said too much already. I just wanted you to know that all this might be tied to something much bigger."

"Dammit, Constance, quit playing games with me. What the hell are you talking about?"

She moved toward the door. "You'll have to trust me on this."

That's what Ethan had said to me over a year and a half ago and it didn't turn out well. I was running low on trust these days.

We moved silently down the hallway and I'm pretty sure she knew I was pissed. "Where are we going?" she asked.

"Stanley's office. Do you still have the master keys?"

She jangled the key ring in front of her. "What do you think you'll find in Stanley's office?"

"I haven't a clue. All I know is that he lied to me about Father Peter, and I want to know why. I think he lied to me about a lot of things. I want to find out what he's hiding."

"Like what?"

"No idea. It could all come down to the fact that he's a pathological liar and he lies because he can. But if there's something more going on, I need to know what it is."

Constance stopped in front of the women's restroom twenty feet from Stanley's office. "I have to pee." She hurried into the bathroom, keys and all.

I sat down on a leather chair by a marble statue of St. Thomas, and pulled out my cell phone. I was reading the article again about Father Peter's death, and remembered I still had the phone number of the last person to text Ethan Jr. I found the number in my call log and hit dial. The phone rang in my ear. A second later a phone rang in one of the nearby offices. I got up and moved to Stanley's door. The ringing was coming from in there. To make sure, I hung up, waited a few seconds and dialed again. A phone rang again in Stanley's office, a half-beat off the ringing I heard on my cell.

Constance came up behind me. "Who are you calling in the middle of the night?" she whispered.

"No one." I nodded toward the locked door. "Let's get inside and see what we can find."

Unlike the HR office, Stanley had windows. I didn't want the troopers assigned to the campus to see where we were. Instead we moved through the darkness with Constance's flashlight and the lights from our cell phones.

Constance found more keys and started going through the filing cabinet, while I searched his desk.

She pulled a file out of a drawer and thumbed through the papers. "Why do you think people murder?"

"You mean like *ever*?"

"Yeah. What drives them to murder. If we could come up with a motive, wouldn't it be easier to piece this together?"

"Probably."

"So?"

"You're looking for an answer?"

"Yes."

I stopped what I was doing and looked at her. "From what I've observed, there seem to be mostly generic reasons like money, love, sex, revenge, blackmail."

She sat down on the arm of a chair. "I wonder which one applies to that young man?"

She still wouldn't say his name. I wondered if she ever would. "We have no way of knowing until we find out who did this."

Constance turned her attention back to the files she was holding. "Well look at this."

I walked around the desk to where she was sitting. She handed me a thick file and shone her flashlight on it so I could read—bank statements going back several years for an account in Mother Abigail's name. Activity was sparse and some months there was nothing, but the money that moved through the account was substantial. Occasionally, smaller amounts filtered through, but some deposits were for ten to twenty thousand dollars.

I looked at Constance. "What the hell?"

She shrugged. "I have no idea."

Cleared checks, usually written the month after a large deposit, were divided between the college and an investment account in Mother Abigail's name.

"I don't get it," I said. "Is this part of the fundraising she was so good at?"

"I don't know. I wonder why Stanley would have any of this information. It has nothing to do with his job."

I took the bank statements and handed the empty folder back to Constance. "File this wherever you found it."

She handed me another file. Inside were several birth certificates, Ethan Jr.'s sitting on top.

"What is going on here?" I said.

Constance found a large mailing envelope and put the birth certificates in it. I handed the bank statements back to her to add to our growing collection.

There was a closet door across the room. I walked over and opened it and shone my cell phone flashlight around inside. On the floor, pushed to the back, was a cardboard box that had once held copy paper. I pulled it out and removed the lid. I knew right away that everything in that box had once belonged to Father Peter.

I couldn't carry it all the way back to the dorm without being seen and I really didn't want Constance in on this yet. It was important to find out first what exactly I was dealing with.

The contents of the box looked, perhaps, like they had once been the contents of the dead priest's office. I extracted the few file folders among the personal memorabilia and pushed the box back into place.

Constance had her back to me and I slipped the folders into the envelope that held the copies from the HR Department.

"We need to get going," I said. "We've been here too long."

She locked the file cabinet and returned the keys to the desk, then stepped out into the hall. I took one last look around the room, then walked over to Stanley's desk, opened the top drawer, reached in, removed the Mizpah and put it in my pocket.

CHAPTER EIGHTEEN

W E STARTED DOWN THE DARK HALL, back the way we'd come, each of us carrying an oversized mailing envelope. At the restroom, Constance put out a hand and stopped me. I looked at her, she put a finger to her lips. I heard a footstep behind us—soft breathing.

We walked another twenty feet and Constance pulled me to a stop. Another footstep behind us and Constance yelled, "Run."

She took off. A foot came from behind and hooked around my ankle. I went down hard, the envelope slid across the floor and hit the wall ten feet in front of me. I scrambled forward on my hands and knees trying to retrieve it. Someone grabbed my right foot, I rolled over on my back and kicked hard, aiming in the general direction of a head I couldn't see.

I heard Constance's footsteps moving farther away. My left foot landed a blow against something substantial followed by a loud groan, my right foot was free.

I belly-crawled toward the envelope, grabbed it, stood and ran to the fire door where I'd come in. The door closed behind me and I leaned my back against it trying to find my breath, trying to find my calm place—afraid that I'd lost it somewhere eighteen months ago when I'd been chased by a maniac with a gun.

Constance loomed out of the darkness, grabbed my arm and we ran to the front of the building and into the RV.

We sat on the rumpled blankets on the couch.

"Did you see who it was?" I asked Constance.

She shook her head.

"Maybe the custodian?"

"There is no nighttime custodian. Like other colleges, St. Jo's is in a budget crisis. I remember when they cut hourly staff back to the bare essentials."

"Then who? And what were they trying to do? Scare us away?"

She pushed the hair back off her face. "It could have been anyone. It might not have had anything to do with the murder. We were in the Admin Building in the middle of the night. Regardless of what we were trying to do, we had no business being there. For all we know, it could have been one of the nuns chasing us out."

"Maybe." But I wasn't convinced.

The clock on the microwave read quarter after four. "Why don't you get some sleep," I said. "I have to be at the workshop to greet everyone and sign them in and I'm exhausted."

"Oh damn. I forgot about the workshop. I'll see you in a few hours." She picked up her envelope and went to her room, closing the door behind her.

I'd get the envelope from her later. Right now I needed sleep. I picked up my own envelope and headed for the dorm, where I thought I'd have a better chance of hiding the information until I could look at it. Once in my room, I slid the envelope under my mattress and crawled into bed.

It was eight forty-five, the next time I opened my eyes. Ethan's workshop started at nine. If I didn't expire from lack of sleep, I'm sure Ethan would gladly finish me off when I showed up late.

I threw on some clothes, combed my hair, ran to the elevator and out the front door. I took off across campus and almost bowled over Mother Abigail, who was coming out of the chapel.

"Sorry," I called over my shoulder and kept running.

Sr. Imelda was sitting at a small table outside the door, with a sign-in sheet. The women were already in the classroom.

She looked at my disheveled self and smiled. "It's all taken care of."

The jog across the compound had helped wake me up, but it took a few minutes to catch my breath. "What about the refreshments?"

She waved her hand toward the large table we'd moved into place the day before. "There's tea, water, fresh coffee, fruit, scones, doughnuts and a plate of cheese and sausage."

"How did you manage that? And when?"

"I'm Mother's assistant, remember? I'm authorized to sign checks and department credit cards in her absence. I got here at seven and realized the women would be coming soon, so I took a check from the office and hustled into town and picked up what we needed."

I put my hand on her shoulder. "Oh my gosh. You're a lifesaver. I can never thank you enough."

"Glad I could help. Mr. Miller has been looking for you."

Mr. Miller was the last person I wanted to see. But I couldn't put it off. We needed to get things rolling. I walked into the classroom. Constance and the women were talking to each other, seated at the circle of desks surrounding Ethan's. Everyone had coffee and a plate of food.

There was an eerie sameness about the group. Stepford wives: each one could have been cloned from Constance, same age, same taste in clothing, similar hairstyles and make-up.

Ethan moved to my side. "Glad you could show up."

"Sorry. I overslept."

The look on his face was far from happy. "Do your thing," he said in my ear, "and let's get this over with."

I walked to the front of the circle, welcomed the group, explained what the workshop would cover, introduced Ethan and headed out the door. My part was done.

I made a trip back to my dorm room, passing one of the State Patrol cars on my way. A woman was sitting on the cement bench when I passed Millie's RV. All the other women were in the workshop, so she was likely a Trooper.

I retrieved the envelope from under my mattress. On my way back out, I ran into Ginny as she was entering the front door. She saw me and stuffed a large envelope, almost identical to mine, into her tote bag..

"The workshop has already started," I said. "Aren't you going?"

"I had some personal business to take care of, I'll make it over there for the afternoon session."

I nodded toward the envelope sticking out of her bag. "Isn't that—"

"Sorry. I'm in a hurry." She pushed the button for the elevator and disappeared behind the closed door. I hoped Constance hadn't been stupid enough to hand her envelope off to Ginny.

On my way to the library, I stopped at the Humanities building, grabbed a doughnut and some coffee off the table and headed out.

The library was quiet. I nodded to Sister Ancient behind the circulation desk and went up the spiral staircase to the second floor, ignoring the sign that said, *no food or beverages beyond this point*.

At a workstation near a window, I opened my envelope holding the copies we'd taken from HR and separated them into four piles—Stanley, Father Peter, Imelda and Mother Abigail.

Abigail's covered over forty years of employment. She joined the faculty part-time as an Instructor in the Nursing Department shortly after graduation and taking her vows while working part-time at the local hospital. Years later, she was promoted to Dean of the Nursing Department. Another ten years and she became President of the College. An impressive rise for a first-generation college student who came from a poor rural family.

Sr. Imelda's file showed that she, too, graduated from St. Jo's, but joined an order out of St. Louis. After taking her vows, she spent some time in Ecuador, and worked in elementary schools and child centers in four different locations in the Midwest before moving to Northern California five years ago. Her transfer papers back to St. Jo's were only a few months old. Her college transcripts were attached to the transfer papers, along with workshop certificates she'd attended over the years.

An unexpected sadness moved through me when I opened the file for Father Peter. He'd touched so many lives, it made his own tragic ending even more poignant.

Peter Greene was a true academic—a bachelor's degree in Art History from Notre Dame, a master's from Georgetown and a doctorate from Stanford with a stint as an intern at the Smithsonian. So, what was the lure that brought him to St. Jo's? There was no way of knowing.

His file held a stack of certificates for spiritual retreats he'd attended over the years, his professional development hours.

I took my time on Stanley's file. His application showed his time at the *Omaha Tribune*, but gave no hint of being fired. His resume stated that he'd left Omaha to pursue job options in San Francisco, where he'd worked at two different weekly publications, but his job history barely covered the time he'd spent out west.

The bottom line is, liars lie. I looked at his application again. He'd lied about how he'd left his job in Omaha. What else had he fabricated to get the job at St. Jo's?

He'd told me that he wanted to come to the college to feel closer to Peter after his death. I logged into the computer in front of me and pulled up the article Bob had sent me the night before about the jogger found murdered in the Presidio—Father Peter.

The dates didn't jive. Stanley's application was submitted a week after Peter's death, yet he'd put Peter down as a personal reference.

My brain kept saying, *what's wrong with this picture?*

Had he not known, at that time about the death of his friend? But, if he'd come to the college to feel closer to his dead boyfriend, then of course he knew. Why use Peter as a personal reference at that point? This was odd, and more than a little creepy.

I felt unsettled, not sure what I was missing.

I looked at the three files of the others—Peter, Abby and Imelda.

Imelda's transfer to St. Jo's was requested a week after Stanley's start date at the college. Was it coincidence? Perhaps, but was it even significant?

Back to Peter's file and again to Imelda's. Both had attended the same twenty workshops on the same dates over the past five and a half years. I couldn't chalk that one up to coincidence.

Six months after the first workshop both had attended, Imelda had moved to California, yet she kept traveling back to the Midwest for spiritual retreats.

A warm hand grasped my shoulder. I jumped.

Constance stood over me peering at the papers I had spread out in front of me. "Sorry," she said.

"You are not good for my heart."

She slid into the chair next to mine. "Did you find anything?"

"I'm not sure. Look at this and tell me what you think."

I showed her Stanley's application, pointing out his start date, listing Father Peter as a reference after he was already dead.

She wrinkled her forehead. "Weird. What do you make of it?"

"I don't know. But it's strange. And look at these." I showed her the workshop certificates for Peter and Imelda for so many of the same workshops over the years.

"I don't know what this means."

"Neither do I. Yet."

She looked up at the clock and stood. "I have to get back. This is all very interesting, Jessica, but I don't see where it has anything to do with the murder of that young man."

I was about to ask her about the envelope I'd seen Ginny with that morning, but she was gone.

I stood and stretched. I hadn't realized how long I'd been sitting there, not sure at all if I'd learned anything new.

I gathered up my files and headed for the stairs, dreading what I knew I had to do next. All I could think of as I made my way out into the heat was, *the devil you know.*

CHAPTER NINETEEN

STANLEY SAT BEHIND HIS DESK, the sun coming through the window at his back. *The devil you know . . .*

My shoulder leaned up against the frame, I watched from the doorway. How had I been so naïve all those years ago? Maybe he'd changed in the time we'd been apart—like he'd somehow wandered down the wrong path. I wanted to believe he really had been the boy I thought he was, that I hadn't been so blinded by my own infatuation that I never really knew him, but whoever he'd been all those years ago, the thing that was so clear to me now was that he couldn't be trusted—whatever he told me. I could never count on him again.

His jaw was clenched as he chewed on the inside of his cheek, his attention fixed on the papers on his desk.

With my hand in my pocket, my finger hit dial on my phone and from his desk drawer, another phone started to ring. Something unsettling flooded his face—fear perhaps.

"Aren't you going to answer that?"

The sound of my voice seemed to startle him. He looked at me. It was fear. He hid it quickly. "It's just my cell phone. I'll get it later."

"Your cell phone is on the desk."

I took my phone out of my pocket, ended the call, then hit redial. The ringing inside his desk started again.

The fear turned to anger. "What do you think you're doing?"

"A little research."

"Where'd you get the number?"

"Off of Ethan Jr.'s cell phone."

"And what exactly do you think that proves?"

"Couple of things," I said, and walked in and sat down across from him. "First, that you knew him before the scene at the social hour the other day when he confronted Ethan. And, secondly, your relationship must have been a little slimy if you communicated on a burner phone."

He leaned back in his chair and put his hands behind his head. "So? You've proven nothing."

"The sheriff might think differently."

He laughed. "The sheriff will never know."

"You texted Ethan Jr., asking him to meet you at the cemetery."

He raised an eyebrow.

"Traceable to the number of the phone in your desk drawer."

He smiled and nodded slightly. The anger replaced by arrogance. "The phone isn't traceable to me."

"It would be easy for the authorities to trace where it was purchased, and pull video surveillance from the store to see who bought it."

"That would be Ethan Jr."

"The phone was sitting in your car the day of the murder and now it's in your desk drawer, also traceable."

"I found it lying on the ground and was holding it until someone claimed it."

"You have an answer for everything."

"So it seems."

"I was watching Ethan Jr. that day in your office when Ethan sent everyone away, so he could tell us why he couldn't have been the young man's father. A couple of times, Ethan Jr. looked to you for direction. I thought he was just confused as to what to do, but it was more than that. You had some kind of plan, and he was looking to you to tell him how this was going to play out. What he was supposed to do next."

Stanley looked at me with those deep blue eyes that had lost their magic. Whatever I once felt for him was suddenly gone.

He got up, walked over and closed the office door.

The devil you know . . . Maybe I should have been afraid, but I'd known Stanley for a long time, we'd once been close. He may have been—and probably was—the person Ethan and Bob Elliott and Eric Amundson, my publisher at the *Trib,* thought he was. But he was still Stanley Groveland and I wasn't afraid.

He sat again and leaned forward, putting his elbows on his desk. "We need to talk."

"Okay. Talk."

"Hand me your cell phone."

"Why?"

"Because this is confidential, I don't want anything recorded."

I didn't move.

"Please, Jess."

I wanted to hear what he had to say. I handed him my phone.

He took it and put it on the corner of his desk, out of my reach. "Thank you."

He took his time. "When I met Peter in San Francisco, he was a mess. He was stressed and drinking a lot. At first, I thought it was because he was struggling with his sexuality and the decisions he had to make, and he didn't know what to do."

Stanley watched my face, maybe trying to gauge my response to the story. When I didn't jump in, he went on. "I know that leaving the priesthood was a monumental decision for him, but there seemed to be more. As time went on, I found that he was conflicted about something even bigger than what I saw. He was frightened. He knew something about this college that made him run all the way to west coast."

It was an intriguing tale I'd have to give him that. If I didn't know it was all crap, I would have been on the edge of my seat waiting for the ending.

"And?" I said. "What happened here that scared him halfway across the country?"

"I can't tell you. I'm sorry. I want to break this thing open, for Peter's sake—and mine. I'm hoping to get an exclusive on this when it's all over. You'll have to trust me for now."

"You can't tell me because it's a deep dark secret? Or because you made the whole thing up?"

If I hadn't been watching his face, I might have missed it—a brief flash of anger, right below the surface. "You've very cynical," he said.

"Sadly, I'm not. If I were cynical, I might have seen who you really were years ago. Now, I'm wary."

He smiled. "Of me?"

I didn't want to play this game. "Let's cut the crap, okay? Here's what I know, feel free to fill in the blanks. Father Peter was not leaving the priesthood. He was on sabbatical and was planning on returning to St. Jo's at the end of the semester. You applied for a job here only a week after he died and you used him for a reference, which seems a little odd, don't you think?"

He picked up a pen and started flipping it in the air and catching it. Neither of us talked for a couple of minutes, finally he looked at me. "Oh, sorry. Was I supposed to respond to all that?"

"I'd be interested to hear what you have to say."

He put the pen down. "I didn't know about the sabbatical. I was under the impression that he'd quit his job and was moving to San Francisco. Yes, I applied for the job here when it opened up. The timing was a coincidence. I told you that he spoke of the school often and I visited the website, so when I saw the job posting I applied. I put Peter as a reference, for my sake. I thought his name, and the fact that he was a personal friend, might carry some weight in their selection process. Satisfied?" He smiled.

No, I wasn't. "And how did you get hooked up with Ethan Jr.?"

"He thought Ethan Miller was his father—hence the junior part." He smiled again, thinking he was pretty funny. "When he heard Ethan Miller was going to speak at the college, he contacted me, he wanted to meet him."

"Ethan's visit to St. Jo's wasn't publicized. How did he know?"

He shrugged. "Beats me."

He was so glib about all of this, and the two murdered men whose lives had touched his so very recently. I wanted to reach across the desk and slap him. I stayed put. "What was the deal you had going with Ethan Jr.? Were you two planning on blackmailing my boss?"

"Jessica! I'm shocked."

"To be perfectly honest with you, I'm not really enjoying this game. You had a copy of Ethan Jr's birth certificate. Why?"

"He brought it to me when we met the first time, to show me that his father truly was Ethan Miller. We had no plans. No extortion. Just a young man wanting to meet his father."

I stood and walked around the desk and planted my butt against the corner, so he had to look up at me. "Then why the burner phone? Why the secret rendezvous in the cemetery?"

"The burner phone was his idea. I told you he bought it. That's how he wanted us to communicate, I don't know why. He was an odd dude. Yes, we had a plan for him to meet Ethan Sr., but it was merely for him to meet his father. We'd planned to do it discreetly so as not to cause any awkwardness for anyone. Ethan Jr. bungled the whole thing when he confronted him at the social hour. I wanted to meet him and talk things through."

"At the cemetery?"

"It's private."

"And secluded."

He stood quickly. The glibness had been a temporary cover for the anger seething below the surface. Now I had to look up at him. "If you think I murdered him, you're wrong. I had no motive whatsoever. And I never even made it up there, I overslept."

I pushed away from the desk and straightened up to my full height, still not a match for his, but he needed to know that I wasn't afraid. "It's interesting that there is a trail of murdered men wherever you go, Stanley."

He bent so that his face was only inches from mine. "What the hell are you talking about?"

"Father Peter didn't have a heart attack while he was jogging. He was murdered."

His eyes shifted ever so slightly, as he searched his brain for the next lie. He straightened up and his voice was tight. "You're right. I couldn't deal with that part of it. I told you about the heart attack, because the other made the loss feel so much more painful. So senseless."

I picked up my cell phone and walked to the door. I had my hand on the knob when he said very quietly, "Don't get in my way, Jess."

The devil you know . . .

CHAPTER TWENTY

To anyone who knew Millie, there was no question why Ethan had her on his payroll. As housekeeper at his estate, she kept everything in quiet working order. She took care of the house and she took care of us. She was the calm we counted on in the midst of any storm.

As much as I needed her comfort at the moment, I needed more to be alone—to process what had just happened, to figure out where to go next. To find that one thread that would keep the people I loved out of jail.

I probably should eat, but for once, I wasn't hungry. And, as lovely as it would have been to relax in an air-conditioned space, Millie's presence would be a distraction.

I bypassed the RV and headed for the dorm.

The room was hot and I lay down on the unmade bed.

I thought about secrets. Not that many years ago, although it felt like a lifetime, when Stanley and I were starting out, he would occasionally sleep over at my apartment. Sometimes—when we'd been out too late and he was too tired to drive home—he'd climb into bed with me. There was never any sex, or even the hint of sex—which should have been a tip-off. Right?

But we'd talk until we fell asleep, sharing secrets. The secrets back then had been innocent hopes for what the future would hold. Now we were in the middle of the biggest secret of all and someone had been murdered because of it, whatever it might be.

I sat up and reached for the papers we'd taken from Ethan Jr.'s apartment, the emails from the unknown source.

They'd started last May, tentative at first as if testing the waters, looking to set up a meeting regarding important family information. A second, then a third email, both more insistent than the first. When Ethan Jr. finally responded, he said he wasn't interested.

They didn't stop. Ultimately there was a dialogue. A meeting set up. But in every one of Ethan Jr.'s responses, all he wanted to do was meet his father. If this was a blackmail scheme, it was clear he didn't initiate it. He may even have been naïve enough to have missed the plan altogether.

This was where Ethan Jr. had gotten his information that Ethan Miller was coming to St. Jo's, but who was behind it? Was it Stanley, or someone else from the college?

I took a picture of the IP address and sent it to Bob Elliot. As resourceful as he and his contacts could be, I didn't hold out much hope that they could trace it back to its source. The internet was a convenient place to hide.

It was time to talk to the sheriff. I found his number and called and was put through immediately.

Before I had a chance to bring him up to speed on what I'd found, he cut me off.

"It's not my case, Ms. Kallan, you'll need to contact Sergeant Andrews with the Violent Crimes Support Unit."

"And how do I get hold of Sergeant Andrews?"

The heavy sigh of an overworked County Sheriff came through the line. "I thought you had the number. Just a minute—here it is."

He gave me the number and then he was gone.

I called Sergeant Andrews and was rerouted to another trooper. I gave him a brief message and my contact information and he told me Sergeant Andrews would be in touch—and that was that. An active murder case and no one to connect with, something about this felt very wrong.

I lay back on the bed, closed my eyes and fell asleep. The next thing I knew, Constance was shaking me awake.

I opened my eyes. "What time is it?"

"Six. You were dead to the world." I must have made a face. "Sorry. Poor choice of words."

I sat up and pushed my hair off my face. "What are you doing here?"

"Just checking on you."

"How'd day one of the workshop go?"

"Ethan killed them."

I must have made the face again.

"Sorry. Ethan was awesome. I knew he would be, but he's back in his RV rumbling around like a bear coming out of hibernation. I couldn't take it anymore and had to leave. Millie has a headache and wanted to rest. My son and Dan are bingeing on some stupid vampire show. So, it's you and me."

I made a point to keep all expression off my face. "What about your college chums?"

"I think we've bonded enough for one day. Come on, get up. I'll buy you dinner and you can tell me all about what you learned today."

That was the best thing she'd said since I woke up. I was ready to go in five minutes.

Constance climbed into the driver's seat of the RAV4 and I got in the other side. She drove for about twenty minutes to a small diner on the outskirts of town. The sign by the front door told us to seat ourselves and we found a booth overlooking the parking lot.

I looked around. "Is this it?"

She wrinkled her forehead. "Is this what?"

"Is this the place you and Ethan came the night you met?"

She smiled. "No, that's about four miles west of here."

I was kind of disappointed.

When our food arrived, I told Constance about my conversation with Stanley, and finished the story with his cryptic words as I left his office, *don't get in my way, Jess.*

She put her fork down. "That borders on a threat."

"That's how it felt."

"What do you think he's into?"

"I don't know. There's something significant about his connection to Father Peter, but I don't think it has anything to do with the story he tells."

"But you don't know what that significance is, do you?"

"Not yet."

She started in on her omelet again. I waited before I said, "I saw Ginny this morning with an envelope that looked like the one we put the birth certificates and bank statements in last night."

She didn't even look up as she put strawberry jam on her toast. "I imagine most envelopes look alike."

"Constance?"

She poured creamer into her coffee. It seemed she was doing everything she could to not look me in the eye. "What?"

"Constance, look at me."

She finally made eye contact.

"Did you give that envelope to Ginny?"

She kept her gaze on mine and said very softly, "Don't ask me that, Jessica."

Of all the things that had happened in the last few days, even the threat from Stanley, her voice frightened me the most. "Did you give her the envelope?"

She closed her eyes. "Yes, I did."

"Why?"

"I thought another pair of eyes on the information we found would be helpful."

"I don't believe you."

"I know Ginny grates on you, but she's incredibly bright, and insightful. We need her help right now. Don't worry about it."

"Tell me about the workshop."

She broke eye contact with me and went back to the task of eating—and stalling. "What do you want to know?"

"You and Ginny dreamed this up when you got together in Florida. What was behind that?"

"Not sure what you're driving at, but I thought it would be good PR for Ethan and we both thought it would be good for the college. And, I guess, we were a little nostalgic, wanting to see some of our old classmates again."

The waitress came, took my plate and refilled our coffee. I waited until she was gone. "Whatever money is raised this week for the college, you could easily have written a check for."

"That's not how fundraising works." She looked at me with her big blue eyes and it was easy to see how she manipulated Ethan. I, however, was not Ethan Miller, it had no effect on me. But I also knew she was digging in her heels and I'd gotten as much out of her as I was going to for the time being.

Constance went to pay our bill, then caught up with me as I was walking back to the car. She took a detour on the way back to the college, the scenic route down memory lane, showing me all the places, the girls used to sneak off to, to meet boys, smoke pot, drink and have parties. I turned around once in my seat and thought I saw Ginny following us. I said something to Constance. The car hit a pothole and I grabbed the dashboard. Constance told me I was being paranoid and by the time I turned around again the other car was gone.

Apparently, the best place for the girls from St. Jo's to have private time with their boyfriends was an old deserted rock quarry. Constance aimed the car down an entrance road, that was falling away on one side. I looked out the passenger window. Clods of dirt rolled into the ditch and something slithered off into the weeds. A huge chunk of mud and asphalt slid away from the rear tire.

"Is this safe," I asked.

"Don't be a worry-wart. We're fine."

About fifty yards in, we came to the opening for the quarry.

She stopped the car. "This is it."

It was a rock quarry. It held no special memories for me as it did for her, yet I tried to share her enthusiasm for what a cool place it had once been. I could tell it hadn't been used for a while, but piles of rusty beer cans and stained mattresses expelling their stuffing onto the ground told stories of times past.

"Did you and Ethan ever come here?"

She laughed. "Ethan courted me at his estate and in upscale hotels. He didn't need a rock quarry and the back of a pickup."

It was getting dark out. She slowly turned the car around, careful to avoid the soft spots where we could get stuck, and we headed back the way we'd come in. As she waited to turn back onto the county road, a black Lexus drove by.

We both looked at each other. "Was that Mother Abigail?" I said.

"I think so. Nice wheels."

"Wonder where she's going so late at night?"

I think the trip to the quarry had put Constance back forty-some years, she was in the mood for adventure. "Let's find out." She turned left, the RAV4 chasing a black Lexus driven by an old nun, down a county road in Missouri

"I didn't know nuns could afford cars like that."

"You'd be surprised the gifts that rich grateful Catholics give to their favorite priests and nuns."

"Isn't there like a vow of poverty or something?"

"That's probably not as strict as it used to be. Besides, if you put a good spin on it, it's not an issue."

"How would you put a spin on a car like that?"

"It's necessary for the day to day functions of the convent."

Constance hit the accelerator to close the gap between Mother Abigail and us. I grabbed for the dashboard again. "Sounds like a pretty flimsy rationale."

"Probably."

She was having fun, enjoying the chase.

We drove for fifteen minutes, Constance hanging back just enough for us not to be obvious to the car ahead. Abbigail slowed, took a left turn into the driveway that led to a one-story brick house.

Constance took her foot off the gas and I heard a deep intake of breath. Even in the darkening car, I could see the look of horror on her face.

She applied the brake, steered the car onto the shoulder of the road and cut the lights. The Lexus come to a stop in front of the house.

Constance put her head against the steering wheel and cried softly.

I reached over and patted her back then rubbed her shoulder. "You okay?"

She sat up, wiped away the tears and took a tissue out of her purse. "Sorry. I didn't think it would hit me like that."

"What?" I asked as we watched Mother Abigail walk up the front steps to the house, but I already knew the answer. "Is that the house where your friend, Barb, died?"

"Yes. All those feelings just hit me out of the blue."

"You haven't been here since it happened?"

"No. I don't think I even remembered how to get here. Maybe I blocked it out of my mind. It was the most terrible night of my life."

"So, this is the old doctor's house?"

"Yes."

"That was a long time ago, he's got to be dead by now."

"He'd be over a hundred if he was still alive."

"Then what is Abigail doing here?"

She opened the door. "I don't know. Let's find out."

CHAPTER TWENTY-ONE

DURING HER COLLEGE DAYS, Constance must have been a pistol, she was up for anything. She had more than thirty years on me and I was the one holding back—but then, I was the one who'd once been shot.

She was across the road by the time I caught up with her.

I grabbed her arm. "What the hell are you doing?"

She pulled away. "I'm trying to find out what's going on."

"We just found a dead body, remember? I don't think we should be going off half-cocked in the dark, when no one knows where we are."

Our conversation consisted of stage whispers while trying to see each other's face in the darkness that surrounded us.

"It's Abby. I'm not afraid of her."

"Really? Then why didn't you pull up into the driveway? Why are we sneaking across the road and talking in whispers?"

She stopped and let out a deep breath. "Okay. I'm not afraid of Abby, but I do think something odd is going on around here and I'd like to know what it is, *without* her finding out."

"Why?"

"Trust me, Jessica."

People kept saying that to me, and I was getting tired of it. Trust, to me, had to be earned and none of them had displayed anything to my mind that was remotely trustworthy.

I took her arm again, mostly to keep her tied down until we could come up with a game plan. "What are you going to do?"

"I'm going to find out why Abby is at this house, who lives here now, and what, if anything this has to do with Ethan Jr."

She pulled free of my grip, took my hand and led me up the driveway, just off to the side, close enough to the bushes to keep us from being spotted.

It wasn't really a game plan, just a bunch of unanswered questions that could get us both shot.

Mother Abigail switched on lights as she moved through the house. The living room curtains were open and from where we were, we could see the small living room, the dining room, and part of the kitchen. Constance inched forward, pulling me along as we progressed up the flat asphalt driveway.

We were maybe fifteen yards from the building itself. Constance dropped my hand, made a head bob in the direction of the house and took off running. She crouched down in front of the living room, then motioned for me to follow.

As I sprinted toward the house, all I could think of was that Ethan owed me a raise, and I'd have to find new friends when we got home—maybe a nice, sedate knitting group.

I scooted in behind Constance and knelt in the flower bed, watching for any movement behind us. The yard, at night, with no streetlights was just a big blob of dark, but I was certain, if I wasn't vigilant, someone would sneak up behind us.

Constance batted at my shoulder. "Look."

I didn't want to turn around, just in case . . . "What's she doing?"

"Look."

I peered through the bottom of the picture window. Abigail was coming out of the kitchen with a cup of something and seated herself at the head of the dining table in front of a stack of papers.

I looked at Constance. "What the—"

She put her fingers to her lips and shooshed me.

"This is stupid. We followed an old nun through the night to a farmhouse to watch her do paperwork at the dining room table. Let's go."

"But why is she here? We don't know that yet."

"Does it matter? Everything that happens isn't tied to some big conspiracy theory. Everything that happens at St. Jo's isn't related to Ethan Jr.'s murder."

"I know, I know. But there's something about this house."

"I think the thing about this house is that you experienced the biggest tragedy of your life here and you never dealt with it."

Light from the living room glanced off the side of her head. I could tell she was exasperated. "But I did deal with it. I've been in therapy. You don't think I didn't talk about it? There was a good three months where that's all we talked about. I came to terms with it. I worked through my guilt. I miss my friend, but I don't carry that around with me anymore. It was forty years ago. What I want to know is what is Abby doing here *now*? In *this* house? It doesn't feel right."

"I don't know, but what are we supposed to do?"

"Find out why she's here?" Even in the dark, I could see her smile.

"You going to go knock on the door?"

She grabbed my arm again. "Don't be silly."

The house looked like it was really two structures stuck together. A small brick rural farm house with a large addition tacked on. Maybe that's where the doctor had his clinic or practice.

Constance moved across the front toward the addition, pulling me along behind.

Around the corner was an entrance door with plate glass windows on either side.

"This is it," Constance said.

I knew she meant, this was the place where she and her dorm-mates brought her friend, Barb, the night she died.

"You okay with this?" I asked.

"Yes. I think so." She stood up straight sucking in big gulps of air. "Yes. I'll be fine. Seeing this place for the first time in forty years took me by surprise, but I'm okay now."

She jiggled the door handle, which was locked. I found that of no consequence. Between Constance and her son, I didn't think there was any door, short of a bank vault, that they couldn't get in.

We were hidden from the front windows of the house, so it was doubtful Abby could see us. Constance turned on the flashlight on her cell phone and scoured the ground, all the way to the edge of the woods that bordered the property. Finally, she found a small piece of metal, like a piece from an old wire coat hanger.

She straightened the hard wire as best she could, then inserted an end of it into the door lock, wiggling it around until we heard a click. She looked at me and smiled.

If Ethan ever lost his fortune, Constance and John, could easily support the family as burglars.

We stepped into an office space with a chest-high reception desk on one side of the room, a waiting area on the other. It looked like a doctor's waiting room.

Moonlight filtered through the clouds and came through the window in patches on the floor. We both turned on our flashlights.

"Is this the way you remember it?" I asked.

She made a slow three-hundred-and-sixty-degree turn. "Mostly. Of course, there was no computer back then." She pointed to the computer and printer on the desk in the corner of the reception area. "But it looks a lot like it did back then. We sat over there. And waited. For hours. I think we were all numb with shock. I know I was." She pointed to the tan vinyl chairs up against the wall that was adjacent to the side of the house.

The room looked clean, and smelled slightly of disinfectant.

I picked up a couple of magazines, only a few months old. "Another doctor must have taken over the practice."

"Uh huh." She walked to a door on the wall opposite from where we'd entered, and turned the knob.

"What are you doing?"

"I want to see what's back here. We weren't allowed beyond this door the night Barbie died. We never had a chance to say good-bye to her or the baby."

I knew this was an emotional moment for her, maybe even therapeutic on some level, but we were trespassing. We were already guilty of breaking and entering and had no idea if Mother Abigail—or someone else—would hear us and call the sheriff.

I was coming to understand, what Ethan already knew about his ex-wife. When Constance had something in her head, there was no stopping her. All I could do was follow and hope we'd make it out alive.

Beyond the reception area was a private office and two sterilized, well-equipped exam rooms. It obviously was a functioning medical facility.

At the end of a short hallway was a janitor's closet, a supply room and a door that appeared to lead to the main house.

In the main hallway of the exam area was a door at the end of the corridor, almost to the back of the house. Constance moved toward the door.

I grabbed her arm. "We are not going any further," I said in an emphatic whisper.

"I have to see where that door leads."

"No, you don't. We have no business being here and we have to leave."

I was about two inches taller than she was and had maybe fifteen pounds on her, but as hard as I pulled, she didn't budge.

She pried my fingers off of her forearm. "Go back to the car if you want to, but I'm not done here yet."

In that split second when you have to make a decision you know you'll regret, a million thoughts ran through my head, not the least of which, was that I'd promised Ethan I'd do what I could to keep Constance out of jail. I didn't think being her prison cellmate was what he had in mind, but I couldn't let her go on alone. I followed her to the door, which opened onto basement steps.

We kept our flashlights aimed at the stairs, all the way to the bottom. Egress windows faced the back of the property. We continued on with flimsy lights illuminating only a few feet in front of us. There was another wall with two more doors.

Constance opened the nearest door. We stepped into a small, clean five-bed infirmary.

"Dammit, Constance, we have found nothing—absolutely nothing—except the medical practice of a country doctor. We are courting jail time if we get caught. I'm out of here."

"One more minute. Come on. We've already come this far."

"There is nothing here to see."

She backed out of the infirmary and opened the other door. There was an enclosed room, no windows here, big enough for a small office, but actually filled with linens. I think she was disappointed. I turned and headed for the stairs.

We made it outside and crept down the driveway the way we had come, moving slowly, as close the bushes as we could get.

"That was a total waste of time and adrenaline," I said, once we were in the car.

"Maybe." She started the engine and drove maybe a quarter of a mile with the headlights off, before she switched them on and made a tight U-turn in the middle of the road, pointing us back in the direction of St. Jo's.

Neither of us spoke on the long drive back to the college.

She pulled to a stop behind the RV. "You staying with us tonight?"

"No, I think I'll sleep in the dorm."

I left her sitting there and headed back to my private room. Ginny was sitting alone in the commons area on the main floor when I entered the building. The lights were out and she was smoking, her cigarette glowing in the dark every time she took a puff.

I nodded to her on my way the elevator.

She smiled. "You two find what you were looking for?"

CHAPTER TWENTY-TWO

I WASN'T IN THE MOOD TO DEAL WITH THE NOSY, ex-homecoming queen, or tell her she was in a smoke-free building. I kept going up to the fourth floor.

A gray tee-shirt was lying at the foot of the bed, where I'd thrown it that morning in my rush to get to the workshop. I stepped out of my clothes and slipped it over my head, then got into bed, exhausted.

I overslept—again. When I opened my eyes at eight-thirty, Constance was sitting in a chair she'd moved from the desk, as close to my bed as she could get it.

"What the hell?" I said when I saw her, then looked at the clock. "Oh crap."

"Settle down. Imelda has already set everything up for the day."

"This is starting to get creepy. What are you doing here? Didn't we spend enough quality time together last night?"

"I want to show you something."

"Now?"

"It's important."

"Do you mind if I pee first?"

"Fine. But hurry."

When I got back to the room, she was sitting on the edge of the bed. "I need to get to the workshop, but I wanted to show you what I found last night."

"What do you mean what you *found last night*? Didn't you go to bed when I left you?"

"Eventually. But look." She patted the bed next to her.

I sat down and she handed me what looked like a real estate deed. To make her happy, I pretended to scan it. "What am I looking at?"

She flipped to the last page and pointed a long pink fingernail at the bottom. "Abigail Vargas."

"Where did you get this?"

"Abby's office, last night."

"Constance, you are bound and determined to get yourself arrested."

It was clear she was losing patience with me. She flipped back to page one and pointed to an address. "This is where we were last night. This is the address of the house where that old doctor lived, and the owner of said property is now, Abigail Vargas."

I stood and started to rummage for some clean clothes. "So?"

"So? That's all you can say? How did Abby come into possession of the property?"

I pulled on some white shorts. "Maybe she bought it. Maybe the old doctor left it to her. Maybe he left it to the monastery and she's the executive in charge, or whatever she would be. I don't know."

"First of all, how could she buy it?"

I found a yellow cotton blouse, slightly wrinkled, but clean, took off the tee-shirt and put on the blouse. "I don't know. Maybe she inherited money."

"Her family was dirt poor."

"Okay. The doctor left it to her."

"Why?"

"Constance, I *don't know*. You told me last night that people sometimes give expensive gifts to favorite nuns or priests. I could probably come up with a million plausible answers, but the truth is, *I don't know*. And I don't care. I don't know what you're searching for here and I don't know why it matters. I don't find it all that interesting. Or mysterious."

"You saw it, Jessica. There's a fully equipped medical practice there."

"Maybe she rents it out to a doctor. Don't you have a workshop to get to."

She glanced at her watch. "Okay, I'm leaving. But I think this is important. Just think about it, please."

She handed me the deed and left.

The problem with amateurs getting involved in investigations was that everything to them was a possible clue. Not that I'm not an amateur, but I did have some experience and was trying very hard not to be led down a dead-end path. We didn't have time for that.

Constance had left and I finished making myself presentable, like combing my hair, a little mascara and hiding the dark circles under my eyes with some concealer. For four days, I'd been running on empty.

I headed toward the Humanities Building, hoping Ethan would see me and take note of my professional dedication—or that Ethan would see how exhausted I looked and have enough compassion not to fire me.

The ladies were all in their seats when I got there. I poked my head in the door, smiled and waved. The ladies smiled back. Ethan did not.

Imelda was straightening up the coffee area in the hallway. I grabbed some paper towels and started wiping down the table. There was more food that she'd picked up in town.

"Thanks for doing that," I said. "Sorry I haven't been here for the setup."

She smiled and pulled a credit card out of the pocket of her black skirt. "No problem. Compliments of St. Jo's and Mother Abigail. Besides, it's been kind of fun to have a purpose so early in the morning, to run into town, and it gets me out of morning prayers."

I raised my eyebrows. "I never thought a nun would say that."

She shrugged. "We're human, believe it or not."

She bent over to pick up some napkins that had fallen to the floor, the gold chain and the Mizpah fell out of her blouse; she saw me notice and tucked it quickly beneath the fabric.

I moved in next to her. "Did you get that from Father Peter?"

She tried to look casual and kept her face blank, but her eyes gave her away. "Who?"

"Father Peter Greene."

"No. I mean, I never met him. He was the Chaplin here, right? I think he died before I came to St. Jo's."

She wasn't a very good liar—her entire demeanor changed the moment I mentioned his name.

"Skipping morning prayers and lying. Not very nun-like behavior."

She wouldn't look at me and busied herself wiping the table that I had cleaned minutes ago.

I caught her arm in mid-swipe. "You don't remember Father Peter from the retreats and workshops you two attended over the years?"

She looked like she was thinking. "Oh yeah. I think I had met him before."

I took the paper towels from her hand and laid them on the table. "We need to talk."

"But . . ."

"It's important."

We made our way down the hall and found an unlocked class-room. I went in and, to my surprise, she followed me. I'd half expected her to bolt, as soon as I turned my back.

I sat at a student desk and nodded to the one next to it. She took a seat, but kept her eyes on the floor.

I put my hand on her arm. "You and Father Greene were good friends, weren't you?"

She looked up at me. "Very."

"Then why did you lie to me about him?"

"I don't know. I didn't want to talk about him yet. His murder was . . ."

She didn't finish.

"When did you meet?"

"Maybe eight years ago, at a spiritual retreat, when I was still in the Midwest. He was part of my small group and he was the kind-est, wisest man I'd ever met. We spent a lot of time talking about our vocations. We saw each other again at another retreat months later. After we left, we kept in touch with occasional emails and our friendship started to grow."

She relaxed some while she was talking. Her words weren't hesitant anymore and I wondered if she'd ever had the chance to tell her story.

"Stanley said Father was gay," I said.

"What? No, he wasn't."

"Are you sure?"

"Well, yes, as sure as anyone can be. Why would he say that?"

As untrustworthy as Stanley could be, that was the one thing he'd told me that I hadn't questioned. And, really, how would Imelda know one way or the other? "Stanley said Father Peter was leaving the priesthood and finally coming to terms with his sexuality and that he was gay."

There was the strangest look on her face and I didn't have a clue how to read it. She shook her head. "No. That's not true. He wasn't gay."

"He said Father Greene was also drinking a lot out there."

Sadness filled her eyes. "Yes, that part's true."

"Any particular reason?"

"He was under a lot of stress. He had a personal research project that consumed him, and I think the intensity of it was taking its toll."

"Was he going to leave the priesthood?"

She closed her eyes then opened them. "Eventually. He was coming back to St. Jo's for a while, because he had things to take care of here."

"What things?"

She shrugged. "Something to do with one of his students."

I felt like I was losing her. "Did you get your half of the Mizpah from him?"

She fingered the pendant around her neck and looked away. When she looked back at me, there were tears in her eyes. "Yes. Last spring, when he came to San Francisco. We were out walking one day, and passed a small jewelry store and went inside. He found these and thought they were beautiful, so he bought them and gave one to me. I told him they were too expensive, but he insisted. It was my fortieth birthday, April fifth. He wanted to do something special for me and said we should wear them every day and we'd always be safe. But . . ."

"But?"

"But then he wasn't."

"Wasn't what?"

"Safe. Two days later he was murdered."

"I wonder if he was wearing it then?"

"I know he was. I saw him when he left to go jogging and he had it on."

"Did you know Stanley before you came to St. Jo's?"

She shook her head. "Father talked about him sometimes. They met in a bar I think."

"Isn't it interesting that you both ended up at the college."

CHAPTER TWENTY-THREE

Imelda left and I headed back to the dorm. She was pretty upset and sometimes I wondered if I did more harm than good.

Immediately following Ethan Jr.'s murder, there was an overt law enforcement presence on the campus, but now, as I crossed the quad area, it seemed like they'd blended into the scenery. I rarely noticed them anymore, wherever they were. I wondered how close they were to an arrest, if they had sufficient evidence to implicate anyone. It just made me feel like I had to work harder if I was going to protect Constance and also, Ethan. He may not be high on their radar, but anyone looking for a motive could easily find one.

I'd never heard back from Sergeant Andrews and called the number the sheriff gave me—again. And, again, I reached the sergeant's partner, underling, friend. I was never really sure who I was talking to or why I couldn't get through to the person in charge of the investigation. I left another message.

From under my mattress, I pulled out my stash from the Admin Building from two nights ago and the files I'd confiscated from Father Peter's box in Stanley's storage closet.

I'd told Sister Imelda it was interesting that both she and Stanley had ended up at St. Jo's, but it really wasn't. There was no coincidence, the common denominator was Father Peter. He was the reason they both were here. What that meant, I hadn't a clue.

The folders, which appeared to have been taken from his office, held old sermons and sermon notes, class lecture materials and syllabi. One folder contained a stack of personal emails from friends, his brother and possibly a lover—romantic, borderline steamy and unsigned. No way of knowing if the sender was straight or gay—only that whoever it was, was very much in love with him.

A final folder held Father Peter's handwritten notes from counseling sessions with one of the freshman students, Franny Pohlson.

Franny and Father Peter started meeting last December. At the time she was six months pregnant. Her boyfriend had left and she was terrified to tell her very religious parents of her situation.

After only a few meetings, Franny went AWOL. She never registered for second semester, and Father Greene hoped that the girl had gone home.

In the early spring, she was back, emotionally distraught. She told Father Peter that she thought she'd found the help she needed through one of the nuns who offered her a place to stay for the final months of her pregnancy. The sister tried to encourage her to give the baby up for adoption, but Franny was determined to keep her child.

After she delivered, the baby wasn't breathing and was whisked away. Franny was given a sedative and slept for almost two days, but every time she awoke, she could hear her baby—she was sure it was her baby—crying. She wasn't sure how many days later she was given the sad news that the baby died. Franny was convinced the nun had killed her baby.

It wasn't clear whether or not Father Peter believed the girl's story, but he convinced Franny that she needed to talk to the authorities and made arrangements to drive her the next day to the Missouri Violent Crimes Support Unit. And then the notes stopped, with no follow-up on Franny or the investigation.

Father Peter had scribbled names and years on the back of the file. I took a picture of it, then picked up the file and headed toward the computer lab at the library.

Sister Imelda was coming out of the chapel when I passed.

I stopped her on the walkway. "Can I ask you a question?"

She looked wary, maybe because my questions always brought her to tears. "Sure."

"You said that Father Peter was coming back to the college because he had something he had to take care of."

"Yes."

"What was that?"

"It had something to do with one of his students. Why?"

"A student who'd recently had a baby?"

She hesitated. "Well, I guess it doesn't matter now. There's no confidentiality here to breach. Yes, the girl had had a baby."

"Franny Pohlson?"

"How did you—"

"What was he coming back to do?"

"I'm not entirely sure. He'd talked to the authorities before he left for the west coast and they wanted him to come back. Maybe they wanted more information from him. That's all I know, Jessica."

"Thank you."

SISTER ANCIENT WAS AT HER POST at the circulation desk and I waved as I hurried past and up the stairs to the second floor. Constance and Ginny had taken up residence by the window, engrossed in some serious conversation.

Constance looked up as I approached. Ginny scooted around in her chair to face me.

I pulled up a chair. "What's up?"

Constance glanced at Ginny, then back at me. "We're on our lunch break."

"And you wanted to spend it in the library?"

Constance stood. "As good a place as any, I guess. Sorry to run, Jessica, but we need to get back now."

I looked at Ginny and realized who she was and why she was here. I don't know why it took so long, maybe because I'd been so distracted—sidetracked by Ethan Jr.'s murder. "Ginny Clude."

She smiled. "I haven't been that since college."

I moved in a couple of inches. "What is it now? Andrews? Are you related to Sergeant Andrews? From the state Violent Crimes Support Unit?"

"We need to be going," Constance said.

Ginny stopped her as she moved past us. "It's okay, Connie," Ginny said and looked at me. "I'm Sergeant Andrews. I'm the one you've been leaving messages for."

It was one of those moments when you kind of want to kick yourself for not seeing the obvious. "Do you work undercover?" I asked.

"Sometimes."

Which may have been why Bob Elliot couldn't find any information on her.

"Were you ever going to return my calls?"

She smiled. "Eventually. I'm sure you can understand that I've been busy these past few days."

It's not that I don't believe in coincidences. I just think they're rare. "You being on campus when Ethan Jr. was murdered seems rather fortuitous."

She didn't respond.

"Were you here for another reason?"

"The workshop."

Constance was getting antsy, but Ginny stayed put, watching my face. "What is it you want to ask me?"

"Did Father Peter talk to you about Franny Pohlson?"

"Yes."

"Is that why you're here?"

She paused. "Yes. Ethan Jr.'s death was an unforeseeable event. The fact that it happened while I was on campus was a coincidence."

"I don't believe in those. What happened with Franny Pohlson?"

"It's an active case. We're still investigating."

"I'd like to talk to you later."

She nodded. "That's a good idea. How about six? I'll be in the commons at the dorm."

They left.

I did a web-search on Franny Pohlson. Not much history on her, she was only eighteen. I clicked on the first two links connected with her name. She was a cute girl from a middle-class family in Kansas City. An Honors student in high school, she won a partial scholarship to St. Jo's to study Elementary Education. Her parents owned a hardware store and Franny and her three brothers all worked there during high school.

I opened a link to the Mossberg Weekly, little expecting to see an article about how she died in a hit-and-run accident. I checked the date, then looked at Father Peter's file. Franny died the night before she was going to report the death of her baby at the Violent Crimes Support Unit. She was struck from behind by a car while she was walking on a rural road outside of Mossberg, a hit and run. The driver never even stopped to help her. By the time, she was found and paramedics were called, it was too late, she died at the scene. Another coincidence?

THE AFTERNOON SLID AWAY. At three-thirty, I walked over to Ethan's RV, knowing he was done for the day, and knocked on the door.

He plodded his way through the shaky metal structure and swung open the door.

I stepped in and he handed me a drink. "What's this?"

"Screwdriver. It's how I'm ending all my days after answering inane questions for two hours every afternoon, and reading character descriptions for another hour of my life that I will never get back, written by a bunch of women with too much time on their hands about their third grade teacher or their first love."

I sat down in the recliner. "So, you're having fun?"

He glared at me and poured himself a drink, then came and sat down across from me. "If anyone ever tries to talk me into doing something like this again, please remind me how much I hated it, and then shoot them."

"Really sounds like you're having fun to me."

"If you say that one more time, I will take back my vodka and personally throw you out the door. I'm guessing you wanted to talk to me about something. What is it?"

I brought him up to speed on everything I knew. When I started, it didn't seem like there was much to tell, but once I got rolling, it turned out to be a lot.

He listened. I finally got his attention when I got to the part about Father Peter's and Franny's cases being handled by the same officer investigating Ethan Jr.'s murder. Sergeant Andrews, previously Ginny Clude, Constance's former classmate.

He wrinkled his forehead. "Interesting."

"Did you know that Constance and Ginny got together in Florida, before Constance came to see you at the estate?"

"Where are you going with this?"

"Did they set up this week's activities when they met in Florida and then pulled you in? And, if so, why?"

He looked out the window. I'd spent enough time with Ethan to know when he was working something through in his head. "They wanted me on campus for some reason," he said without looking at me.

"Why?"

He turned back toward me. "I don't know, but I intend to find out."

"I think you should wait, Ethan. If there's something Constance doesn't want you to know, there's no way you're going to get it out of her until she's ready. I think we need to keep doing what we're doing and watch to see what happens."

"You're right, but you know what makes my blood boil? If Constance and Ginny had some scheme to get me here, for whatever reason, then she was manipulating me and I will not tolerate that."

I raised an eyebrow. "Really? Isn't that exactly what you did to me last year to pull me into the investigation on your estate?"

"That was different."

CHAPTER TWENTY-FOUR

M ILLIE FED ME HOMEMADE CHILI AND GARLIC BREAD. It was
wonderful and I didn't want to leave. But, at five to six I forced
myself out the door and headed to the dorm and my meeting with
Ginny, Father Peter's file on Franny Pohlson under my arm.

She was sitting on a plush gray sectional and hung up her cell
phone when I walked in.

Her first words were, "I don't have much time."

I sat next to her. "Okay. Then let's talk."

"Jessica, I am currently working two active cases. If you think
I'm going to give you an interview you're wrong. Ask me what you
like. I may or may not answer."

"So much for full disclosure."

She smiled. "I never promised that."

I handed her the file Father Peter had on Franny Pohlson, she
pulled her glasses down from the top of her head where they were
perched and flipped through it, scanning pages as she went. "Can
you tell me about Franny?" I asked.

She put down the folder. "No. I told you before I will not give an
interview. Your questions need to be more direct."

"From what I understand, you and Constance met at her condo
in Florida last spring to plan the activities here on campus for this
week. Correct?"

"Correct."

"And Ethan had not been consulted at that point?"

"Also correct."

"Was your purpose to have a reunion this week?"

She looked at me without blinking—stalling. "No."

"So, you wanted to be here for another reason?"

"Yes."

I felt like I was playing twenty-questions and I was getting frustrated. "Why did you need to be here? And why pull Constance in?"

Again, she was slow to answer. "After Franny died, Father Peter was my only source for the investigation regarding her allegations on the death of her child. After he was murdered, I had no one. It was important for me to be on campus, but I couldn't get a search warrant, I didn't have any evidence that a crime had been committed."

"But you believed a crime *had* been committed?"

"It's my job to investigate. I have to have an open mind. The story Father Peter told me seemed plausible."

"But what would be the motive?"

"You're putting the cart before the horse. First I had to prove that there had been a murder."

"Okay. So, why the workshop?"

"As I said, I was unable to obtain a search warrant. I was told I could interrogate people, but unless you have a substantial lead, that often goes nowhere. My next option was to get here by some other means. I met with Constance and this is what we came up with. An unobtrusive way to be present with a small select group who would not get in the way of my investigation."

"And you wanted to use Ethan?"

She smiled. "He was merely the vehicle to get us in place. I brought it up to Constance, and she jumped on board with that right away."

"Do you think Franny was murdered."

"I do."

Her answer was quick. It certainly wasn't a surprise, but it was disturbing. "So, you were here investigating the case of Franny Pohlson, and Ethan Jr. just happened to get murdered."

She nodded. "Essentially."

"And were you the one who took the case away from Sheriff Allen?"

She did a funny kind of head bob. "I pulled a few strings."

"He didn't seem very happy about it at the time."

"Law enforcement can get very territorial. I understand his feelings. We've talked recently and he understands why it's best for me to be here. He's a competent sheriff and he would have done an excellent job on this case, but I needed to take over as a matter of logistics. Besides, the man is woefully overworked. Once he accepted my position here, he was glad to have one less thing on his plate."

Her cell phone rang and she looked down at the caller ID. She stood. "I have to take this." She picked up Father Peter's file on Franny, walked out into the front reception area and outside.

I moved to the glass front door of the building and watched her light a cigarette and pace up and down the sidewalk, talking to whoever it was. The bubble-headed former homecoming queen had been replaced by a serious law enforcement professional. The look on her face indicated the conversation was not going well. Finally, she put the phone in her pocket, stubbed out her cigarette, got into her car and drove off campus.

Even now, knowing who Ginny was, I still didn't know what to make of her or how much to trust her. As Constance's friend, did she still consider Constance a suspect in Ethan Jr.'s murder? For whatever reason, I didn't trust Ginny. She was all too eager to use Ethan to get on campus, which seemed less than ethical to me?

I turned and headed toward the elevators when John caught up with me.

"What's going on with my mother?" he asked.

I realized that I hadn't talked to him for a while. "Nothing at the moment."

"I saw you two leave together last night."

"We went out to dinner."

He looked disappointed. I wasn't sure what he expected, what he thought I was going to say. "You got back pretty late."

"She took me on the grand tour of all her illicit college party sites."

"I don't need to hear about those. So, you don't know anything?"

"Not yet. I'll keep looking, but you need to stop worrying."

"That's what Ethan says too."

"Maybe you can help me with something."

"I'm up for anything. What is it?"

We rode in the elevator to the air conditioned second floor. The few women we passed didn't seem to mind another of Ethan's sons wandering the hallway.

"Where are we going?" he whispered.

I stopped in front of Ginny's door, and looked down the corridor to make sure we were alone. "We're there." I turned the knob, but it was locked. "I need you to get me in here."

He didn't even question it. He pulled a credit card out of his wallet and slid it through the separation between the flimsy door frame and the molding that surrounded it, until he hit the lock, then maneuvered it up and down, until he hit the sweet spot that released the lock.

We were inside in less than a minute. All I wanted was the envelope with the birth certificates that Constance and I had taken from Stanley's office.

It was crammed into a top desk drawer. Once I retrieved it, I nodded toward the hallway. John opened the door a crack to check for anyone in the hall outside. He inched it open slowly, then motioned me out. He clicked the lock behind him, closed the door and we were free.

He followed me to the elevator. "What's in there?"

"Just some paperwork I found in Stanley's office."

"How'd it end up in that room?"

I pushed the button for the elevator. "That was Ginny's room. Your mother gave her the envelope."

"Because?"

"Long story, but I want to check what's in here and compare it to something else I have."

He didn't question me further. "Do you need me for anything else?"

"Not right now. Thanks for your help."

I rode down to the lobby with him and before he got out, I put my hand on his arm. "Please don't worry about your mother. Everything will be okay."

He looked like he might be fighting back tears. "Thanks."

In addition to breaking into Ginny's room, I'm sure there were other laws I'd just broken, like stealing stolen evidence back from a law enforcement officer. I wondered how long it would take for her to figure out it was missing.

I pushed the elevator button to take me up to the fourth floor. My phone was ringing when I walked into my drab dorm room.

"Have you found a murderer yet?" Matt asked.

"If that's your lead-in to phone sex, I can see why you've been single for so long?"

"Really? Maybe it's my delivery."

"I miss you."

"I think when this is over, you need to come stay with me for a few weeks, you interested?"

"More than you know."

We talked for a while, said *I love you*, and then hung up. I stretched out on the narrow single bed and fell instantly asleep.

IT WAS DARK WHEN I WOKE up. I hadn't intended to fall asleep.

I went to the restroom, splashed cold water on my face. Back in my room, it took a minute to remember what it was I'd planned on doing before I zoned out.

The envelope I'd taken from Ginny's room lay at the foot of my bed. I dumped the contents onto the desk, wondering where all the birth certificates had come from and why Stanley had them in his office.

There were twenty of them, all local births, all signed by the same doctor, covering a span of years, most of them ten or more years old. I pulled up the picture I had on my phone of the names Peter had written on the back of Franny's file.

The names from the file all corresponded to a mother listed on one of the birth certificates, but there were more certificates than names.

I stuffed the papers back in the envelope and took off for John and Dan's RV.

All the RV's had the same layout, with the bedrooms at the back. I went to John's bedroom window and scratched on the screen. Getting no response, I scratched louder. Still there was nothing. Finally, I tapped on the window. When that didn't stir him, I pounded loudly, hoping Dan wouldn't hear.

John's face appeared at the window, his hair tousled from sleep. He slid the glass open. "What the hell are you doing here?"

"I need you to break into one of the buildings for me."

"Now?"

"No. Let's wait until the middle of the day. Oh wait. Everything would be unlocked and I wouldn't need you. Of course, *now*."

"Yeah. Funny. I should have remembered from our trip to Mossberg how cranky you get in the middle of the night."

"Are you going to help me or not?"

There was enough light shining against the back of the RV that I could see him roll his eyes. "Let me get some clothes on."

I sat down on the curb to wait. Five minutes later he emerged from his air-conditioned bedroom carrying a plastic grocery bag.

"What's in the bag?"

He reached out a hand to help pull me up. "Just some tools I might need. Where are we going?"

"The library."

"We're breaking into the library?"

"Yup." I started walking.

He caught up with me. "Why?"

"I need to check on something."

"And it can't wait until morning?"

"No."

We walked across the campus surrounded by an eerie silence.

When we reached the library, John squatted down to examine the locks on the two heavy main doors. The moon over his shoulder provided enough illumination for his nefarious deeds, so I walked around the building looking for other entrances, hoping for an unlocked fire door like there'd been at the Admin Building a couple of nights ago.

There was a door on every side of the building, but all were locked. By the time I was back in front, John had the entryway unlocked, a look of accomplishment on his face, wires and knives and screwdrivers on the ground by his feet.

"Want to know how I did it?" he asked.

"No." I pulled open the heavy door and walked inside.

The door closed behind me. Two minutes later, he caught up with me as I started up the spiral staircase, my cell phone flashlight, leading the way, his bag of burglary tools in his hand.

"Where are we going?" he whispered.

"Third floor. I don't think we need to whisper."

"What's on the third floor?"

"Old yearbooks."

I was expecting a response, but there was none.

We reached the bookshelves filled with old yearbooks, where I'd found Constance, the day Ethan Jr. had been murdered.

"What now?" John asked.

I showed him the picture on my phone of the back of Father Peter's file on Franny Pohlson.

"I want to see if these girls were students here at St. Jo's. I think the number next to each name is either the year they attended school or the year they graduated. You start at the bottom and I'll start at the top. Find the corresponding yearbook and see if the girl is in there."

"What is that going to tell us?"

"I'm not sure yet."

Unlike Matt, who questioned everything I did, John, seemed perfectly willing to go with the flow, whether or not he understood what the flow might be. It made my life easier.

It didn't take long to get through the list. All the names Father Peter had written on the back of his file were former students at St. Jo's. We moved on to the birth mothers' names on the birth certificates, who hadn't made it to Father's list.

I gave half to John and looked up the other half myself. We went by the year the birth certificate had been issued. We found most of the mothers in the yearbook corresponding to that date. We had to go back to the previous year on a couple of them, to find them in one of the yearbooks. When we were finished, all the names were accounted for as previous students at St. Josephine's College for Women.

John had stretched out on the floor between the stacks. "Do we know anything yet?"

I looked at him, he was half asleep. "We know that all these girls attended St. Jo's."

"Sounds inconsequential."

"You may be right. Let's get out of here, before you fall asleep and I have to carry you out."

CHAPTER TWENTY-FIVE

IT WAS TOO LATE TO DO ANYTHING ELSE and I was too tired to care. I dropped John off at his RV and went back to the dorm and my hot, lonely room.

I set my alarm for six and went to bed.

At seven the next morning, I was showered and dressed and sitting on the edge of Constance's bed when she opened her eyes. I smiled. "Good morning, sunshine."

She rubbed her eyes and glared at me. Even waking from a deep sleep, she looked gorgeous—another reminder that life isn't fair. "Good God, Jessica. What the hell are you doing here? What time is it?"

"Tell me about Ginny."

"What?"

"Is she a close friend of yours?"

She scooted up in bed until she was resting her back against the wall. "I don't know what you're talking about. Go away."

I moved up closer. "Tell me about Ginny."

"What is it you want to know? And why do you need to know it at this hour of the morning?"

"Why didn't you tell me who she was and that she was investigating a murder?"

Constance reached for the blue metal-framed glasses on her nightstand and put them on. "We thought it best that you didn't know."

"Why?"

She swung her legs over the side of the bed until we were sitting side by side. "We thought the fewer people who knew what was going on, the better. If people got in the way, it could impede her investigation and possibly be dangerous."

"Then why let me run around doing my own investigations and even helping me, when she was here, supposedly doing the same thing? Isn't that supposed to be her job?"

Constance ran a hand through her hair. "Legally, there are some things Ginny can't do."

"Like breaking and entering and stealing information from private offices?"

"Exactly."

"I was being sarcastic."

"I know you were, but it's true. If Ginny obtained the same information illegally, she could not use it as grounds for an arrest and it would never be admissible in court if there was a trial."

I shook my head. "Something's not right here."

She raised an eyebrow, but said nothing.

I stood and looked down at Constance sitting on the edge of the bed. "I don't trust Ginny. I don't know what the two of you are up to, but this doesn't feel like a legitimate investigation."

I moved toward the door in the small bedroom, she didn't bother to deny what I'd said or try to stop me.

Millie was cooking breakfast and I sat down to eat, my first real breakfast in days that didn't consist of pastry and coffee.

While I visited with Millie, I heard Constance in the bathroom, moving back and forth between the bathroom and her bedroom. I finished my bacon and eggs and left before she made it to the kitchen.

I was in the Humanities Building when Sister Imelda walked in, carrying boxes from the bakery and bags from the local deli. She seemed surprised to see me.

I helped her set out the food, filled the humongous coffee urn with pitchers of water from the sink in the restroom and had it going before the first of the ladies showed up for the workshop.

By nine, Ethan and his gaggle of women were all settled in the classroom for the day. I looked at Imelda, "I need to talk to you."

The look on her face told me she was still wary of me. "Now?"

"Do you have other plans?"

"I should get over to my office, I have a ton of paperwork on my desk—"

"Can it wait?"

She opened her mouth, closed it and finally said, "Yes, it can wait."

We walked down the hall to the classroom where we'd talked the other day and sat at the same desks.

"Tell me about Father Peter," I said.

"I thought we did this the other day."

"Tell me about *you* and Father Peter."

Her eyes filled with tears. The tears spilled over and ran down her cheeks. She put her face in her hands and cried. I waited until she'd finished crying and took a tissue from her skirt pocket and dabbed at her eyes.

"I'm sorry," she said.

"It's hard to lose someone you love, isn't it?"

Her eyes filled with tears again, but the crying jag had passed. "He was a good friend."

"He was more than a friend, I think. Am I wrong?"

She drew in a breath. "No, you're not wrong."

"You were in love with him."

"Yes. And he was in love with me."

I reached out and put my hand over hers. "Tell me what happened."

"We met at a retreat outside of Springfield, maybe eight years ago. He was the most spiritual man I'd ever known. We went for long walks and would talk for hours. Then the week was over and we both went back to our lives."

I removed my hand from hers. She didn't seem to need my reassurance any longer. A peaceful calm had settled on her face. "Did you keep in touch after that week?"

"No. I thought about him often, but we didn't communicate."

"When did you see him again?"

"A year later, we were both back at the same retreat, it was almost as if no time had passed. We picked up where we'd left off, like two comfortable friends," She smiled. "We spent every moment we could together. And when we left, we exchanged email addresses so we could keep in touch. At first it was maybe once or twice a month, then once or twice a week. Eventually we were writing every day. I wasn't sure about Peter, but I knew I was falling in love. I tried to deny it, I tried to fight it, but it was there. We'd never done anything wrong, but I felt as if I'd broken my vows. I didn't know what to do."

She looked out the window for the longest time.

"Sister?" I finally said.

She turned to look at me, a sadness came over her features, as if I'd pulled her back from a place she'd rather be than sitting in an uncomfortable student desk in the Humanities Building at St. Josephine's College. "Yes?"

"When did you and Father Peter see each other again?"

She smiled a sad, lost smile. "Any time we could. We made a point to attend as many of the same retreats as we could. And every time, we'd find a way to be alone together to talk. The first time Peter kissed me, we were on retreat in Nebraska. I'll never forget it. I don't know which one of us said it first, but being able to finally say, *I love you*, out loud made it real."

"Were you planning on leaving your orders?"

She shrugged. "We talked about it. We both fought it. We'd made a lifelong commitment and neither one of us expected this."

"So, what were you going to do?"

"We thought maybe if we had some distance between us, our feelings might change. That's when I went to California. And even though I loved my new convent out there, and loved the sisters, I still missed Peter. More than before. I think he felt the same way."

It was starting to come together. "Tell me about last spring when he was in California. Had he planned, by then, to leave the priesthood?"

Her eyes filled with tears again. "Yes, he'd finally made his decision. And his strength gave me the courage I needed to leave my order. We were trying to plan the best time to make the transition, neither one of us wanted to put our schools in a bind. But we were going to get married."

"If all this good stuff was happening, then why was Peter drinking so much?"

"I'm not entirely sure. He'd planned on coming out in the spring so we could make plans, but when he arrived, he wasn't himself. He told me about Franny Pohlson and he told me that he thought she'd been murdered. As bad as that was, I always felt like there was more to it, and I couldn't get him to tell me what it was. He was stressed, and he was drinking. At first not a lot, just regularly."

"Could it have been from the stress of leaving the priesthood?"

"Possibly, but I don't think so. His decision had been coming for a long time and I think he'd reconciled himself to that."

"And how did Stanley come into the picture?"

Her face got dark. "He met Stanley one day while I was teaching. They may have met in a bar, I'm not sure. All I know is they ended up in a bar. Every time he met with Stanley, there was more and more drinking. In fact, we even started fighting about it. We'd never fought before."

"And you're certain he wasn't having an affair with Stanley?"

Anger flashed through her eyes and then it was gone. I wasn't sure if I'd offended her. "He was not having an affair with Stanley, I'm certain of that. But I was working every day and Stanley somehow became his outlet for . . . . well, I honestly don't know what he was an outlet for. I felt that he was sharing more with Stanley than he was with me about what was going on here. Maybe he didn't want to upset me."

"And you don't know what it was that was eating at him?"

"No."

"Tell me about the day he died."

She hesitated, looking down at the floor. "We'd spent the night together." She looked at me, to see perhaps, if I was shocked.

"How did you mange that?"

"I made up a story about out-of-town relatives visiting the area and I was going to stay at their hotel and show them the sites. We didn't sleep together. We just talked all night. In the morning, I had to get back to school and Peter left to go running. I never saw him alive again."

Oddly enough, there were no tears. Maybe she was all cried out. She pulled herself up in her chair, as if willing some kind of strength into her body.

"What happened when you didn't hear from him again?"

"That night, I called the police department. He hadn't been gone long enough for them to do anything. I called all the area hospitals. Nothing. Even though I didn't want to admit it, somewhere inside, I knew he was dead."

She stopped talking and looked down at her hands. The silence hung between us.

"Was he wearing his Mizpah when he went running?"

She smiled. "Of course. It was supposed to protect him."

I pulled Father Peter's Mizpah out of my pocket and handed it to her.

She clutched it to her chest. "Thank you. Oh, thank you. But where did you—how did you get it?"

"We can talk about that later."

I DIDN'T KNOW WHAT TO DO NEXT—where to go from there, so I wandered aimlessly around the campus, into the woods behind the dorm, up over the hill, until I found myself, eventually, sitting in the cemetery on the monument for Barb Baker, Constance's friend.

By late afternoon, I was back in the RV, letting Millie feed me. I was trying to give Imelda her space, it had been an emotional morning.

When I finally left Millie, it was almost four. I headed back to my dorm room, stripped off my clothes, put on a tee-shirt and lay down on the bed. I fell into a deep sleep and didn't wake up until the moon was shining through my window.

I lay on the bed in the dark, trying to sort through everything Imelda had said. How her relationship with Peter had developed and blossomed over the years, the plans they had for the future. Peter, by some cosmic fluke, meeting Stanley.

I thought of Stanley and Peter spending all those hours together, drinking. What was it that Peter had shared with Stanley? What did he know? And why couldn't he share his secret with Imelda—whatever the hell it was?

A part of me felt cheated that I'd never met Father Peter. A part of me was jealous, that he'd touched so many lives and now our paths had crossed only after his death.

He was strong, compassionate and deeply spiritual. Even in death, Stanley and Imelda wanted to feel close to him—so close, they were willing to give up everything to come to St. Jo's to be near him.

No, that wasn't right. There was that niggling in my brain, when the pieces just didn't fit—when the obvious was too neat, too predictable, too, well, obvious.

Stanley had told me why he was here, but Imelda never had. I'd assumed that she came here for the same reason as Stanley, to feel closer to Father Peter. Something else brought her here. Stanley was here because of Father Peter, but Imelda was here because of Stanley.

CHAPTER TWENTY-SIX

I GOT UP, WASHED MY FACE and slipped back into my clothes. I was spending more time roaming the campus in the dark, it seemed, than I was during the day.

The fire door on the back of the Administration Building was unlocked and I moved into the building, turning on the flashlight on my cell phone. The key ring in the janitor's closet was back where Constance had put it the other night. I lifted it off the hook on the wall and carried it down the hall, trying not to let it jangle as I made my way.

Once in Stanley's office, I moved around his desk and looked out the window at the vacant campus below, a feeling of sadness settled over me.

I sat at the desk, searching methodically through every drawer, not rushed as I had been with Constance, taking my time. There was nothing.

In the closet, I pulled Father Peter's box out into the office and lifted off the top. It appeared to be mostly personal items that he may have had in his office, but too much to examine thoroughly by flashlight.

I hefted the box up, looked around to make sure nothing seemed out of place and headed for the door. In the hallway, I placed the box in the alcove and went back to lock up.

There was a footstep behind me. Too close, then the click of a gun being cocked, a sound I could never forget. I leaned my head against the doorframe, unable to make myself turn and look.

The gun barrel poked into my back, then harder.

"I thought we were friends," he said.

Finally, I turned to see Stanley's face, half illuminated by the moonlight shining through the front windows of the building, half from my flashlight. The hairs on the back of my neck stood up, the look on his face was evil. Adrenaline crept up my spine. It was Stanley's face, but not Stanley's face. It was a look I'd never seen before.

With more conviction than I felt, I said, "Put the gun away."

He raised an eyebrow. "I don't think you're in a position to tell me what to do right now."

"Stanley, what are you doing? It's me. Jess. Whatever trouble you've gotten yourself into I can help. Just tell me."

"You don't have any idea." He waved the gun in the direction of the far end of the hall. "Let's go."

"Where?"

His voice grew harsh. "No questions. Let's go. Now."

I moved past him and headed toward the other end of the building.

"We'll leave the same way you came in," he said.

We walked through the darkness toward the fire door. All I could hear in my head was Constance, the night we'd been in here together, *run!* she'd yelled. I didn't have a gun pointed at my back that night.

With every step, I was calculating a way out, but he was too close.

My flashlight still in my hand pointing the way, I pushed open the fire door, then reached up and pulled the fire alarm. I was out the door and turned to push it closed behind me. Stanley pushed from the other side, he was strong. The door opened a crack, then inches. I took off running, up the hill toward the woods, the fire alarm blaring behind me, strobe lights from the top of the building flashing through the night.

I didn't think Stanley would chance a shot when we were out in the open, visible to anyone in the dorm or cloister, looking out a window. And I was hoping someone was looking out their window. Someone would see us.

I ran harder than I'd run in a long time; probably not since the last time I'd been chased through the night by a crazy person with a gun.

He was gaining on me. He called for me to stop. I kept going. I was almost to the woods at the top of the hill. The trees would give me the cover I needed, only a hundred yards away.

I could hear his feet hitting the dirt, closing the gap between us. Only fifty yards to the woods, I heard a sound and looked over my shoulder. He dove for my legs and hit me in the back of the knees. I went down, hard. We skidded across the dried grass, but he didn't let go.

He flipped me over on my back, straddled my abdomen and clocked me across my jaw.

His breathing was erratic. "Don't. Try. That. Again."

He slid off of me, sitting in the grass, trying to catch his breath, while I tried to catch mine.

There was some commotion at the bottom of the hill, but I couldn't see it—only the strobe lights throwing blinding rhythmic flashes through the night.

He pushed the gun into my ribcage. "That was stupid, Jess. Really, really stupid. Don't try it again. Do you understand me?"

I nodded.

"Let's go." He stood and waited for me to get to my feet. I don't think I could have taken off running if I tried. There was nothing left inside me.

We moved off into the woods, the noise and the lights from the building below fading, as we moved farther away from the tree line.

I don't know how far we walked or where we were headed. In the dark and the unfamiliar terrain, I didn't think I could find my way back to Ethan even if I could get away from Stanley now.

Five, maybe ten minutes later we came to a clearing. Boulders perched haphazardly around the perimeter of a misshapen circle.

Neither of us had recovered completely from our run up the side of the hill in the heat, both of us still breathing hard. Stanley waved me toward a small rock to sit down, He leaned his back against an ancient oak tree.

I couldn't hear anything from the bottom of the hill, not even sure anymore, how far we were from the campus buildings.

I looked at Stanley in the dark. "What are you going to do with me?"

"I'm not sure yet."

"Not much of a plan."

"Doesn't matter. I've got the gun."

I didn't need to be reminded. "Are you going to kill me?"

"Probably."

"You'd kill a friend?"

"We haven't been friends for a long time, Jess."

"No, I guess not."

He moved out into the clearing and squatted down in front of me about ten feet away. "This all would have been fine, if you could have stayed out of it."

"Ah. So, this is my fault?"

He smiled. "Mostly."

"Tell me what happened in San Francisco. Tell me what happened with Father Peter."

"Not sure what you want to know."

"You weren't having a relationship with him, were you?"

"Nope."

"And he wasn't gay?"

"Not as far as I could tell."

"Then why the lie? I would have had no way of knowing either way. Why did you have to make up that story?"

He stood and stretched, but his eyes were on me the whole time. I couldn't make a run for it. "You were asking too many questions, you wanted to know what brought me to this hell-hole. I had to come up with something plausible. No one would come here without some draw. And I thought it would shut you up, especially a sad tale of a broken heart."

"Okay, so you met Peter in a bar, right?"

"That part was true. I found out early on that he wasn't much of a drinker. And when he was drunk, he liked to talk. At first, it was kind of funny to get him drunk and hear him ramble on, but after a while, I started paying attention."

"What did he tell you?"

He laughed. "All the dirty little secrets that are hiding under the rug at St. Josephine's College for Women. When he was drunk, I could ask him anything."

"So? You learned all the gossip."

"That I did. But, the more I listened, the more I realized that it was more than gossip, this could well be worth my while."

My butt was going numb. I stood, and Stanley took a step closer. "Are you talking embezzlement?"

He relaxed a little, when he realized I wasn't going anywhere. "Embezzlement takes too long and gets too messy. Too many red flags along the way. I was thinking more about blackmail."

"And did Peter know what your plans were?"

"He figured it out. Even drunk, he wasn't stupid. And he realized, eventually, that he'd tipped his hand too much. After a while, he caught on that my questions weren't just idle conversation, that I was actually pumping him for information. He tried to clam up at that point, but it was too late?"

This was not the man I'd fallen in love with. Or maybe it was but I was too young and naïve to realize who he really was. I didn't want to hear the answer to the next question, but I had to ask. "What do you mean too late?"

Stanley moved over to one of the smaller stones and sat on it. He smiled. "I think you already know the answer to that. I had all the information I needed to put a plan in place. When Peter figured that out, I offered to let him in on it. He was suddenly all self-righteous and moral. Said, he'd never let me get away with my plan, that he'd go to the authorities. I didn't really need him anymore. He'd become a liability."

"And you murdered him while he was out jogging."

"Always the reporter, aren't you, Jess?"

"Just putting it all together. Was it really necessary to kill him, Stanley?"

"When he started to threaten me, it was. This was the best gig I'd had in a long time, I wasn't going to let him blow it."

"Why the Mizpah? Why did you steal that?"

"Just a small trophy for a day's work."

Stanley was a full-blown psychopath. There was no doubt in my mind, and if he was remorseless over Peter's death, there was nothing to stop him from getting rid of me too.

I had to think. "So, your plan was to blackmail Ethan Miller with an illegitimate son?"

He nodded slowly. "That was the tip of the iceberg, but it's not what brought me to the college. I didn't know about that little gem until I got here, but when I found Ethan Jr.'s birth certificate and heard Ethan Miller was coming to the college, it couldn't have been more perfect. We had a plan in place to extort a little cash from the famous author, but then Junior had his own agenda and ruined it."

I was looking around now, trying to figure which way to run. After hearing about Peter, I knew I had to try. It was my only chance. Just think. And keep him talking. "Ethan Jr. wasn't really onboard with the blackmail, tough, was he? He just wanted to meet the man he thought was his father?"

"All true. All pretty lame, in my book. We could have made out pretty well on that one."

"Why did you have to kill him, though?"

He laughed and reached up to scratch his nose. "He knew too much, but I didn't kill him. I didn't have to. Someone did it for me. I told you, I overslept. By the time I made it to the cemetery, he was already dead. It was perfect, I got what I needed and my hands are clean. As far as murderers, my money is still on that Constance Miller chick."

He found a great deal of humor in that and kept laughing. He was laughing when the gun went off in the woods somewhere behind me. And in that instant, when he realized what had happened, he stopped laughing, as the bullet tore into his chest.

He hit the ground and I took off running, full bore into the woods. Fragments of moonlight filtered through the leaves, but not enough to help me. Someone was crashing through the trees behind me, there was no time to slow down and look around.

I kept running, hurdled a few fallen limbs and slipped and fell in a stream. I got up and slogged my way to the other side, then ran like my life depended on it—which it did.

I didn't know which way I was headed. The person with the gun wasn't far behind. I jumped over a small log, hit a hole on the other side and twisted my ankle. I fell to my knees and my phone flew out of my hand. I lost my balance and went face-first into the moss-covered ground.

CHAPTER TWENTY-SEVEN

I LAY PERFECTLY STILL, MY HEART POUNDED, blood pulsed in my temples.

The footsteps slowed, moved closer. I rolled up against the log, as close as I could get, listening.

For a while there was nothing—no sound, only the woods at night. I lay there. Five minutes passed. Did I hear movement? Was it a footstep, an animal? I couldn't be sure.

And then again, it was too slow, too methodical, too calculating for an animal. I listened trying to gauge the direction from where it was coming, trying to determine the distance between us.

The sound came from somewhere on the other side of the log—quite a way out. The footsteps moved, stopped, moved closer, then stopped. I wondered if they could hear me breathing.

I couldn't wait any longer. Waiting would be my death.

I had to run. I had to find my way back to Ethan.

The footsteps were moving away. I peered over the log, into the darkness. I had no idea where my phone had landed, but I didn't have time to look. I crawled on my hands and knees back into the dense part of the woods, moving in the opposite direction of the footsteps.

Once, I was hidden in the trees, I stood and moved forward. Or I hoped it was forward. I'd heard stories of people lost in the woods, moving in endless circles, never making any progress, guided by some internal dysfunctional compass.

I took my time, step by step, away from the small clearing where I'd fallen next to the log. If I took my time, if I moved slowly and paid attention, maybe I could figure out a direction—maybe.

Every time a twig snapped beneath my foot or I kicked up a pile of leaves that rustled around me, I stopped, terrified, waiting for the footsteps to come back.

It was slow going, but at least I was moving. All I wanted, was to keep moving. I had no way to judge the passage of time. It could have been twenty minutes, maybe an hour. Finally, I made it to the edge of a clearing.

Rocks and boulders formed that erratic circle. This is where Stanley had taken me. I scanned the ground and saw his prostrate body. In the covering of the trees, I moved around the edge of the clearing, until I was as close to Stanley's body as I could be and still remain hidden.

I already knew he was dead. But I also knew I had to check. I had to be sure. I got down on my belly on the dry grass and scooted and inched my way toward him.

As I neared his body, I stopped again, listening for any movement in the woods, then reached out and felt for a pulse. I put my ear to his face, hoping to hear a breath.

He was dead. I wanted to cry for so many reasons, but I didn't have time to cry. There was nothing I could do for Stanley and I had to keep going.

I scooted back to the tree line, stood and moved to the boulder on the far side of the circle, where we'd come from when Stanley brought me to this place.

I moved deliberately through the woods, trying to sense the path we'd taken to get here. I developed a funky sort of rhythm: walk, stop, look at my surroundings, hoping to see something—anything—familiar. I listened for footsteps behind me.

It was a painstaking process. After some time, I relaxed my routine a little, until I was simply walking. I hoped I was headed back in the direction of the buildings and RV's.

There was a break in the trees ahead. Moonlight shifted and gained strength. I was almost at another clearing. It was the edge of the woods at the top of the hill, overlooking the Administration Building.

Relief flooded in. I moved faster. I let my guard down, wasn't paying attention. And then I heard the footsteps moving in quickly behind me.

I heard my name. "Jessica," someone whispered. I wanted to run. I should have run. Instead I stopped, turned.

Ginny stepped toward me, a gun in one hand, and reached for my wrist with the other.

I pulled away hard enough that I almost lost my balance, then bent over, and rammed my shoulder as hard as I could into her abdomen. She groaned and fell backwards. Her head snapped back and smacked up against a maple tree with a thud, before she slid to the ground. I think she was unconscious. I didn't stop to find out. I ran.

I hit the tree line, and started down the hill, then stopped. Someone was moving around down there, but I couldn't make out who it was. Then two more people came into view. I looked back over my shoulder to see if Ginny was following me. I couldn't see her. Maybe she was hiding in the trees.

I did a slow zigzag down the hill, moving in a crazy pattern, so as not to be an easy target either from the top of the hill or the bottom.

Eventually, I stood outside the fire door in the back of the Administration Building. It would have been a good place to hide, but I wanted to get to Ethan. I wanted to feel safe and I needed his help.

I stayed close to the building, working my way around to the front. Whoever I'd seen from the top of the hill was now gone. I moved across the open area, past the fountain, toward Ethan's RV.

The door to the motorhome was locked. I moved around to the back, and scratched on his bedroom screen. He didn't stir. I scratched harder, then tapped and finally pounded.

He still didn't respond and I was starting to panic. Ethan was a light sleeper, so he either wasn't there or someone had gotten to him too.

John would help. I was quickly running out of steam. I needed someone with a clear head. I turned away from Ethan's RV. A large heavy object landed on the side of my skull. I started to fall and then everything went black.

MY HEAD THROBBED AND SOMETHING STICKY WAS IN MY HAIR. I tried to open my eyes, but they wouldn't cooperate and I fell back into the black pit.

Consciousness ebbed again. I forced my eyelids up, blinking, trying to clear my vision.

I was inside a building, but it was dark. The only light was a sliver that peaked through the bottom of a door.

My arms were tied down and I could only partially sit up, resting my weight against my forearms. I was lying on a firm surface up off the floor, but it didn't feel like a bed; there was a pillow underneath my head.

When I wiggled my feet, my legs were also in restraints. There was movement overhead. Was there a second floor maybe?

As much as I wanted to fight my restraints, to figure out a way to break free, I didn't have enough fight in me to try. I heard movement again above me and I closed my eyes, slipping back into the vast unknown. I was so tired.

CHAPTER TWENTY-EIGHT

FOR A MOMENT, I WAS LOOKING INTO STANLEY'S LIFELESS EYES—his beautiful blue eyes staring up at me with questions I couldn't answer. Stanley asking, with those unblinking eyes, why it hadn't been me, why I wasn't the one lying on the ground with a bullet in her heart.

I realized that I'd been dreaming, but that line between reality and dream grew hazy as I crossed back and forth between consciousness and the nether world.

The dream was dark, some malevolent figure was chasing me through the trees. It was disturbing and I knew there was something else I needed to do. I finally forced myself awake.

My head ached. When I opened my eyes again, the light seeping through underneath the door had shifted, what had previously looked like a lamp was now, the gray light of morning.

I listened, waiting for the footsteps overhead. But there was only silence. I tried to figure out who had brought me here. There were few people I trusted anymore.

Ginny was the one who came to mind, Ginny walking through the woods, gun in hand. She was law enforcement, I knew that, but I'd never trusted her. And her connection to Constance was confusing.

And what about Constance? We'd started an awkward friendship over the past few weeks, but there was still much about her I didn't know. I knew very little about her past, except what she'd chosen to share. She'd had no qualms about using Ethan to get on campus. Maybe there was more to the story than anyone suspected.

The similarities between the death of Constance's friend, Barb, and Franny Pohlson's allegations about what happened to her, were all too obvious. An investigation might stir up questions that Constance or Ginny didn't want anyone to ask.

I wondered if I'd been missed, if Ethan knew I was gone. Had anyone thought to check my dorm room? And would my absence tell them I was in trouble?

I strained, in the darkness, trying to make out shapes, but it was hard to tell what I really saw and what was an illusion.

I pulled against the restraints on my arms, then my legs. The strap on my right leg had some give to it and I moved my leg, trying to pull free.

I flexed my right thigh, then rolled to the side and was able to maneuver my right leg until it was free. I rolled onto my back, breathing hard. It had been an exertion.

One free leg didn't do me much good. I braced the heel of my right shoe against the toe of my left, then slid my foot toward my body until the heel of my shoe was off and I could kick it to the floor.

My free foot rubbed against the restraint on my left ankle. It felt like a wide leather belt with a large metal buckle resting on top. My right leg crossed over the left, until my toes reached the excess end of the strap that had been pulled through the buckle. I tried to push the excess up and through the buckle. After several tries, I stopped in between to catch my breath, and rest my leg muscles that were on the verge of a major cramp.

Minutes passed. The light beneath the door, changed as daylight took hold. I maneuvered my free foot until I was finally able to push the loose end of the strap up through the buckle. I took a break, then went back to the task of grabbing the end with my toes and pulling it back far enough, releasing it from the center prong holding it in place.

Eventually, both feet were free. I was still stuck, but now I had hope that, somehow, I might be able to remove myself from the arm restraints.

The room was cool and I fell asleep again. Sadly, it was the best sleep I'd had in days. I was tired, frustrated, hungry, scared and had a head wound, so until help arrived, it wasn't a bad way to pass the time.

A door slammed upstairs and jolted me awake. The light under the door was full-on daylight, but what time of day, I had no way of knowing.

I pulled against the arm restraints again.

Upstairs, footsteps plodded across the floor, back and forth in some kind of methodical pattern. Doors opened and closed.

A car door slammed. The footsteps overhead stopped, then softly retraced their path. And then, silence.

An outside door to the building creaked open, then closed again, and I realized, I was in the basement of the clinic Constance and I had found in Mother Abigail's house. Who had brought me here? Was it Constance? Was it Ginny? I'd thought she was following us that night. If this was where Barb had died forty years ago, Ginny would certainly know about this place.

How many other people knew about the clinic and this basement?

There were two people upstairs now, but I heard no voices, only silence.

I pictured what I knew of the layout of the house. The door that had just opened and closed was the front door to the living room.

Who was upstairs? Part of me wanted to know, but part of me knew whatever I'd gotten myself into might only get worse, once one of those people made their way downstairs.

Time passed. I fell asleep again. The front door slammed and I startled awake.

I pushed myself up into a half-sitting position, my forearms flat against the table, my head and shoulders raised, as I looked around in the dark room.

Metal cabinets filled with medical supplies hugged the walls. High up in a far corner, covered by a curtain, was a window edged by sunlight. My shoulder muscles strained, I laid back down. And I waited.

The footsteps started again. The heavy, methodical footsteps, moving across the front of the house. They moved through what I thought was the dining room. Eventually, they were almost overhead.

I was still frightened, but a little hopeful. Maybe help was on the way. The door at the top of the stairs creaked open and someone made their way down the basement stairs.

Just as quickly as the hope had risen, it slipped away. Now there was only terror. With all that had happened in the past few days, I couldn't kid myself that this was going to end well.

My breath became erratic. There was a loud noise, like someone falling down the stairs, a hard thud, silence and then a groan followed by swearing.

I called out, "Ethan. I'm in here."

I wasn't sure if he'd heard me, he was still swearing. I waited.

"Ethan? Are you all right?"

"No, I'm not all right! I just fell down these damn stairs. Where the hell are you?"

"Open the door. I'm right here."

He grunted. "Oh God. I think I broke something."

"Can you get up? Are you okay?"

"Jessie, I'll get there as soon as I can."

He panted and grunted and there was more swearing, but eventually, the doorknob turned and the door swung open. Sunlight blasted my retinas. It took a while to adjust. Ethan's silhouette should have filled the doorway, but he wasn't there.

"Ethan? Where are you?"

"Jessie. Shut. Up. I'm moving as fast as I can."

It sounded like he was dragging himself across the tile. An arm came into view and he reached up and flipped on a light switch.

He was on the floor. "What are you doing down there?"

He glared at me. "I told you, I think I broke my ankle."

"Are you sure you didn't sprain it? Can you stand up?"

His head was bleeding. There was a lot of blood.

We weren't saved. We were still in a shitload of trouble, but Ethan was here. He'd come for me and I felt a sense of relief.

He scooted over to a heavy lab table and pulled himself up.

"Can you put weight on your foot?"

"I don't know." He put his foot on the floor, tried to take a step and almost fell. "Dammit!"

"I don't think you could have done that much if you'd broken it. It's got to be a sprain."

A sprained ankle or a broken ankle were the same to Ethan. Either would be another of life's annoyances. He was not happy.

He braced himself against the lab table, and closed his eyes. I could see the pain on his face.

He opened his eyes and looked at me. "Are you all right?"

"I think so. I got hit on the head last night, but I'm probably in better shape than you are right now. Stanley's dead."

"I know. I found him in the woods."

"How did you know I was here?"

"I didn't. Everyone's out looking for you. Constance dropped me off here and is headed for the rock quarry."

"Can you move at all?"

"I'm not sure I can walk." He looked around and saw, a few feet away, one of those stools on wheels that doctors sit on when they're doing pelvic exams. He pulled it up next to him then lowered himself onto it.

"Who was upstairs with you?"

"I don't know. I hid when they came into the house."

"What do we do now, Ethan?"

"We've got to get out of here." He scooted toward me on the stool, and pulled himself up, leaning against the table I was on while he unfastened my restraints. I sat up and rubbed my wrists.

Ethan examined the top of my head. "You've got quite a knot back there and a pretty deep cut. You didn't see who did this?"

"No."

He cleaned up my head with wet paper towels and gauze and I cleaned up the gash on his head from the fall down the stairs. Then I made him get up on the table so I could look at his ankle. It was swollen and already starting to turn black and blue, I didn't think it was a break. I found an Ace bandage in a metal cabinet and wrapped it tightly to give him some support.

I helped him stand. He put a little weight on his foot.

"Are you going to be okay?" I asked.

"Yes. Let's go."

"Is Constance coming back for you?"

"I don't know. Doesn't matter, we need to get out of here."

I found a cane leaned up in a corner and handed it to Ethan, then got on his other side, so he could put some of his weight on my shoulders.

We took exactly four steps forward, when Mother Abigail appeared in the doorway.

Ethan and I exchanged looks.

"Mr. Miller is hurt," I told her as we inched toward the door. "We need to get him to a doctor."

"Where are you hurt, Mr. Miller?"

"I sprained or broke my ankle."

"I see," she said.

She was very calm. Too calm. She stood watching us and the pit in my stomach grew tighter. We inched forward again. Ethan couldn't move quickly, and it was obvious that if she didn't move out of the doorway, once we got there, we had nowhere to go. Ethan was big and strong. But in his present state, Mother Abigail, could easily reach out and push him over.

We moved a few more feet. She didn't budge.

We were in trouble and we both knew it. I felt Ethan's hand tighten on my shoulder and I sensed him assessing the situation. But it didn't change our odds.

We were halfway across the room, when Mother Abigail took a gun out from beneath the folds of her habit.

As only the great Ethan Miller could, he looked at Mother Abigail and said, "Put that thing away."

"I'm afraid I can't do that, Mr. Miller."

He removed his arm from around my shoulders and tottered forward a few steps, positioning himself between me and the gun. "And why not, may I ask?"

She actually looked very sad. "Too much has happened here recently. I need to protect this college, our sisters, our students.

That is my responsibility, so you see, Mr. Miller, the gun is necessary for the protection of St. Josephine's College."

"I don't understand what the hell you're talking about." And it was obvious he didn't. Ethan was a brilliant man, but had limited skills in reading other people—or the motives that drove them to take drastic measures, and when it came to reading women, he was clueless. I don't think he believed for a second that Mother Abigail would hurt us. Even though, she'd said very plainly that she needed to protect the three things that meant most to her in the world.

He took another step forward. "Jessie and I are not a threat to anyone or this college and if you have any compassion at all, you will see that we both need medical assistance. Immediately."

She raised the gun and pointed it at his heart.

I took a few steps forward and caught hold of Ethan's arm before he could make any more advances toward the gun-toting nun. "Ethan, stop. Please. She's the one with the gun. She's in charge right now."

He looked down at me, and even though, he still didn't entirely understand the situation, he saw the look on my face and could see how serious—and frightened—I was.

"Okay. Fine," he said and turned toward Abigail. "What is it you're going to do with us?"

Her hand never wavered. "I'm going to protect this college."

A car door slammed and we heard voices outside. For the first time, Mother Abigail looked flustered.

Someone was pounding on the front door. She motioned us back to the exam table where I'd spent the night. "Hurry."

Ethan couldn't hurry. I helped him to the table.

She had us straddle the table, back to back, placing the leg restraints around Ethan's wrists and the arm restraints tightly around mine. She found adhesive tape in one of the cabinets and placed it over our mouths then moved to the doorway and turned to point the gun at us again. "Do not make any noise."

She turned out the light, closed the door behind her and we were in darkness again.

CHAPTER TWENTY-NINE

Ethan pulled against his restraints and eventually wore himself out. I leaned my back up against his. If there was another alternative, we needed to figure it out before Abigail returned. It might have helped if we could have talked to each other, but she'd taken that option from us.

The front door opened and closed. New footsteps entered the house, maybe more than one set. Muffled voices filtered through the floorboards, too indistinct to make out what was being said, too muted to even tell how many people were involved or if they were male or female.

I looked around the room from a new angle, but in the darkness it was difficult to see anything that might help aid an escape.

Ethan pulled against the restraints again, his back muscles flexed and released with each futile attempt. I wanted to tell him to give up, but I couldn't speak, and maybe, just maybe, he was strong enough to break free.

The conversation upstairs went on for quite some time. They moved into the dining room, chairs scraped across the floor as if they were all taking seats at the table. Twenty minutes or more passed. The conversation continued.

At least, for the time being, I knew where Mother Abigail and her gun were. A small comfort, it was just a matter of time.

Ethan had finally given up pulling against the restraints. We'd settled against each other, back to back. Occasionally, one or the other of us would butt the other one with their shoulder. I wasn't sure if Ethan's shoulder butts were to keep me awake or give me some kind of reassurance that he was in this with me. Whatever his motivation, it helped just knowing he was there.

I wondered what kind of threat Abigail thought we were to her college or her nuns or her students. When she came back for us, and it was obvious she would, we somehow had to let her know that we were the good guys. Whatever was going on, we were not the ones to be afraid of.

Hopefully, she would turn us over to the sheriff, but I didn't trust anyone these days.

I bent over as far as I could, my face close to my right hand, pinned against the table. It was an uncomfortable contortion. I leaned in farther until the tape on my lips brushed against my hand. Ethan grunted a question.

The muscles in my back tightened on the verge of a spasm and I moved back into an upright position until the tension passed.

I tried again, bending as far from my waist as possible. The tape touched my fingertips again. It took a couple of swipes to move my cheek in the necessary angle to grab the end of the tape with my fingers. I finally loosened the end of the adhesive and slowly turned my head to peel it off.

I sat up, breathing hard, but at least I could talk. "I got the tape off."

Ethan grunted again. He attempted to bend as I had done, but he wasn't as limber as I was and he eventually gave up.

Even though I could talk, what was there to say, if we couldn't figure this out together?

I pulled my legs up from the sides of the table and sat cross-legged, leaning against Ethan. I felt myself starting to doze.

Something bumped against the basement door and I was suddenly alert. The muscles in Ethan's back tensed. We both turned as the doorknob twisted. The conversation upstairs was still going on and I think we'd settled into a false sense of security. As long as they were talking, Mother Abigail was not going to shoot us.

The door slowly opened. Sunlight blared in from the window and it took a moment to recognize the figure standing in the doorway. Sister Imelda stepped into the room, closed the door quietly behind her and switched on the overhead light. She put a finger to her lips and moved toward us.

"What?" I whispered.

She didn't say anything until she was up against the table. She walked over to Ethan and ripped the tape off his mouth. "Are you all right?"

"Jessie has a wound on her head and needs to see a doctor. I've sprained my ankle and not sure I can walk. Where's Mother Abigail?"

Imelda went to examine Ethan's ankle. "She's still upstairs."

She released Ethan from his restraints and undid mine. "Let me see your head," she said.

I bent over. She touched it gently, but it still hurt. "You might need stitches."

I slipped off the table. "We need to get out of here. Mother Abigail has a gun. I know she's scared, but I really don't trust people with guns."

Imelda put up her hand to stop me. "We need to be careful. You both need medical attention and Mr. Miller can't walk. Do either of you have cell phones?"

"I lost mine in the woods," I said.

Ethan patted his pockets. "I must have forgotten mine. I was in a hurry to find Jessie when I left the RV."

"Then I need to go for help," she said. "If Mother comes back and you're gone, she will come looking for you and in your present conditions, I'm afraid she'd find us."

I started to protest.

Things upstairs were changing. Chairs scraped across the floor, voices moved toward the front of the house.

Imelda nodded toward the table we'd been tethered to for so long. "Quick," she said. "We need to make this look like everything is just as she left it. I'll attach the restraints—loosely. But she needs to think she is still in charge of this situation. I'll go for help. There's a house not far from here. I'll call the sheriff and an ambulance."

"No," Ethan said. "We need to get out of here now. We'll go with you. Or hide in the woods." He took a step forward, his ankle gave out and he grabbed an exam table to keep from going down.

Imelda's voice was firmer than I'd ever heard it. "No, Mr. Miller, there is no way you can escape Mother. She knows every inch of these woods. She's really quite fit and we can't take the chance."

Ethan looked at me and then at her. "Take Jessie with you and I'll stay behind so I don't slow you down."

"No." There was no room for argument in her mind. "The longer Mother thinks she's still in charge, the more time I have to get help out here. If Jessica is missing, it will be obvious to her that her plan is falling apart and she will kill you."

I didn't want to stay behind, but I was not willing to leave Ethan. What Imelda said made sense. I put my hand on Ethan's arm. "We'll be okay. We just need to sit tight a while longer."

The voices upstairs were more sporadic, as if the conversation was over and they were wrapping things up.

Ethan listened. Then he looked at me. "All right, but hurry."

Imelda had us strapped down again, with our mouths taped shut. The restraints weren't as tight as they had been and I hoped we would be able to pull free if we needed to.

The front door closed and a single set of footsteps moved through the house toward the clinic. A car started up outside. Imelda patted my leg, walked over to the door, turned out the light and left the room.

I don't know how Imelda escaped the building without passing Mother Abigail, but after a few minutes without any commotion from above, I assumed she was on her way to get help. I hoped like hell she would hurry.

Abigail took her time coming for us. Minutes passed, maybe ten, maybe twenty. It seemed like a long time. For once, I didn't doze off. My back pressed up against Ethan's. I listened, for every sound, real or imagined, that filtered through the door.

Ethan's back muscles were tighter than they'd ever b
he was poised for action. Under normal circumstances, th

have made me feel safe, but with his hobbled leg, there wasn't much he could do and win.

We were wound tight, hyper-vigilant to our surroundings. Still, when the door opened, we both jumped a little as if taken by surprise.

Abigail walked into the room and flipped on the light switch, looking around. I scanned the room, trying to remember if Imelda had touched or moved anything that might be noticeable, but there was nothing.

She walked over to Ethan. Even though I couldn't see what she was doing, I figured she was examining his ankle. I felt him flinch. She moved up the table and I think she ripped the tape off of his face. He flinched again.

She moved toward me and removed the tape from my mouth.

"What happens now?" I asked.

"I haven't decided yet."

"We're not a threat to you, Mother Abigail," I told her.

She looked me in the eye. "Oh, but you are." She pulled the gun from inside her habit. "I should have taken care of you that night you and Mrs. Miller were in the Administration Building."

"That was you?"

"Of course. I know everything that goes on at my school."

Insight was dawning. "And the clinic belongs to you now?"

She'd moved to one of the medical cabinets and was searching the contents, every few seconds, she looked over at us. "Yes, Dr. Kline left it to me when he passed away."

"This is where Barb died," I said.

"Who's Barb?" Ethan asked. "Oh right, Constance's friend from college. Were you here then too, Abigail?"

She found a box of syringes and put them on a table. "We were all in the same graduating class."

She was answering our questions. I wasn't sure if she was distracted by what she was doing and not paying attention or if she didn't care at this point how much we knew—because, perhaps, we wouldn't be around long enough to cause her any problems."

"So, who started the baby selling business? You? Or Dr. Kline?" I asked.

She finally looked up at me. The look on her face was acknowledgement that I was a good student and had figured out the problem on the blackboard before anyone else.

She hesitated.

"Just fill in the blanks," I said. "After all that's gone on, I have a right to know."

The last time, I'd been in a situation like this, I kept the killer talking until help arrived. Even if it wasn't a foolproof plan, it bought us some time. I hoped like hell, that Imelda had made it to a phone and help was on the way.

Mother Abigail put the box she'd been rummaging through on the table in front of her. "It was Dr. Kline's idea. He'd actually been doing it for years before I came along."

Ethan's back muscles were tensed again. I pushed my shoulder into his, hoping he understood that now was not the time to try to wiggle free from the restraints. "How did you get to know him?"

"I did a rotation at his clinic my junior year. I didn't know at the time what was going on. A couple of his patients, young, unmarried women lost their babies. I was surprised because they were all healthy young women. None of them were high-risk pregnancies."

Ethan must have picked up my signal, I felt him relax a little. "The night you brought Barb here, did you know what was going on? Did you know the doctor was selling babies?"

She pulled out the stool Ethan had used earlier and sat on it. "No. I didn't know then. All I knew at the time was that Barb was in a lot of trouble. She needed more help than I could give her and I didn't think she'd make it to town, so we brought her here."

Abigail stopped talking and looked at the far wall, as if she was thinking. As if she was remembering that horrible night, she shook her head at the memory. "She didn't make it. She'd lost too much blood. It was the first time I'd seen someone die. And the fact that it was someone I'd known for so long— it was devastating."

"But the baby didn't die, did she?"

She looked at me. "No. The little girl was beautiful and healthy."

Ethan was surprisingly silent through all of this. I was pretty sure he was thinking. The sad part was, we really had no options available; he was disabled and I couldn't carry him. Keep her talking, that's all we had. "Who decided to say that the baby was dead?"

"Dr. Kline."

"Why? Why would he do that?"

She took a deep breath. "He told me that the baby was conceived in sin—Barb wasn't married when she got pregnant. That the best thing we could do for the child was to find a good home."

"She had grandparents."

There was a flash of anger in her eyes as if I'd challenged her decision. "And every time they looked at that child, for the rest of her life, they would be reminded of their daughter's sin. Taking the baby was the kindest thing we could do for her."

How do you argue with decades of twisted logic? Or a morality so judgmental, it left little room for being human.

"So, you went into business with Dr. Kline. You and he must have made some good money over the years. You must be a rich woman today. How much do babies go for these days?"

Ethan must have thought I was goading her, and maybe I was. He hit me in the back with his shoulder.

She smiled. "Grateful, childless couples can be very generous."

"Five thousand dollars a kid? Ten thousand?"

"Jessie," Ethan said. His voice was low and full of warning.

Abigail's smile grew tight, she wasn't amused. "Let's just say that the sinful acts of some of our less reputable students payed to keep this college going."

"And what were their sins, Mother?"

"Premarital sex. Promiscuity."

"All the girls you stole babies from were students at St. Jo's?"

"Not all. There were a few girls from the area, but most were students at the college. Girls who came from good religious homes who should have known better."

"And was whatever sin you think they committed, a greater sin than what you did?"

"Jessie, stop." Ethan's tone was sharp.

"No, Ethan. If she's going to kill us, I want her to know that she had no right to do what she did—"

She moved quickly across the room, so fast, I didn't have time to think. She pushed the gun into my ribs. "What I did? I was trying to rectify what they had done. I was trying to put things right. They didn't deserve those sweet innocent babies. I found good homes for those children—good Catholic homes. They were all raised by honest, religious people."

I stared into her eyes. "You had no right to do that. It wasn't up to you."

The gun pressed harder into my ribs.

I didn't blink. "The birth certificates we found were just the tip of the ice berg weren't they?"

She took a step back. "You found those? Where?"

"In Stanley's office."

"I knew he had them. But I couldn't figure out where he got them."

"My guess is from Father Peter."

She nodded. "You're probably right. Father was sticking his nose into things. I was grateful when he took his sabbatical. He got what he deserved in San Francisco."

"How many babies have there been over the years?"

She shrugged. "I don't know. The business has been dying out for a long time now?"

"How sad for you."

She side-stepped my sarcasm. "People don't think their sins are worth hiding anymore. Years ago, those girls would do anything to keep their pregnancies secret from their parents. Now—well, it's a whole different world. They want to flaunt what they've done."

She moved back across the room and pulled another box out of the cabinet. My growing fear was not that we were going to be shot, but that she was planning some kind of lethal injection. She had the medical training to know what she was doing.

I knew I'd pushed too far. But I had some perverse need to know what she'd done. And, where the hell was the sheriff? "Did you kill Ethan Jr.?"

She didn't even bother to look up, and it was obvious we were dealing with a more than a religious zealot. Like Stanley, Mother

Abigail was a psychopath. "I had to. Even though, the young man was not one of *ours*, he was only going to raise questions that would start people looking into what went on at our college. I was on my way to chapel that morning, when I saw him heading up over the hill. It was almost as if an opportunity were being given to me. I went inside and grabbed the closest thing I could find, a small replica of a sword in the narthex and followed him to the cemetery."

"And Stanley? Did you shoot him too?"

She looked up, startled. "No. Is he dead?"

She seemed genuinely surprised by the news. "I thought you knew."

She shook her head. "I did not. But, really, it's just as well. You saw the birth certificates. You must have figured out that he was trying to blackmail the college. He was trying to blackmail *me*."

That apparently made his death justifiable. But if she wasn't lying, there was another killer out there somewhere. "You're an evil, bitter old woman. And whatever wrong you think those girls committed is nothing compared to what you have done."

"I saved those babies. I saved the college."

"You had no right—"

She raised the gun and aimed it at my chest. "I think that's enough, Miss Kallan."

A shot exploded in the basement room, so loud it hurt my ears. Ethan yelled my name.

Mother Abigail clutched her shoulder, blood spurted through her fingers.

Ethan yelled my name again as he struggled to pull free of his restraints.

When the noise that echoed through the room stopped, I looked to see Imelda standing in the doorway, her smoking gun still aimed at Mother Abigail. Tears ran down her cheeks.

"Imelda," I said, but she seemed not to hear me.

She walked over to Abigail, who was sitting on the floor, her back up against the cabinets, her eyes wide with fear and shock.

Imelda held the gun inches from the other nun's head. "It was you. It was all your fault. Peter is dead because of you. A beautiful man died, because of what you'd done."

Abigail found her voice, although, it wasn't very strong. "I never hurt Father Peter."

Imelda crouched down beside her. "He's dead because of you, because he found out what you did. He mistakenly shared that information with a very unscrupulous greedy man, but you're the one who started all of this. You might as well have pulled the trigger that killed Peter, that killed the only man I've ever loved."

Abigail opened her mouth.

Imelda stood and tried to wipe away tears with the back of her hand. "Don't. Just don't. I can't stand to hear your excuses. Jessica was correct when she said you had no right to do what you'd done. You had no right to ruin the lives of all those young girls."

She took a step back and Abigail reached for her gun that was on the floor two feet away. Imelda kicked it across the room.

"Imelda," I said. She turned toward me. A look of absolute brokenness that I will never forget, filled her eyes. "Could you please release us?"

She was in shock it took a minute for her to answer. "No, I don't think so."

She fingered the necklace she was wearing and I noticed that she'd put both halves of the Mizpah on the same chain. Both halves of the broken heart—hers and Peter's.

"It was you who shot Stanley? Out in the woods tonight?"

She started to cry again. "Please don't judge me, Jessica. I had to. I had to do it for Peter."

"You followed him here to Missouri, you obviously wanted to kill him. Why not do it weeks ago?"

"I needed to be sure. I needed to know he was the one. When he told you what he'd done, I couldn't take it anymore. All I could see was Peter's face out on that jogging trail. Peter dying all alone so far from home."

"Please release us."

She smiled a very weak smile. "Don't worry. You'll be okay."

There was a free exam table and she had Abigail get up on the table, then used the restraints on her wrists and ankles. She walked over and patted my leg like she'd done earlier.

"I'll send help this time. I promise."

And then she was gone.

CHAPTER THIRTY

SHE LEFT THE LIGHT ON. I glanced over at Abigail on the exam table. She'd lost some blood and her coloring was starting to fade.

Ethan pulled on his restraints.

"Stop," I told him. "She said she'd send help."

"And what if she doesn't? She said that last time too."

I let Ethan continue with his attempts. Mother Abigail's eyes were closed, but I could hear her breathing.

I thought about Imelda. There was no way to justify what she'd done, but love and loss can take over our lives in unexpected ways. They can drive us to do things we never thought we'd do. Her love for Peter was great and her loss was traumatic.

If something ever happened to Matt, if someone hurt him like that, would it push me to that place, from which there is no return? Because, once you take a life, you can never undo it.

I understood more of what had happened as if the pieces were falling into place. Everything wasn't totally clear yet, but most of it made sense. Still, my suspicions about Ginny lingered. How does a law enforcement officer let things get so out of hand? Two people were dead and another lying six feet away might be next if help didn't get here soon. Did Ginny have a hand in all of this?

And did Constance? The writer's workshop with Ethan had been engineered by the two of them. Was their motive really to get

Ginny on campus to investigate Franny Pohlson's murder and the allegations of the child she's lost?

Interesting, the thoughts that roam through your head when you're locked in a basement with a crazy old nun and a narcissistic author.

Ethan finally stopped struggling. I leaned into his back, closed my eyes and fell asleep.

The next thing I knew footsteps were pounding down the basement stairs, voices shouted. The door banged open and Ginny charged in, gun drawn, sweeping the room in its arc looking for perpetrators. When she realized that Mother Abigail was lying on an exam table with a bullet in her shoulder and Ethan and I were strapped to the table, and were the only people there, she holstered her gun. A look of disappointment slid across her face.

Constance ran into the room and stopped. I'm not sure what she expected to see.

Ginny checked on Mother Abigail's wound. She found some gauze in one of the cabinets and pressed it against Abbigail's shoulder, holding it firmly. Abigail opened her eyes.

Ginny looked over at us. "You two okay?"

Before we answered, she looked at Constance then motioned toward us with her head. "Release them."

Constance undid the clasps on my restraints, then went over to Ethan.

"It's about damn time you got here," he said almost under his breath.

"Don't start with me, Ethan," Constance said.

I rubbed my wrists. "Would you two stop? Please."

Constance undid Ethan's restraints. "See what you started? The children don't like it when we fight."

Ethan actually laughed.

Sirens approached from somewhere in the distance. "Wait out front and show them where to come," Ginny said to Constance.

Mother Abigail was loaded into the ambulance on a stretcher. Ethan and I rode to the Emergency Room in the back of Sheriff Allen's squad car.

The ER wasn't busy, but it still took longer than I thought was necessary. Two hours later, the wound on my head had been cleaned, some of my hair cut away and I had eight stitches where Mother Abigail had banged me over the head. Ginny told me they'd found a piece of firewood on the ground outside Ethan's RV with blood on it, so we assumed that had been her weapon of opportunity.

Abigail was strong and had a good arm, so I was grateful that I didn't end up with a concussion.

After I'd been discharged, I went to find Ethan.

Two exam rooms over from mine, I found him lying on a gurney, eyes closed, hands folded across his chest, he looked relaxed. His shoeless, sockless foot was propped up on three pillows and even beneath the bandages, I could tell there was a great deal of swelling.

"Will you ever walk again?"

He didn't even open his eyes. "Very funny."

"What did the doctor say?"

"That a lesser man couldn't have withstood the pain I've endured."

"Uh huh. What did the doctor really say?"

"That I need to keep it elevated and stay off of it for four to six weeks." He finally opened his eyes and looked at me. "How are you doing?"

"I'm okay. A little tired of head trauma, but I've had worse. By the way, I'm taking a two-week paid vacation, starting now."

"Paid? I'm paying you for doing nothing for two weeks?"

"Yes, you are and thank you."

He sat up on the gurney and slowly moved his legs until they were hanging over the side. "Are you really okay?"

"I will be." I climbed up on the gurney next to him. "Ethan, did you know Ginny was a cop? That she was here on official business?"

"Not until this morning when we were all out looking for you. Was it only this morning? Anyway, Constance finally came clean about the whole set-up."

"They used you, you know, to get on campus. How does that make you feel?"

"Not so crazy about being used or manipulated." His voice was gruff and I had no doubt he and Constance would go a few rounds over this.

I opened my mouth, but he cut me off.

"I know what you're thinking—that I did the same thing to you at one time—that I manipulated you and others for my own ends."

Which he did when he pulled me into that twenty-year old case. "Yes, I was."

"For the record, that was totally different."

Ethan Miller's world, apparently, had its own rules.

He looked at me. "So, are we even now?"

"Even how? What are you talking about?"

"I know you haven't completely forgiven me for getting shot last year, so I figure the injury I incurred coming to your rescue finally makes us even."

"You're kidding right?"

"I'm very serious."

"I got *shot*. You fell down the stairs. How is that *even*?"

"I was coming to rescue you."

"For all I know, you fell because you're a klutz. That does not make us even."

He grunted. "You're very difficult to please."

CHAPTER THIRTY-ONE

THERE WAS MORE COMMOTION ON THE SECOND FLOOR than there'd been all week. The ladies were moving out and obviously in a hurry to get home.

My own bags were packed and I carried them to the elevator and rode down to the main lobby. Women were crying and hugging each other, saying they didn't want to wait another forty years to do this again. They were all in their sixties. I wondered how long they thought they were going to live.

I dropped my bags by the front door. I half-expected to see Sister Imelda standing there, but she was gone. She hadn't been seen for two days.

I wandered into the commons area and watched as the members of Constance's graduating class bid good bye to Ginny. When the last one left the room, I walked over to the table where she sat and pulled out a chair across from her.

Her glasses were perched on top of her head; two stacks of birth certificates sat on the table in front of her. There must have been at least seventy-five, maybe more.

"Is that all of them?" I asked.

She looked up at me. "All that we've found so far."

"Did you find the one you're looking for?"

She didn't break eye contact with me, but tears filled her eyes. "No. Not yet. How did you know?"

"Just a hunch. I'm sorry for what happened to you. I'm sorry for what happened to all those other girls and to Franny Pohlson."

She took the glasses off of her head and placed them on the table. "Thank you. You know, Franny Pohlson has become my new hero. She did what the rest of us didn't have the courage to do. She told someone."

"Courage at eighteen or nineteen isn't easy to come by. Was your story much different from hers?"

She passed a hand across her face and I saw how tired she looked. I wondered if retirement loomed on the horizon for Sergeant Andrews. "Her story was my story. All the details were there. Just a different generation."

"What happened?"

"Well, I got pregnant. I was young and thought I was in love. The most mature thing my boyfriend and I did was to realize we weren't ready to get married."

"So, you took a year off from school and went home?"

She laughed. "Oh God no. There was no way I was going to tell my dad I was pregnant. As I said, it was a different generation. I had a friend in Mossberg who'd graduated the year before and got a teaching job at the elementary school. We shared an apartment, I worked at the grocery store. And, the biggest mistake of my life, was visiting kindly old Dr. Kline."

"How'd you get hooked up with him? His office was quite a drive from Mossberg."

"A girl from my class, who'd been pregnant recommended him. I was afraid to go to a doctor where I lived. I thought maybe they'd contact my parents. My friend told me Dr. Kline was used to helping girls who were *in trouble*." She actually did the air quotes.

"Were you going to put the baby up for adoption?"

"That was the plan, but the closer I got to my due date, the harder it was to think about that. If I'd actually had to make the choice, if Kline hadn't made that decision for me, I don't know what I would have done."

"Kline told you the baby died?"

She looked out the window. "Yes. That part of the story was exactly like Franny's. They took the baby right after I delivered, told me she was having breathing problems. I saw her for one brief second as they carried her away. They gave me a shot of something and I was gone. Out for maybe two days. I don't know if they had Rohypnol or any of the other date rape drugs back then, but I have snippets of memory. I'd wake up and hear her crying. Whenever I asked about her, I'd get another injection."

"Her?"

She looked at me and smiled. "It was a little girl."

"If you find out where she is, will you contact her?"

"Probably not." She picked up her glasses and started playing with them. "I'm not saying I wouldn't do that creepy stalker thing and drive by her house just to see what she looks like—just to make sure she's okay—but I don't want to intrude on her life after all these years."

"She might want to get to know you."

Ginny closed her eyes, took a deep breath, then opened them. "Maybe."

"If you hadn't had your baby taken away, would you have believed Franny's story? Or would you have just chalked it up to an emotional young woman."

"To be honest, I've wondered for years—decades—what's been going on here. The night Barbie died it took me back to my own delivery. Barb had lost a lot of blood, but that didn't mean the baby wasn't healthy. Even at the time, it didn't make sense that they'd both died. And then, over the years, I'd hear stories of other girls here, who were pregnant and lost their babies. This has been going on for a long time."

"Wasn't it a little convoluted to bring Ethan into this? To set up this whole scenario?"

If I'd just met Ginny, if I didn't have my previous opinion of her lurking in the back of my head, I would have felt quite differently about her. The look on her face—in her eyes—was intelligent and thoughtful. No dithering Homecoming Queen, clinging to her lost youth. She was a professional.

In answer to my question, there was the slightest shrug. "It couldn't be helped. I had to get in here and I couldn't think of any other way."

"Did you think Franny might not be telling the truth?"

"That never crossed my mind. Father Peter had his own suspicions about what had been going on here over the years. When he came to see me about Franny, he already had his own list of names. Girls who'd come to him for counseling. The autopsy showed that Franny had given birth, but we didn't have enough evidence for a search warrant. The judge argued that maybe the girl changed her mind after she signed adoption papers. We were hitting road blocks everywhere we turned."

"So, you came in the back door?"

She laughed. "I like that. Yes, we came in the back door."

I picked up a pile of bank statements and stock papers. "How much money did she make over the years?"

"Hard to say at this point. I'll have a forensic accountant figure it out. Conservatively, I'd say she brought in at least half a million dollars. Business started to dwindle about ten years ago. More and more girls were keeping their babies, I guess. But Abby invested well, there is—or was—ten or twelve million there."

"Lucrative business. What do you mean *was*?"

She leaned back in her chair and stretched. "Sister Imelda, cashed in much of it before she left. She's been transferring funds for a few months now."

I wasn't sure I wanted to know what happened to Imelda. No one had spoken of her. What she'd done—killing Stanley—was so very wrong. I knew she should pay for that. But part of me hoped . . .

Curiosity got the better of me. "Do you know where Imelda is?"

"I do."

"And?"

"She left the country. Flew to Ecuador that night after she shot Abby. She's sitting on a butt-load of embezzled funds, hopefully on a tropical beach. I'm sure she'll have a very nice life."

"She might not think it's such a nice life, the price she paid for it was the man she loved."

"True."

"I'm guessing there's no extradition from Ecuador?"

She shook her head. "No there isn't."

"She must have had it all planned."

"Doubtless."

"How do you feel about her getting away with murder."

She looked at me for the longest time, her gaze never wavering. "Probably the same as you."

"I'm not sure I'm sorry she got away," I admitted.

"Neither am I."

I raised my eyebrows. "I'm surprised."

She smiled again. "That I'm human?"

"What will happen to Abigail?"

The glasses went back on the top of her head. "I don't like to bet on cases, you never know what might derail you along the way, or what a jury will do—but I think this one's a slam-dunk. We have a paper trail like you wouldn't believe and victims will be lined up around the block to tell their stories."

"And what will happen to Sergeant Andrews?"

"She will go home to her adoring husband and play with her grandchildren and have a much-needed rest. I'm getting too old for this. By the way, that shoulder-butt out in the woods, although inspired, left me with some colorful and very tender bruises."

"Sorry."

I picked up a stack of birth certificates and looked at each one, checking the dates.

Ginny watched me. "They're all in chronological order."

I found the one from forty years ago. "May I borrow this?"

"That's police evidence."

I looked up at her and saw her smiling. "I'd like her to see this."

"Just make sure I get it back."

CHAPTER THIRTY-TWO

I STEPPED OUT THE FRONT DOOR OF the dormitory into the heat. The temperature seemed cooler than it had been all week, or maybe I'd become acclimated to it from my nights in the sauna-like dorm room.

Cars carrying the workshop ladies headed toward the county road, they honked their horns and waved at me.

Matt's truck was parked behind the RAV4. He was saying good-bye to his father and then he was taking me home with him. It would be two weeks together, two weeks as far from the insanity as I could get.

Constance was heading up over the hill and I had a pretty good idea where she was going. She too, needed to say her final good-byes. I followed the path up over the rise, keeping my distance to give her some privacy.

She walked into the cemetery, heading for her friend, Barb's grave. I perched myself on a monument by the wrought iron arch-way, with the seraphim above keeping guard over all who entered there, and waited.

Twenty minutes later, I went to find her. She stood in the middle of the neglected area and looked around. She smiled when she saw me. "You found me."

"Actually, I followed you. Are you ready to go?"

She took a deep breath as if breathing in her surroundings.

"I just need a minute. I love this place. Well, not the cemetery so much, but the college. You know, this is where I grew up. The worst thing in my life happened here. And the second-best thing in my life started here."

"The night your friend died was the worst."

She nodded.

"Meeting Ethan, I'm guessing, was the second best."

She smiled. "Yes."

"What was the best?"

She turned to look at me with tears in her eyes. "My son. He is the best thing that ever happened to me. I think of all those young women—girls really—whose children were taken from them. Stolen from them. And I'm grateful for my son."

St. Josephine's College for Women had left its mark on me too. In a different way than it had Constance, but life-changing nonetheless.

For the past two days, I'd been wrestling with the inconsistencies of Mother Abigail's life, but I think it was going to take more than a couple of days, to understand the impact of what she'd done, of what had happened at this place, and now, coming to terms with it in a way I could comprehend.

I think I'd made my peace with Stanley, with who he turned out to be. But Abigail confused me. On some level, she had a deep moral conviction, that what she was doing was right. And then it had gone all wrong.

"Constance, you knew Abigail, what do you think happened to her?"

She wrinkled her forehead. "I wish I knew. I've been trying to figure that out, but honestly, I don't know what happened. Abby always had a deep faith. It was who she was. Knowing her back then, I believe in the beginning that maybe she thought she was doing what was right. Maybe she thought she was truly helping people—the girls, the babies, the adoptive families. But, over time, the money seemed to become the driving force. It became the goal, and whatever goodness she thought she was doing for others, must have fallen by the wayside. We learned it in Sunday School, Jessica. *The love of money is the root of all evil.* It's all very sad."

"I don't think I'll ever understand what took over her."

"I don't think any of us will. Abigail grew up dirt poor. Maybe the money filled some hole in her life—or she got greedy. We should probably head back. I think Ethan's itching to get home."

"It's nice that you offered to take care of him while he convalesces."

She groaned. "I have no idea what I've gotten myself into."

"Did you know that Sister Imelda was adopted as an infant."

She looked at me, an unreadable expression on her face. "No. Why are you telling me this?"

"She grew up not too far from here."

"Okay."

I handed her the birth certificate I'd taken from Ginny's pile of evidence. "I thought you might want to see this."

Her eyes never left my face, as she reached out, very slowly, to take the paper from me. Then she looked down at it. She put her hand to her heart and bit her lip, tears ran down her cheeks."

"It's the birth certificate of Barb's baby—her little girl."

It took a while for her to get the words out. "It says *Live Birth*."

"It also says date of birth was April fifth."

"Yes, I knew that."

"Sister Imelda was born on April fifth. She turned forty this year."

Constance didn't even try to hold back the tears. She sat on Barb's monument, clutching the birth certificate to her chest. Minutes later, when she was all cried out, she dried her eyes and looked up at me. "Do you really believe Sister Imelda was Barbie's daughter?"

"We'll never know, but it's a very real possibility. And wouldn't it be ironic, if it was Barb's daughter who finally brought closure to this whole thing? A little justice for all the girls who lost their babies."

WE HEADED BACK DOWN THE HILL and stopped in front of the Administration Building. Millie stepped out of the RV and shook out a kitchen rug. Constance moved over to the fountain, watching the water erupt from an artesian spring onto the colored tiles at the bottom of the pool. She seemed lost in nostalgia.

Millie walked over to me, she nodded toward Constance. "She's coming home with us," she whispered. "I don't know if I can take it."

I patted her shoulder. "It's a big house. And it's only for six weeks."

I thought she might cry. "Another six weeks."

Dan and John emerged from Ethan's RV, followed seconds later, by Matt. There were days I didn't want to admit it, but I loved these people and all their insanity. This was my family.

Ethan hobbled down the two steps from his motorhome, teetering on his crutches. "Constance! Are you ready or not? I can't wait all day. I've been injured you know."

Matt hurried over, grabbed my arm and moved me in the direction of his truck. Millie disappeared into her RV, moving faster than I ever thought she could. John headed for his vehicle. Dan sprinted toward the RAV4.

No one I knew could clear an area faster than a grumpy Ethan Miller.

I looked back over my shoulder. Constance rolled her eyes. "Lord, help me. Six weeks of Ethan Miller's recuperation. What did I ever do to deserve this?"

Author Photo by Steve Mattson www.zenithcityphotos.com

Born in Omaha, Nebraska, Susan C. Richards has lived throughout the Midwest and the Pacific Northwest. She currently resides in Northern Minnesota.

Dead Write, which takes place on the campus of a private college in southern Missouri, is the second in her Jessica Kallan series. As the daughter of a roving college professor, Susan knows firsthand, that almost anything can happen at a small liberal arts college.

Her manuscript, The Edge of the Moon, a novel of psychological suspense, was a finalist in a national writer's contest.

For more information, visit her website at: SusanCRichards.com

CPSIA information can be obtained
at www.ICGtesting.com
Printed in the USA
LVHW020320031121
702213LV00010B/627